TIMEKEEPERS

By Catherine Webb

Mirror Dreams

Mirror Wakes

Waywalkers

Timekeepers

The Extraordinary and Unusual Adventures
of Horatio Lyle

Praise for Catherine Webb

'*Waywalkers* is an exciting fast-paced tale . . .
Highly entertaining fantasy'
THE BOOKSELLER

'Assured, well-sustained and engages directly with the
reader . . . If I were a teenage fan of Terry Pratchett
or Philip Pullman I would love *Mirror Dreams*'
SUNDAY TELEGRAPH

'A brilliant book!'
WHS ONLINE

'*Mirror Dreams* is a splendid book . . .
I want to read the sequel. Now!'
THE ALIEN ONLINE

TIMEKEEPERS

Catherine Webb

www.atombooks.co.uk

ATOM

First published in Great Britain by Atom 2004
Reprinted 2006

A CIP catalogue record for this book
is available from the British Library.

ISBN-13: 978-1-90423-343-5
ISBN-10: 1-90423-343-0

Typeset in Cochin by M Rules
Printed and bound in Great Britain
by Bookmarque Ltd, Croydon, Surrey

Atom Books
An imprint of
Time Warner Book Group UK
Brettenham House
Lancaster Place
London WC2E 7EN

Contents

INTRODUCTION

Sam Linnfer

Where to begin? So many minds, drowning out my voice, filling my soul, no escape. So many places blending into one, all these memories, no more individual, no more alone. The Light has brought this on me, always the Light. So many voices filllng my ears, yet they speak as one, and they say the same. We are the intention and the act, the strength and the weakness, the light and the dark, the individual and the whole, the magic . . . the magic and the what? What is the opposite of magic, why doesn't it know? Surely the Light, that compasses so many minds, feels so many thoughts, is so much in so little, so much in me, knows all answers. Where to begin?

Even here the Light knows, although it is hard to tune down all the voices to one single sound. A thousand minds that are not my own, a thousand souls imprinted on my soul, just as mine is imprinted on theirs, whisper the answer, and even as I understand, I feel myself slipping from the One into the Many, and not even the magic can hold me up. Not any more.

To begin . . .

In the beginning there had been Cronus, and under his iron rule there was no change. All was suspended at one point, endless existence with no death, but no life either. Then came Time, who fought with Cronus and imprisoned him beyond the veil of physical worlds, locking him away for all eternity and hiding the key to his jail that no man might find him. And under Time came life, and with life came the other Greater Powers, his Queens of Heaven. Night, Day, War, Wisdom, Light, Love, Chaos, Order and Belief brought forth children to Time, and these children grew many and powerful. Immortal and magical, they used their gifts to walk between worlds, through the Ways of Hell, Heaven and Earth.

But all was not well in Heaven, and the Children of Time warred among themselves, each house fighting for rule of that magical land. And Time feared that his children might free his enemy, Cronus, so he created a weapon of such power that even the Greater Powers themselves trembled at its passage. And he took this weapon, called it the Light, and placed it in the heart of his favourite child, his golden son, Balder, the only Son of Light, Time's most honoured Queen. And Heaven rejoiced to see this great man hold this great power, for none feared that he might use it for evil, and he was most loved in all the worlds. So much so, it was rumoured that Balder was the only child truly beloved by Time himself, who ever used men only as tools.

Yet there was one, Loki, a Son of Night, who did fear. He struck a bargain with the sleeping god Cronus, and slew the Bearer of Light, Balder, striking dread into the heart of Time once more, for, without the Light, Time feared the return of Cronus. Loki himself was imprisoned like his master, Cronus, who remained locked away, plotting and scheming in the darkness. All feared that without the Light, Cronus should escape and destroy Time for ever. So all of Heaven wept for the death of Balder, the shining child of Time. None more so than his father, who feared that with the death of his son he had lost the greatest weapon he possessed; for Time did not wish to meddle directly in the affairs of men.

Then one day, out of the shadow stepped a new Bearer of Light. A Son of Time and Magic, illegitimate Prince of Heaven, this child had been created for the sole purpose of serving Time against his enemies, and in his heart was locked the power of the Light for ever. He was made suspicious, cunning, clever, so that should another Child of Time decide to act against him, he would survive, where Balder had died. But he was also defiant in the face of his father's purpose, and he turned away from Heaven and was banished to Earth. There for thousands of years he schemed and watched and waited, aware constantly of the Light inside him, and wishing it were not his burden to bear.

He walked Earth and Hell under many names. Sam Linnfer, Luke Satise, Sebastian Teufel, Satan, Lucifer, the Devil. And few dared challenge him, for fear of Magic, his mother, and the power of the Light that he guarded inside him, so he and his power endured.

The time for action came unexpectedly, from three of Lucifer's brothers – Seth, Son of Night, Jehovah, Son of Belief and Odin, Son of War. These, their houses weakened by war, drew together and swore to find and free the Pandora spirits, banished and imprisoned by Time for the danger they posed to his realm: Hate, Greed, and Suspicion. However, their sister, fair Freya, Daughter of Love, discovered what they planned. But she was betrayed to her death and the spirits were freed, their powers answering only the commands of Jehovah, Odin and Seth.

Lucifer, seeing what had been done, drew the Light to himself and attacked the spirits, though using the Light at all brought him great danger. The Light tapped the minds of men, and from their thoughts drew its power. But in the process his mind, channelling all those other minds, could become lost in a sea of thought, and to recall it to its rightful place was hard. With the spirits weakened, if not destroyed, he fought his brother, Seth, leader of the three who had conspired to unleash this evil. But neither won and both, wounded, had to flee the field.

Yet through this battle Lucifer had learned one thing that made what had gone before seem trivial. His brother Seth was mustering an army in Hell to seek the thing no one had dreamed he would look for. The key that locked Cronus in his prison was buried somewhere in the sands of Hell and Seth, driven almost to madness by his lust for power and by hatred of his kin, was determined to find it.

Protected by the Light from the spirits' power, by injuring Seth Lucifer had averted disaster. But not for long, as well he knew. He looked to Heaven, and felt the eye of his father fixed on him. All the while Time had waited. As King of Heaven he had created the Bearer of Light with just one possible purpose. To destroy Cronus would mean channelling with the Light, through Lucifer's mind, everything that lived. And Lucifer knew, as well as Time, that such a use of the Light would not only bring down Cronus, but take the Bearer with him too.

It was, as Lucifer himself concluded, a piss-poor situation.

ONE

Son of Magic

This, thought Sam Linnfer, *is a piss-poor situation*.

Amid the squalor of his Clerkenwell flat, Adam, shapeshifter spirit and part-time spy for Sam, passed a mug of coffee and said, 'I've checked up. All our Heaven sources are utterly silent; not a creature stirring up there. Most of Hell has gone hush-a-bye too, although rumour has it that Seth has obliterated Hades. The capital, though, Pandemonium, seems intact.'

Sam sipped the coffee, scowling at his own thoughts. As ever, Adam's sitting room was a tip: empty Coke cans everywhere, unread newspapers stained with food, stacks of books more than slightly foxed, a carpet looking like an outsize pride of lions had used it as substitute cat litter. Adam himself, a small man with ginger hair and freckles, looked dwarfed by the piles of rubbish.

None of this was important to Sam Linnfer. What counted right now was the knowledge sitting inside his head, where it looked thoroughly unhappy. Indeed, the more he considered his situation, the less hopeful he felt.

Yeah, wake from a week's regenerative trance after getting pounded to a pulp by Seth, and, as a last resort, releasing the Light – it was always bound to be a bad day.

'What will you do?' Adam's gaze was mild but attentive.

'What can I do?' sighed Sam. 'I can't even stay and talk to you for more than a few hours. As soon as Jehovah remembers my existence, he'll dispatch the Pandora spirits to destroy me, but when they find themselves unable to get through my head they'll target yours. And you know well enough that, depending on which spirit is sent, you'll either hate, suspect or be jealous of me, and it'll get messy.'

Adam blushed at the memory of his own recent dominance by one of the Pandora spirits. Jealousy, who'd made him try to kill Sam.

A week. A whole week in a trance of regeneration. The thought of that much time gone by disquieted Sam. Even injured, Seth might have got closer to releasing Cronus. Anti-Time, the end of life. Sometimes Sam wondered whether he shouldn't just fulfil his apparent destiny – to die discharging the Light against Cronus. Yet always that single word 'destiny' hardened his resolve. If that was the purpose of his father in creating him, then he would do everything in his power to defy Time, and live.

But not at the cost of letting Cronus go free.

The one nagging question that remained was simple: how?

And to that he had no answer. At least no satisfactory one.

'One man, a mortal working for Freya, found out where Cronus was imprisoned,' he said. 'He was killed by Seth, but not before revealing to Seth that same location. Therefore Seth is now the only person who knows where Cronus's key is hidden. Correct?'

Adam looked uncomfortable. 'Correct,' he admitted with reluctance, as if such disaster could somehow be falsified by its sheer scale.

'I can't confront Seth, because with an army, the Pandora spirits and Odin, probably Thor too, on his side, I'd be flattened before I could say "Sorry, wrong door". I can't forge new alliances because, let's face it, the Pandora spirits would break them in a second, and I can't draw on old ones for exactly the same reason. I'm stumped.'

'But,' ventured Adam, 'I don't think you're about to give up, are you?'

Sam gave a weary smile. It was unlike his usual boyish grin, on a young face made old by the knowledge in those black eyes, but it was still a smile. 'Whoever said anything about that?'

He was packing his bags, when it came. He froze where he stood and frowned, trying to concentrate on the itch in the back of his mind.

Lucifer . . .

<Who's there? Who calls on Lucifer?>

A laugh, suddenly loud in his head. <Hello, brother.>

He sighed. <Seth. And to think I stabbed you.> The suave Son of Night, with his nearly always perfect manners.

<And to think I beat you to a pulp.>

<I guess we're even. Still planning to take over the universe in a sea of blood and death?>

<Actually, I was thinking the subtle touch. A lake, at the most.>

<Ah, the restraint of my fellow Waywalkers. Anyone's blood in particular?>

<Yours, as a matter of fact. There's probably a good five pints, isn't there?>

<More than in you; the state of my dagger testifies to that. And why are you scrying for me, brother?>

<Just seeing if you were dead.>

<Well, great news! I'm alive, well and looking forward to round two! So why don't you get down here and we'll settle this like immortals. Otherwise, stop this now, Seth. Because I *will* come after you. I *will* seek to destroy you.>

<Likewise, brother, likewise.>

<You don't get it, do you? I'm the Bearer of Light. If the worst comes to the worst I'll discharge everything I have against you and hope it fries your mind. I'll take all the fear, hate, anger, resentment, bitterness, jealousy in the universe and I'll blast it right into the centre of your twisted little consciousness.>

<And I control *your* one-time Hellish army *and* the Pandora spirits. How does the situation stand now, Bearer of Light? Little Lucifer? You'd never dare discharge on that scale. You're too afraid.>

For a second behind Seth's voice, Sam felt something else. His mind struck something cold and hard as he lashed out at it, and he heard Seth laugh.

<Is that the best you can do, Son of Magic? I expected something more from you!> Seth's counter-stroke came,

flaring across Sam's senses like fire. Sam closed his eyes against it, crawling along the afterburn of Seth's magic to find his brother's mind, and hammered back with mental darts of ice that tore at it for all it was worth.

<You bastard!> he screamed. <You did this! You killed them!>

He felt Seth fall back. <Freedom, brother! Freedom from Time, freedom from death, freedom from tyranny!>

<You bastard! You killed Freya, you killed *my* Freya!>

<She was never yours!> Light flared against Sam's eyes and he instinctively shielded, repulsing the spell and lashing out again at Seth.

At where Seth's mind had been.

The scry was broken. Seth was gone.

Sam sat down slowly on the flat's ruinous sofa and groaned.

Problems . . .

Had he managed to push Seth back in time? Scrying was a spell designed to locate physical objects and obtain information – had he managed to push Seth back before his brother had found his location? And even if he had, Seth had other ways of finding him, hadn't he?

Seth had the Pandora spirits . . .

There was a knock at the door. Sam stood up, wobbling slightly as blood rushed from his head. 'Adam?'

The door opened, and Adam stuck his head round. 'Hi. I wondered if everything was okay.'

Sam opened his mouth to answer, and hesitated.

There was something . . . like . . . singing? Very far off?

He stared at Adam in slow dread. 'Oh, Time,' he muttered.

'What's the matter? Sam, what's wrong?'

He looked at the expression of concern on Adam's face. 'They're here,' he answered with a little shrug. 'I shouldn't have stayed.'

'Who's here?'

He smiled wanly. 'Everyone.'

At which point, in accordance with the universal laws of plan-screwing, the windows exploded inwards. A bit showy, thought Sam; assassins should, by rights, simply knock on the door and murder whoever answers it. Coming in through the windows was unnecessarily flash, especially since they were on the first floor.

He heard Adam exclaim, 'Shit!' – and spun in time to see one of the assassins of Heaven, a Firedancer, all in red, his dragon-bone knife already out. Sam yelled, 'Adam, get out of here!', but heard no answer from his comrade. Backing up against the wardrobe he looked around for Adam and saw him standing stock-still, a little smile across his face. The music in Sam's ears roared in triumph, the song of the Pandora spirits, of . . . Hate? Was it Hate that Seth had sent to fill the room? But why, then, hadn't Adam moved yet?

No time to contemplate such details. A Firedancer lunged for Sam, who caught the man's wrist – if indeed you could call Firedancers men – and pulled him down towards an upward-bound knee. Firedancer and knee collided, and the Firedancer sagged. There was a hiss of metal as Sam drew his small, silver dagger that, though looking no more interesting than a sharpened pencil, still had the gleam of something designed for killing. He looked round the room. Three Firedancers – one doubled over and in no condition to fight, judging by his groans – and Adam. Standing motionless. Smiling at nothing.

The other two Firedancers decided to try killing from a range. They raised their hands, fire flashing around their fingers. Sam warded quickly as fire flared, tearing through the room and around him. It struck the wardrobe behind him, blackening the chemical-tanned wood. At the top of the bed, the pillows ignited, burning slowly and quietly to themselves. Sam waited until the fire had cleared from the shields in front of his eyes and retaliated. The principle of fighting fire with fire, though basically sound, could fall down badly when taking on Firedancers. Fire could put them briefly out of action, but it certainly wouldn't kill them.

Therefore the light that Sam called to his fingers was bright blue, streaked with silver, and shimmered around him with a quiet hiss. He saw the Firedancers back away and grinned. 'Shouldn't have come looking, should you?' he asked, and threw the coldfire. It struck the Firedancers, splattering out on impact in every direction. Frost crawled along their red robes, turning them pure white. In ordinary people – ordinary immortals – it would have inflicted little more than stiff joints and drastic inconvenience. With Firedancers, the reaction was very different. They screamed. In the moment of deafening distraction Sam leapt forwards, spinning round to bring his dagger down hard into the shoulder of one Firedancer. He heard something uncomfortably like the crunch of someone walking on glass and yanked his blade free, trailing orange-red blood.

Pain exploded in the small of his back and he staggered, almost falling into the bed, which was by now burning fast, filling the room with noxious black smoke. He coughed, eyes watering, and heaved himself to one side. The shattered remnants of the stool Adam was swinging slammed down on to the bed next to him. He saw the hatred twist Adam's face. This was what happened when the Pandora spirits came; they consumed your mind, bringing in its place just a single emotion. Sam was the only one they couldn't touch, because, with the Light filling him from inside out, they had to pass through the shards of too many other minds.

Even his closest allies, however, could be affected. Like Adam. 'Adam!' he yelled, knowing all the while that it was futile to try and reason.

One of the frost-encrusted Firedancers had crawled to the window, blood soaking through his clothes. Sam watched as the Firedancer bodily tossed himself out of the window and fell. Falls wouldn't kill a Firedancer either. Not nearly as effectively as the kind of magic Sam could muster. Another Firedancer had made for the door and was trying to drag himself downstairs. The third . . .

The third . . .

Sam pitched himself on to the floor. Which was lucky, as it meant the Firedancer's blade sliced the air instead of his throat. A knife of dragon-bone, one of the few weapons guaranteed to kill a Waywalker like Sam. He put his back against a wall and raised his hands as Adam brought the stool swinging at his face. The air rippled, catching the stool where Adam held it, suspended motionless. With a wrench Sam pulled it from Adam's grip and tossed it across the room.

The third Firedancer gave a screech like nothing human, nor even immortal, and dived for Sam's throat, hands blazing fire. Sam kicked out, striking the Firedancer in the chest. Heat crawled along his shins, and his feet slid on impact with the floor, the soles of his shoes rapidly melting. He pushed the Firedancer back, who staggered and fell on to the now roaring bed. There was a scream, barely audible over the noise of the fire and the humming of the Pandora spirit.

Adam grinned as he advanced towards him. 'Adam!' Sam yelled, coughing through the smoke. 'Don't be stupid!'

Adam drew his hands back, fingernails lengthening into claws. Sam acted on instinct, twisting his hands round each other in a tight, rapid circle. Adam's feet were pulled off the floor and up, even as his body seemed to be knocked to one side by an unseen force. For a second he spun on empty air, then crashed down hard against the opposite wall, by the shattered windows.

Sam got to his feet and held out his hands. On the blazing bed the bags he'd packed, themselves already smoking, leapt up and flew into his grasp. He trod out the few small licks of flame that threatened to consume them and tossed the bags out of the door. Then he clambered over to Adam, tears streaming down his face, holding his jacket across his nose and mouth. He felt for Adam's pulse, sensed its weakness. By now the fire on the bed had spread to the curtains. Sam seized Adam by the ankles and dragged him out of the room and down the stairs, thankful that at least his friend had resumed a fully human form. Kicking open the front door, he pulled the little spirit out into the street.

A small crowd of mortals had already gathered,

gawping in what struck Sam as an exceptionally unhelpful manner at the fire now clawing its way out of the shattered windows.

When they saw him, covered in soot and looking battered, the silence rang. Of course, thought Sam. A Pandora spirit could affect far more than one person at a time. But the more people it affected, the thinner its powers would stretch. Perhaps, if he hurried . . .

He grabbed his bags and was halfway down the street before someone behind him yelled, 'Fucker!' By then he was unstoppable. Let the world rise up against him at the spirits' command. He was used to being alone. Let them take his allies, let them turn even mortals against him. He was the bastard Son of Time. His entire life had been spent in preparation for this.

Sam no longer felt care. He worked best when alone. And now, he knew, there was serious work to be done.

TWO

Soho Square

He carried two bags – one a large leather satchel containing almost everything he owned in the world, including money, a few hastily purchased clothes, a crown that was nothing more than a band of plain silver, a phone card, and a slightly spongy chocolate bar that had been there for longer than was healthy. The other was a plastic hockey-stick bag of the kind that sporty types carry to demonstrate to the world that they're professionals. Sam had neither played hockey for several decades, nor did he carry a stick. In the bag was a short, very light silver sword that hadn't tarnished in the thousands of years he'd owned it; and somewhere in the recesses of his left sleeve he also enjoyed the ownership of his thin silver dagger. Though neither of these items was particularly flashy, they had the power to kill other Waywalkers, the Children of Time, where ordinary weapons of iron and steel might fail.

He had, to date, never killed one of his siblings. Which was remarkable, because they'd tried to kill him on numerous occasions and he'd even returned the favour a couple of times. But neither side in the endless Heaven v. Sam conflict had scored any major points. Until now.

Now the battle wasn't about the fact that he was the only bastard Son of Time ever to be acknowledged with a sword and crown. He had been caught up in this conflict because within him he had the power not only to destroy Cronus, but any Incarnate in the universe, even Time himself. It gave the battle an almost impersonal feeling, as though being Bearer of Light was only a title: a ball in a pinball machine, bouncing around dangerously, but still just something for scoring points.

So he was determined to show *Them*. *Them* with a capital letter, *They* who thought he'd die to destroy Cronus, or that he hadn't the guts to fight, or that he'd fight and die and lose anyway. Above all, he'd show Time. No matter what it took, he'd fight back.

It seemed, therefore, an anticlimax to start the fight with a trip to the local chemist.

He bought some tubes of toothpaste, in two different colours, which was important. He also bought a bottle of surgical spirit, a large box of talcum powder, and a small plastic-framed mirror. From the newsagent next door he bought several cans of Coke, some bottles of beer with screw tops, a ball of string, a bottle of the cheapest whisky he could find, a pad of paper, a biro and a packet of J-cloths.

He walked to Kensington Gardens and sat by the lake

under a plane tree. Children were playing football, people were feeding the geese. They were really trying to feed the swans, but the geese were that bit faster. Above the red dome of the Albert Hall the sky was blue with the occasional white, fluffy cloud. Young lovers dawdled along the paths between Marble Arch and Queensway, and a pair of schoolgirls picnicked on damp sandwiches and too much chocolate while gossiping in conspiratorial voices. Sam laid out his booty and set to work with a calm, careful air. The Coke cans he carefully shook, before writing ignition wards on their thin metal sides with a finger trailing red sparks. At a thought, the already pressurised can would get red hot. He then placed one of the Coke cans inside the box of talcum powder.

Sam opened the whisky bottle, on the inside of which he traced another ignition ward, this time leaving the end of the ward untied. Concentrating hard, to keep the ward from firing spontaneously, he picked up the ball of string and wrapped the end of the ward round the end of the string. He was careful to keep the string in contact with the bottle, and thus not damage the ward as he tied it round the mouth of the bottle and screwed the lid back on. He then wrote 'Do not touch, signed Lucifer' on a piece of paper and tied that down to the bottle with the same piece of string. The bottles of beer he emptied on to the grass and replaced the tops.

His miniature magical arsenal prepared, he walked towards Marble Arch. Beyond Hyde Park, and several streets of expensive hotels, he found a petrol station and went over to a pump. He didn't bother with a properly thick illusion but simply stood at the pump, unconcernedly pouring petrol into the beer bottles and soaking the J-cloths as well. People passed him by without a glance. When anyone did look his way, all they saw was a man standing by a pump: Sam was very careful to make sure of that. Sure, the nearby CCTV cameras wouldn't be deceived by the tiny tendrils of thought he was manipulating; but they were the least of his worries. Screwing the lid back on the last bottle, he walked away stinking of petrol and feeling satisfied. He'd studied arson at the feet of masters. And just because he usually found magical means more efficient, it didn't mean he hadn't listened.

Sam made his way beyond Bond Street and its grand antique shops, and crossed Regent Street into the byways of Soho with their bizarre mixture of Georgian architecture, clubs, offices and prostitutes. It was beginning to get dark, which was good; he liked darkness, especially when forced to call attention to himself.

The streets grew narrower. Some were heaving with young fashionables in black, others were all but deserted. On one a lady clad in leather asked him if he wanted to come inside – 'Looking for business, love?' – on another a drunk in a soiled anorak told him he was the devil in disguise, and an inferior one at that.

Reaching Soho Square he looked at his watch, which he kept perpetually on GMT no matter what plane he was on. Ten to nine. A good time, neither busy with office workers struggling to commute home nor with clubbers thronging back out on the streets. The gates to the square were locked, so he dropped his bags on the other side and climbed over the railings. He'd chosen this place, a small haven of green in a maze of shops and office blocks, for the particular reason that it was where two Ways, of Heaven and Hell alike, formed Portals that opened on to Earth.

Sam went over to an area of grass beneath a flowering cherry tree, its pink blooms unappreciated in the dark by all but the most sensitive of beings. There he collected four sticks and stuck them into the ground at intervals around him. Having positioned the whisky bottle behind his back and towards the Hell Portal, he trailed its string towards the sticks, winding it round each one a little above the ground. He then placed the box of talcum powder in front of him and towards the Heaven Portal, careful to judge the range of any potential explosion. To be doubly sure of his weaponry, he also lined up five of the Molotov cocktails of petrol and foul-smelling rag within reach along with seven of the Coke cans.

He then took out the tubes of toothpaste. These were in two colours, unattractive red and sickening green, and smelt so disgusting they had to be good for you. He drew a long green circle of toothpaste around him, tying it off at the end in a traditional ward pattern. Wards were always stronger when they had an artificial line to follow, but it was up to the practitioner to decide which materi-al to use to write the line. Sam had long ago discovered that chalk was too insubstantial and easily washed away, ink just seeped into the earth, and trying to draw your line with a stick usually resulted in a lot of turned up mud and no real indentation that could serve as a path for magic. He'd switched to less likely warding materials, finally hitting on toothpaste as a suitable catalyst for magic. The red toothpaste he squeezed out in blobs at strategic points around the green circle, and filled them with magic – not much, just enough so that if, say, someone trod on it, Sam would immediately know in time to react. The green toothpaste he infused with an altogether more active form of magic, a warding dome of his power to protect against outside attack.

The toothpaste began to glow a pale, pale white. With luck, any attackers should see the toothpaste as his only defence, and notice neither his warning system nor the explosives he'd left lying around. The whisky bottle he expected to go off with an impressive bang, which was why he'd positioned it behind him. If anyone did decide to attack him, they'd want to sneak up behind. And if in the darkness they failed to notice the piece of trailing string – well, that was their mistake, wasn't it? Alternatively, if their eyes were keen enough to see the whisky bottle and its note warning them from touching the string, chances were they'd do exactly what they were told not to, and the effect would be much the same. Never say he left anything to chance.

Sam drew out the mirror. It was pretty tacky and might as well have worn a badge saying 'Does the red lipstick really go with the green eye liner?', but it would serve. He settled cross-legged inside the circle, sword half out of the hockey case, and released a slow sigh.

Scrying, his mother had once said, long ago in Heaven, was a loud business.

'Loud?' he'd responded.

The Incarnation of Magic had nodded sagely at her son. Though never an acknowledged Queen of Heaven and therefore not a legitimate wife of Time, his mother was a Greater Power. Magic had been rejected because she could make the impossible come to pass, and Time didn't like that. Time looked at billions and billions of futures and could see which future was most likely to happen, how many repercussions of one event would lead to the same outcome – the one to which he'd then try to guide the universe.

Magic never wore one particular face when walking in a mortal form; that day she'd looked stern but kind. A teacher, helping her child to survive.

'Some spells are quiet. Lighting a candle, touching minds, calling to the animals, whispering to the winds, listening to the land – these things are quiet. But to send your mind out into the world and actively seek answers, this is a loud process. It draws attention. And if that attention doesn't want those answers found, it will send people to stop you.

'A scry will give you the position of your enemies. But it will also give them your own position, because the power necessary to sustain it properly will blaze out. And all the worse if they are watching for you. Sometimes you can pass unnoticed, for example if you are scrying for something that cannot scry back, or for something that does not watch for magic. But if you are scrying another magical being, it will most likely turn on you and hunt you down, and whilst in the scry you will be powerless to prevent it.'

'So what can I do?'

'You can use your common sense, and assume the worst. Assume you are hunted. And prepare for it in advance. Trap the hunters.'

Waiting, Sam let his mind drift. He heard his father's voice. *You cannot defy me, Lucifer* ... But it faded and passed, without him responding.

He had no desire to call on Time.

He heard Freya's voice, but it was nothing more than a memory as his mind tried to focus. *Sebastian, I'm so sorry.* They'd loved each other only briefly, before she'd been called away by duty to defend her failing House of Valhalla. Even to the last she'd called him Sebastian, the name he'd worn when they'd first met. It was as if it embarrassed her to admit a love for the exiled, traitor Prince of Heaven. Though all he'd done was stop the Eden Initiative, a project that to his mind had been evil.

Sebastian, what do you do now?

Sorry, Freya. You're dead, you see; I can't stop to chat. You died trying to prevent Seth freeing Cronus. I'd love to speak to you, but I need to find answers.

He was ready. But what should he focus on? It would be pointless to try and find Seth; as the guiding force behind the scheme to free Cronus, Seth would almost certainly be defended against every kind of scry. And trying to find Jehovah would run him up against a prodigiously tough mind. Odin he also ruled out, for though the Lord of Valhalla was to Sam's mind a less powerful figure, who'd only allied himself with Seth and Jehovah out of desperation, he was nonetheless a Son of Time.

There were others he could look for, though. He sent his mind out, carrying the thought of Buddha, who with the archangel Gabriel had been one of Freya's secret allies against Seth. What had become of them both, after an attack by the Pandora spirits that only Sam had been able to resist?

For a brief moment his brother's face appeared on the mirror – then the image flickered and died. Sam searched again, felt Buddha's mind.

Cold, dark, pain. Voices, in the shadows of the prison that has been a home for days on end. Whispering in Buddha's ear. *You tried to do the right thing, but you did it for all the wrong reasons, brother mine. You came close to spoiling everything, you don't understand what is happening. Cronus will be freed. The Bearer of Light will fight his destiny, but it is all for nothing, he will die . . .*

Buddha's mind stirring at the sensation of Sam. <Who's there? Who seeks me? . . . Sam? – Time have mercy, Sam, it's not what it—>

Interception. Another mind ramming between them. Dizziness, falling, a second presence shutting Buddha out, a voice roaring in Sam's mind. <The exile has come! Find him!>

Minds tearing at him, trying to attack him through his own spell.

Sam pulled away, spinning wildly out of control. He felt them reach after him, try to drag him back, but he was already gone, dancing far away, leaping out of their reach. When the world steadied, his own face was drifting in the mirror, a thousand images of himself mournfully looking back at him.

Steady. Focus. Breathe. Reach again, a different direction now. Buddha is a prisoner, beyond you. Reach. Try Freya's other ally: Gabriel – Gail.

Cold outside, warm within. Bright light. A full stomach. Heavy hands, a steady gaze. Voices, always voices. *Whom do you serve? I serve you. I have always served you, master. Will the Bearer of Light come? Yes, he will come. He cannot help it, he seeks you even now.*

Mind, stirring. <Sam?>

<Gail, I'm here . . .>

<Where are you?>
<Earth.>
<You're in danger.>
<I know.>
<People seek you.>
<I know that too.>
<Some would help you.>
<Who?>

Intercession, a mind breaking through, always a mind breaking through, interrupting the scry. It won't stop hunting, not now that it knows he is scrying.

<Brother mine!> it declares.

Sam recognises it. Jehovah, Son of Time and Belief, has a very distinct mind, precise, ticking over like clockwork. Sam has always suspected that Jehovah's blood-line has done more for him than others appreciate, because Jehovah believes in himself almost as much as he demands everyone else believe.

Jehovah has sensed his scry and even now seeks him.

<You cannot escape your destiny, Sam, don't even bother to try. Sooner or later you will die . . .>

<You bastard!> yells Sam, hardly aware of what he says or does. The mirror is turning red, fire sweeps across its silver surface. <You murdered Freya, you murdered your own sister!>

<You fool! Seth, Odin or Thor are bound to kill you. Yet before that happens, you still have a destiny to fulfil!>

<You bastard!> he screams again, and lashes out with his mind. He feels Jehovah recoil, shocked. Then his brother strikes out again. A blow rings across Sam's shields and makes the wards around him flare up in alarm. Sam's mind recoils and flees. He doesn't want to exhaust himself in a drawn-out battle that can benefit him nothing.

Drifting. Steadying. Waiting. Breathing. No sense of being followed. Voices. Another mind slipping towards his own, also drawn to the sense of his scry. But this isn't Jehovah, nor is it Seth or Odin. Sam doesn't recognise it, nor for a long while does it speak. But he can feel it play across his mind, tapping against his shields. Not forcefully, but with a child's curiosity.

He sits on a park bench in Rome, in high summer, eating ice cream. Freya is staring at him, a faint strawberry moustache round her lips. She is frowning, trying to remember something she wants to say. He waits, only half aware that this isn't real, that it's just another vision turned up by the spell as the foreign mind works to communicate with him through all these thick, thick wardings.

'Hello, Sebastian,' says Freya finally. She is as beautiful as he remembers, the light catching her hair and making it glow, her delicate hands holding the ice cream as if it were made of glass, her eyes frowning expressively.

Unsettled already, Sam wishes the vision weren't this good. 'And whom do I have the honour of addressing, that intrudes on me in Freya's shape?' He takes another lick of ice cream. It tastes real, which is good.

'Why do you fight?'

'Because the alternative is the end of the universe.'

'You're a selfless man deep down, Sebastian. I know that you would gladly die for certain things. For me, you would die.'

'For Freya, perhaps, but she reached the end of life before I did,' Sam replies.

'You would die to save the lives of mortals, if they were threatened. So why do you fight, instead?'

'Are you asking,' says Sam, 'why don't I just let Cronus be freed, and sacrifice myself heroically to save the universe from his horrific powers?'

Freya, or whatever it is that occupies Freya's face, seems to consider this. 'Yes,' she/it says finally.

'It isn't necessary. There is no reason why Cronus should ever be freed. Time simply wants me to destroy him in the event that he does get out.'

'You're wrong. Cronus will always be freed, he'll always escape. There is no future where he doesn't. So if your death is inevitable, why not accept that fact now?'

'Would you?' asks Sam. 'Hell, why do I ask such a daft question? I don't even know who you are.'

'You searched for me, didn't you?'

'No.'

'But you did, Sebastian. Somewhere, you haven't given up hope yet. That's what makes you defiant. And you thought you could defy death, and find Freya. So you did. And I answered.'

'Freya is dead.'

'Yet still you searched. Thank you.'

'For what?'

'Trying. But it is for nothing, I'm afraid.'

'This conversation is pointless.'

'You don't listen.'

'I listen, I just don't believe it.'

Freya faded, taking the taste of ice cream with her. She went a bit at a time, first the bench, then the ice cream, then the legs, then Rome, and finally the rest of her vanished with a shrug, leaving just the voice hanging on the air. A whisper in the darkness of Sam's mind. *I'm so sorry, Sebastian . . .*

He steadied himself. The visions faded, leaving only the mirror. Once more he searched. He wasn't entirely sure what he was looking for now, but he let the spell drift, whispering his name, calling. It was less of a scry and more of a divining, a complicated, dangerous spell that had a mind of its own.

But a divining was no less loud than a scry. *Sam is searching today, who wants to answer?*

And there it was. A voice. Confident, strong.

'And if he gets in the way?'

'Stop him. But don't let him die. He mustn't die, that's essential. Nor must he be allowed to interfere.'

'I serve.'

Brief flashes of vision. A room, a table, a chair, a figure in the darkness, a window, a dome, a river, a bridge, a boat, a golden cross, a red bus.

Recognition. Voices, more urgent. 'I feel . . . something . . .'

'He scrys, the fool scrys!'

Repulsion, minds slamming in front of him, shoving him away from his quarry. Spinning again, struggling to centre himself as visions flash across his eyes, glimpses of a dome, a golden cross on top of it, a red bus passing the nave, a pigeon sitting on a cherubim over the transept, a long, white footbridge like a suspension bridge, only the joins have been knocked out to each side as if something heavy had fallen on them, rather than standing proud, the River Thames . . .

The sudden sense of danger, and voices filling his head. *Sam, why do you run? Sebastian, Sebastian, what are you trying to do? Luke, is it really worth it? Little light, little fire, little Lucifer, little Satan, danger comes . . .*

His eyes opened with a start and stared at the darkness of Soho Square. The mirror in his hands was hot to the touch, but he didn't move. Someone had trodden on a dollop of red toothpaste and thought it was bird poo. He extended his senses. Behind him and slightly to the right; they'd probably come through the Hell Portal. Maybe six of them, he wasn't sure. He kept utterly still, the pressure of the dagger against his forearm suddenly noticeable.

Voices, whispering. Someone stepped forward, trod on more toothpaste and fired alarms inside Sam's mind, then swore very quietly. Sam, keeping his movements shielded with his back to them, lowered the mirror and reached very slowly for his sword.

Someone touched the string. Jerked it. The end of string tied with the ignition ward moved very slightly, pulled from its place on the bottle. The ignition ward, its delicate matrix disturbed, fired. Sam pitched forward and rolled, coming up with his sword raised as the whisky bottle exploded, showering glass everywhere. In the sudden light he saw four Firedancers and two valkyries, Odin's personal guards. No angels, he noticed with interest; Jehovah clearly hadn't been able to send anyone to join the hunting party.

As the flames subsided, he called the talcum powder to him, then threw it towards the valkyries, triggering the ignition ward in mid-air. The box exploded in a blizzard of metal and plastic shards, throwing white powder and red-hot Coke into the valkyries' eyes. They fell back, yelling. Then the Firedancers, having recovered from the initial shock of the attack, lunged towards Sam. They reached his toothpaste circle, and sparks flashed as the wards fired, repulsing them.

Sam grinned and picked up a Molotov cocktail in his free hand, holding it near the top of the bottle where the J-cloth stuck out, soaked in petrol. Firedancers, for all they were well-trained assassins in Heaven, simply didn't have experience of Earth methods of fighting. Sam watched unmoving as a Firedancer stepped forwards and drove his dragon-bone knife into the ward. It flickered and began to die. Sam waited until the ward failed and flicked a spark from his fingertips to the top of the J-cloth. It lit, the flame rushing down the blue cloth towards the petrol within. The Firedancers were staring at the bottle as if Sam were mad, wondering what it was. The valkyries, having a better sense of survival, began to back away. Sam shrugged and threw the bottle overarm at the nearest Firedancer. It struck him and exploded. The darkness was lit up as the Firedancer's red clothes erupted into flame and he screamed.

Firedancers aren't sympathetic creatures. As one of their comrades staggered around howling and burning before collapsing in a smouldering heap on the ground, the others stood staring at Sam, as if nothing had happened. The valkyries, eyes red and streaming, edged towards the circle. Sam backed away, calling a Coke can to his hands. As one, the valkyries and Firedancers attacked.

Nothing, in Sam's opinion, was quite as scary as being attacked by ten pairs of hands and ten pairs of legs, when you only had a healthy two of each. He threw the Coke can, turned and ran, blowing the ignition ward as he sprinted away across Soho Square as fast as he could. Behind him he heard a satisfying bang and a yell. Someone had clearly been on the wrong end of several jagged shards of metal.

Sam kept on running, sword in hand. He reached the far end of the square and turned, already in the full throes of casting a spell. Around him, the air ignited in blue fire, ice formed on the grass below his feet, his breath emerged in clouds of steam. The Firedancers faltered and stopped. Keeping the coldfire burning, Sam drew his silver dagger and threw it. It wasn't designed for throwing, but there was enough of his magic in it to ensure that it travelled as level as the course of a bullet. It struck a Firedancer square through the heart, and the assassin crumpled.

A valkyrie was drawing something out from behind her back. Sam saw a small, light crossbow, the shot tipped with enchanted silver. He swore and swept his hand up and across. The valkyrie was lifted off her feet and went flying back, but the disruption in his concentration was enough to make the coldfire curtain flicker. A Firedancer made it through and Sam was forced to parry clumsily, staggering as he went off-balance. The Firedancer took advantage of this and caught Sam's wrist in his own red-gloved hand, fire flaring round the fingers. Sam's sleeve began to burn, and he hastily stamped down on the flames with his mind.

But that second of lost concentration had almost cost him his right arm; he had to bring his sword across and round, leaving his left side exposed. The coldfire winked out as he tried to sustain too much magic.

The Firedancers leapt forward for the kill. Sam

retreated until his back was pressed against the railings of the square, and summoned a shield of thick blue magic around him. Two dragon-bone blades and two of enchanted bronze struck into the magic, then continued moving towards him with agonising slowness, the shield screaming as the weapons sought to tear through its magic lattice.

Sam heard a faint 'thunk'. He saw a valkyrie collapse, a crossbow bolt in her back. Her partner turned to discover who'd fired. In the darkness Sam made out a hooded figure, calmly reloading as if he hadn't a care in the world. The valkyrie gave a snarl of rage and ran towards the man. She'd got within two paces when he fired again and she pitched back, the quarrel straight through her heart.

The Firedancers, aware that something had gone wrong, disengaged, suddenly uncertain. Sam let his shield go, blinking sweat from his eyes and trying to ignore the wobble in his legs. The hooded man continued to reload, casual to the extreme. With the Firedancers' attention distracted, Sam lunged, his sword going under the nearest assassin's guard and scoring a long slash across his side. The assailants faltered, realising that they were two fighting two instead of six against one. But with Sam as their target they were determined to finish the job.

Sam caught one blade on the hilt of his sword and grabbed the other Firedancer's wrist, twisting both to one side. He summoned his dagger back to him and caught it in his left hand, releasing the Firedancers with a spin that sent them staggering. Now he had two weapons to his name and only four arms to deal with. He grinned as the Firedancers staggered upright and attacked them, making long thrusts with his sword and swift movements with the dagger, keeping it close to his body against the danger of overreaching with the sword.

He heard another thunk, and a Firedancer fell. Sam stepped past the body and went into a full-out attack, his confidence almost restored. The hooded man made no attempt to reload the crossbow, but stood in the shadows as if at some spectator sport. Almost, thought Sam, as though letting him fight on to see if there were any weaknesses in his technique.

A thrust with the sword, barely parried by the dragon-bone. Twist the sword to the right to take the knife with it, leaving the Firedancer's left side exposed. Lunge with the dagger. Wrist caught, no problem, pull down, dragging the Firedancer down too, and as he descends bring a knee up to meet him. The grasp on Sam's wrist weakened. Sam turned to one side, snapping his elbow up to catch the Firedancer full on the nose. The Firedancer fell back and Sam's wrist was free. He stepped forward neatly, a relaxed movement, and rammed the dagger straight into the Firedancer's heart.

The Firedancer fell.

Sam, a weary figure coated in sweat, head reeling from the shock of too many spells too fast, turned to his unexpected rescuer and stared at him. The hooded man stared back.

'Erm . . . thanks.' The man said nothing. 'You've got good timing. But I guess it wasn't a coincidence, right?'

Still the man gave no answer. Sam tried switching languages, to Elysian. 'You don't speak English?'

No response. He tried various Hell dialects, switched

to Arcadian, French, Spanish, German, Russian, Chinese, and got no response to any one. Finally he returned to English. 'Look, I'm really grateful for the impromptu rescue, but do you mind telling me who you are? And what your part is in all this? Please?'

There was a long, long silence. 'I'm . . . here to protect you. From Seth, from Odin. I've been sent.' The voice was deep, slightly accented, but with what Sam wasn't sure. Elysian, after all? An Earth dialect, maybe Gaelic? 'And boy, you look like you need it.'

Sam bridled, but kept his sharp words to himself. 'That's kind of you. But why? And who sent you? Not that I'm ungrateful,' he added hastily.

'I've been sent to protect you also from yourself.'

Sam didn't like the sound of that. 'Uh,' he finally grunted. 'What exactly am I going to do that's so dangerous?'

'You seek to fight Seth? To get to Cronus ahead of him?'

'Perhaps,' Sam admitted, 'but I hardly see why it's your concern.'

'The path you take is dangerous. There are those who would force you to abandon it, for your own sake.'

'And then there'll be no one to stop Seth, and Cronus gets freed and we all get fried, right?' said Sam. 'Excuse me if I don't find this particularly appealing.'

The figure shrugged. 'I will keep you safe, no matter what. Even if you don't want me to.'

'If you won't tell me who sent you, at least give me your name.'

'I will not say.'

'Give me a clue, otherwise it's gonna be Tinkerbell.'

The figure hesitated. He clearly hadn't expected Sam to be so forthright. 'Tinkerbell?' he echoed with a twist to his voice.

'Uhuh,' said Sam. 'I'm sure someone of your obvious standing wouldn't want that for the rest of his days.'

'I have been called worse things,' said the man, turning to go.

Sam ran after him, caught his shoulder. 'Hey, wait!'

The man moved so fast, Sam hardly saw it. One second looking the other way, the next eye-to-eye, his hand locked around Sam's wrist like a bear's jaws around an otter. He twisted Sam's hand behind his back so fast and hard that tears sprang to Sam's eyes.

'Don't be difficult, Lucifer. Only, I have a short temper.'

'No problem, Tinkerbell,' Sam gasped. After a horribly long time the pressure was released, and he sagged forwards. Something hard hit him in the stomach, and he collapsed on the grass with bile burning his throat. When he looked up, Tinkerbell was loping away across the square. Sam didn't bother to follow. He lay on the scorched ground and tried very hard indeed to breathe without being sick.

Very slowly, his head stopped spinning and he felt strong enough to replay the events of the evening in a rational way. What alarmed him was that Tinkerbell had been sent by Someone to protect Sam. A Someone with a scheme of his own.

Voices rose in his memory, fresh from the scry.

And if he gets in the way?

Stop him. But don't let him die. He mustn't die, that is essential. Nor must he be allowed to interfere.

I serve.

A dome with a cross on it; the Millennium Bridge, a silver blade crossing a river, the Thames. He'd seen through a window that commanded a view past the City of London Boys' School, over the bridge and up to St Paul's Cathedral.

Hurting all over, Sam pulled himself to his feet. Somewhere in SE1 he'd find an answer. And he never liked to keep these things waiting.

THREE

Picture Perfect

At six-thirty the next morning Sam Linnfer stood with his arms hanging over a railing beside the Thames and watched the waters sluggishly flow by. He liked tidal rivers where they ran through big cities. No matter in what century he'd been passing through London, the river had been a constant that gave him a sense of contentment. He looked across to the north bank, on the other side of the Millennium Bridge, and tried to match it up with what he'd seen in the scry. Then he moved a few paces to the east, but still it wasn't quite right. The buildings were all more or less where they should be, but he couldn't yet see enough of St Paul's Cathedral. He turned and looked behind him. Above a newsagent's shop was a large apartment block of red brick, whose well-tended balconies had angular shapes and sliding glass doors.

He found an alley that cut underneath the building to

a small, formal square. There was a stairwell, blocked off
by a large metal door. Sam looked at the intercom system
for a thoughtful while, then buzzed a number at random.

An old, quavery voice answered in tones of such aged
innocence that Sam almost apologised and walked away.
'Yes? Who is it?'

'Delivery for fifty-six A,' said Sam in his most formal
tone.

'Oh. Come up.' After a brief eternity, the door buzzed
and Sam pushed his way inside.

There were windows on the stairwell. He stopped on
each storey to peer out, checking what he saw against the
image of St Paul's gleaned from the scry. On the fourth
floor, the view was almost perfect. The first door on the
left was opened by a young woman. 'Yes?'

'Maintenance, ma'am. We've had complaints about the
balconies. It's probably nothing, but there has been
worry about rot.'

Breezing out on to the balcony, Sam made a brief
show of looking around, with more than half an eye on
the view. Still not quite right. Seeing the woman's look of
concern, he scrutinised every surface of the balcony like
an ant told to get that spider or else.

'Everything seems clear, ma'am, but otherwise do
please call . . .' And he was through the door before she'd
even thought of asking 'Call who?'

Next door his knock went unanswered. Glancing
round, he pressed his ear to the door. No sounds came
from inside, so he risked sliding his mind through the
door, gently reaching out for the slightest sign of life. He
felt no one. His mind touched on the lock and he gave it
a mental shove. It clicked, the door opened. He stepped

in, closing the door, and found himself in a flat completely empty apart from a bed, table, and chair – and more photos than he'd ever seen in one place. Overlapping on the walls; standing in piles.

Every picture was of him.

They spanned his entire life from the invention of the camera onwards; most in black and white, many in colour. Here he was with his half-brother Merlin; there he was with the King of Avalon; there again, somewhere in this city, it must have been the 1880s, sharing a pint with . . . He began to rummage through them, still not quite able to believe his eyes.

Gradually it became clear that, whoever had assembled this account of his life, they'd been both thorough and disorganised. On pieces of paper scattered like so much debris he found a record of everything. Addresses where he had a safe house in cities around the world, account numbers, languages spoken, contacts, what weapons he owned, what weapons he was good with, where he kept his dagger, his favourite spells, his favourite warding patterns, his weaknesses with certain weapons, whether he favoured his right or left hand for the cross-draw, a list of his hobbies including juggling, painting, singing badly and card tricks. His favourite books, his favourite films, the films he'd walked out of, his favourite music. Nothing had been left out.

At the bottom of one pile of papers, he found a half-finished letter.

Dear Ma'am and Sir,
Progress Report, 2nd April.
    As you may be aware, last night he attempted to

scry out answers. Fortunately I detected the scry and was therefore able to focus on him, thus re-establishing contact after the unfortunate period of lapse.

By this means I observed an encounter between him and six assassins sent, I believe, by Odin on behalf of Seth. Despite some impressive security measures on his part, I was forced to intervene; however, he failed to discern anything of significance about me. I believe he remains ignorant of my purposes and your organisation and identities; meanwhile we can add to his file a knowledge of Molotov cocktails, and some explosive device that appears to involve Coke cans.

I planted the transmitter on him, and will resume contact tomorrow at seven a.m.

As regards future actions, so far he does not appear dangerous enough to bring in. He knows less than he thinks he does, and it does not yet appear that he has enough to go on with. I will—

And there it ended, as if the writer had just put down the pen and walked away. Sam folded the letter up and put it in his satchel, together with its envelope, already addressed.

The time was ten to seven. Somewhere about his person a transmitter must have been in place all night. It could only have been planted by Tinkerbell, who was already reporting on him to others. The kind of others who had *purposes* and *organisations* and *identities* and everything else that Sam had learned to dread.

If he was bugged, they could be watching him now. He looked around the room; then at length he began to pick up photos and documents in huge numbers, sweeping them into a shoddy pile on the balcony. When he'd got everything in a heap, he ignited it by throwing a small fireball. He watched it burn, making sure everything was destroyed, and rejoicing as the ashes drifted upwards. Then he turned to go.

Just as he reached the door, it began to open. He slammed his back against it, pushing it shut in the face of whoever was on the other side.

A pause. Then a voice he recognised said, 'Where will you go?'

'You tell me, Tinkerbell! You seem to know everything else!'

Silence. Then someone rammed up against the door with the force of a charging ox and Sam felt the wood shake under his shoulders. Silence.

'I'm coming through!'

'Sure, why not?'

An axe buried itself in the wood, protruding about an inch from his head.

'Bloody hell!' Sam leaped back from the door. He drew the chain across it, for what little good it would do, and ran for the balcony, stepping round the ashes of the photos.

The door resounded again under the impact of the axe and the voice yelled, 'How did you find me so fast?'

'Scryed, Tinkerbell, I scryed!' he yelled back, stepping up on to the edge of the balcony and standing there wobbling. It was a long way down, but below him he could see another balcony, just begging for attention. Very carefully he squatted down until his hands grasped the parapet so that he could walk himself down the outside of the balcony. In the flat there was a splintering sound and the hurried approach of footsteps.

He let his feet drop, and dangled for a few precarious seconds. Tinkerbell's face appeared over the balcony, and by daylight Sam saw that really he hadn't given him the best possible name. The man was black, with a square face whose kindly expression was completely contradicted by a steely glint in the eye. The smile said, 'Trust me, I'm your favourite uncle'; the dark eyes said, 'And I can kill nephews, grandchildren and great grandchildren alike'. His hair was all but nonexistent, and his huge, ham-sized hands leant on the edge of the balcony with the kind of nonchalant vastness that suggested here was someone who could strangle a bear before breakfast.

'Sebastian,' he said with a sigh, 'this really isn't appropriate behaviour for a Son of Time, is it?'

Why, of all my names, does he call me Sebastian?

'And,' he added, 'where exactly are you planning on going now?'

Sam opened his fingers.

He fell – but not nearly as far as he'd planned. One huge hand caught his wrist and dangled him there, satchel swinging from one shoulder, hockey bag from the other, legs flailing.

'You want me to let go?'

'Yes, please,' Sam managed to gasp. His arm felt as though it was about to pull loose from its socket.

'Did you have to burn the photos?'

'Yup.' He wanted to say, 'Did you have to bug me?'

But it might be an advantage, knowing something the other guy didn't realise he knew. He thought again about the envelope in his bag with its address. Would Tinkerbell think he'd burnt that?

'You must realise I only did it to protect you.'

'Flattered, I'm sure.'

To Sam's surprise, Tinkerbell was holding on to his right wrist with just one hand. Now he reached down with his other and began to haul Sam bodily up.

'Erm . . .' began Sam.

'Now, no complaints. It's too bad you've seen my face, but we'll have to live with that.'

'Erm . . .' he repeated, and called the dagger to his free hand from its sheath in his sleeve. As the handle flicked into Sam's hand, his sleeve tore on the end of the blade. Tinkerbell saw the movement, and instinctively recoiled as Sam reversed his grip on the dagger and brought it slashing towards the man's arm. At the last minute, Tinkerbell let go.

Sam fell, swinging his legs wildly and calling on magic as he went. His legs struck the edge of the balcony below with enough force to numb them, but he was ready. On impact he flung both his hands up, invisible extensions to his fingers grappling on to the balcony above as the nearest thing his magic could find. Tinkerbell paled as tendrils of magic lashed on to him like rope. Using him as counterweight to his own descent, Sam swung himself in over the side of the balcony below – and straight into a bush full of prickles. Of all the balconies in all the world, he'd fallen on to one whose owner liked roses. He picked himself up, and checked his bags to make sure they hadn't fallen open.

Above him, Tinkerbell was grinning, once more feeling master of the situation. 'Sebastian, what does this hope to achieve?'

Sam considered saying, 'Hell, it'll piss you off which is a good start', but decided the better course was feigning ignorance – in particular of Tinkerbell's 'organisation'.

'You working for just one man or a whole host of idiots?' he yelled.

'Sebastian, why are you so difficult? All I want is to see that the Bearer of Light is safe in these troubled times.'

'Your concern is appreciated, but I'm fine, thanks awfully.'

'You almost got whacked last night.'

'And as I said, I'm terribly grateful for your timely intervention. But this still raises the "why" question. Why are you doing this? And who for? Do they expect you to write reports about me, things like, "Sebastian went to the toilet, Sebastian brushed his teeth, Time have mercy it's serious"? Have you been watching me every day for the past week? Month? *Year*?' *No, you haven't, there was, in your words 'an unfortunate period of lapse', but you think I don't know that, do you? So I'm that much less of a threat.*

'Sebastian, come upstairs. Let's talk this through like reasonable people.'

'Curious thing, but I'm not feeling very reasonable, and I don't mind talking just here, just like this, with a big space between you and me.'

He heard a sound in the flat behind him and turned. Three men wearing black had burst through the front door and were heading towards him.

'You just don't get it, do you?' Tinkerbell called down, still grinning.

'Pal, it's been a pleasure,' said Sam, and stood up on the edge of the balcony and turned and ran.

He ran across empty air, but this wasn't as much of a problem as it could have been. With ordinary magic it was hard to make yourself fly. But you could usually get away with it if you took gravity by surprise. It was flying for more than a few seconds that bothered him. He landed on the next door balcony and looked back.

His three black-clad pursuers had burst out on to the balcony. He grinned, waved, and ran across empty air to the next balcony, then the next, then the next, all the time glancing over his shoulder. The men had gone, no doubt racing after him through an internal corridor. Tinkerbell was still leaning out of his balcony, sighing with frustration. 'Tiresome,' Sam heard him say.

Sam bowed at him, swung his legs off the edge of the balcony and worked his way down. He wrenched open the sliding glass door to the flat on the floor below and rushed inside. A man and a woman, lying in bed, began to scream at the sight of him. Sam yelled, 'Sorry, can't stop', and ran on through their flat. In the corridor beyond a startled old man in a dressing gown saw him, dropped his newspaper, and darted into his own flat as if he'd seen the Devil himself. Sam forestalled him by putting a foot in the doorway. 'Sorry about this.' Grabbing one frail wrist, he used the physical contact to plunge him into a trance. The man sagged.

Once inside the old man's flat, Sam slammed the front door shut behind them, threw his bags to the ground and began searching his clothes. Tinkerbell had to have put the transmitter somewhere there; he'd had no choice. In one of his jacket pockets, buried at the bottom, his fingers closed over a tiny, plastic object. It was a minute, circular circuit board, with two bits of wire trailing from it. He sighed, and wrapped the wires around each other where before they hadn't touched. Something in the circuit went 'beep' indignantly, and everything went quiet again.

Sam muttered an apology under his breath to the old man lying on the floor in his dressing gown, and scurried through the flat till he found a wardrobe. The clothes inside smelled of mothballs and not enough fresh air, but he took out a long coat nonetheless and pulled it on. Its pockets held a half-eaten packet of peppermints, an ancient bus ticket and a mouldy banana peel, all of which he threw on to the floor. In the kitchen he found a bin bag and slung his satchel and hockey stick bag into it. From a hook he grabbed an ancient hat that looked like something out of a 1930s thriller, rammed it on to his head, and, very carefully, opened the front door.

The corridor was empty. Sam started walking, taking pains not to move too fast. He reached the stairs. They were empty. He began slowly descending them, half tempted by an idiotic urge to whistle. There were voices above but he didn't stop. He heard running feet and kept on walking still. A man in black passed him in the opposite direction, glanced at him up and down and went on, taking the stairs two at a time.

A moment later however, the man stopped abruptly. Sam could feel his eyes on him, looking back. Then he heard someone speaking, as though to a radio. 'Possible suspect heading down . . .'

Sam went on down the stairs, slowly and carefully. He

heard footsteps behind him – saw figures ahead – but kept walking. He reached the bottom, put his hand on the door to the street, heard Tinkerbell's voice.

'Excuse me, sir?'

Didn't turn. Opened the door, ran through it, slammed it shut in Tinkerbell's face and grinned a slow, relaxed grin at the sound of shouting from inside. The door shuddered under the impact of various bodies, but no axe could get through metal this thick. Sam waited, back pressed against the door until he was sure the lock was in place, then smashed a hand burning with fire against the intercom system. There was a loud squeal from the circuit as it exploded, and a decisive thunk from the door itself. He turned and ran for all he was worth through the streets of Southwark, no longer following his mental map of London but reaching out instead for the sensation of a Hell Portal through which he could travel. It was hard, very hard, to follow someone through a Waywalk; you had to start out with a good idea of where they were going.

Sam turned a corner as a large white van swung the other way. He slowed, suddenly aware of how noticeable he must look on the streets of Southwark, running in old-fashioned clothes, carrying a bin bag. Walk. Deliberate, calm and, above all, innocent.

He could sense a Hell Portal nearby. Good. It was time to quit this world. He turned on to a road with heavy traffic and huge billboards advertising films that had gone out of circulation months ago. Somewhere on the railway line from Blackfriars, that was where the Portal must be. Portals were often in the most unlikely places, since humans tended to build around them unawares.

He came to a long parade of shops, ranging from the pretentious French restaurant to the traditional kettles-and-wellington-boots hardware store. Facing it was a long wooden fence, several of the struts displaced. He walked along it until he found a gap big enough and wormed through. Beyond were the many railway tracks that led to Blackfriars Bridge, a few abandoned trains sitting among tall buddleia bushes. He picked his way carefully across to a derelict engine shed.

Behind him, he heard a yell. Tinkerbell was at the gap in the fence, but could only get halfway through. Whereas Sam was narrower and more dexterous, the giant black man had got stuck. Sam grinned, waved and scampered towards the engine shed.

At the back of the shed, amid rusted metal debris and thickets of brambles and willow herb, he could sense the Hell Portal. He slowed, mentally calling it to him. The doorway opened, a Portal hanging on nothing, outlined in white fire. White mist poured through it and the temperature around it was distinctly cooler. Sam took a deep breath, then heard another shout.

'Sebastian!' Tinkerbell was there, slowing as he saw the open Portal. 'Let's talk . . .'

Sam shook his head. 'Uh-uh. You're gonna have to do better than that, Tinkerbell. See you around.'

'Wait!' Tinkerbell lunged forward. But Sam had already stepped back. Earth, complete with shunting yards, Tinkerbell and Southwark, was no more.

White mist. Faces in it, voices whispering, calling. Lucifer, Lucifer, come walk with us, Lucifer, come play with us, Lucifer . . .

It was cold in the Way of Hell, like it was cold in every

Way. It was also hard to breathe – you only ever had as much oxygen in the Ways as you took with you. Only the Children of Time could safely navigate the Ways between the worlds. Everyone else got lost. Which was why the Wayspirits, souls of those who'd tried to breach the gap between worlds and failed, dying in the attempt, haunted the Ways, trying to drag travellers between worlds down with them, calling, beckoning, wheedling. They hated life, particularly the kind of life that could succeed in a Waywalk where they had failed.

Sam stumbled through the Way, his destination clear in his head. The Way felt it, responded, linking Portal to Portal, guiding his path. The Wayspirits clutched at his ankles, the white mist was almost suffocatingly thick, his lungs burned from lack of air. A light ahead, silver, forming the shape of a doorway. He ran towards it, bursting from the Way in a shower of mist.

Beyond, it was even colder than it had been in the Way. Hell was divided into two uneven parts. The larger continent was in sunlight for ninety per cent of the year, while for the same period of time the smaller was in darkness. Between them was the huge expanse of the Whirlpool Ocean, the two continents being linked only at a few points by land bridges that, though small, had been the paths of many an invading army.

Sam's area of Hell, the part that he'd founded, shaped, guided, ruled and eventually been betrayed by, was the colder one where darkness reigned, bringing with it eternal cold. The principality that made up the other, hotter part had often sworn his destruction, and numerous times completely failed to bring it about.

He was standing on a snow-covered ridge in the

middle of nowhere, which was the kind of place he liked Portals to be. Here there was no one to remark, 'Hey, a guy's just appeared out of nowhere, how unusual.'

Sam stood there only long enough to get his breath back, however, before turning and facing the Portal again. It was an unfortunate part of Waywalking that you could never go from a Portal on Earth direct to a Portal on Earth. You always had to go from Earth to Hell or Earth to Heaven and then back the other way. The only good thing about this was that, from Hell or Heaven, you could go to whatever part of Earth you liked.

Sam threw off his hat and the old man's coat, fumbled in his bag with increasingly cold hands and drew out the envelope he'd found in Tinkerbell's flat.

It read, 'The Manager, Der Engelpalast, Berlin'.

Well, Berlin was easy enough to find, even if the Angel Palace was a slightly worrying name for someone who'd encountered angels at first hand. And he knew someone in Berlin who might just be able to help.

He turned back the way he'd come, slipping through the Portal, a darker figure in the darkness. It was a strange feeling, but now that he had a plan he was almost happy.

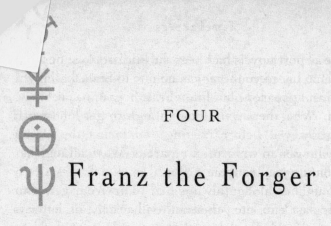

FOUR

Franz the Forger

In a small, dark street in a small, dark suburb of Berlin, in a small, dark house with a small, dark basement, sat a man called Franz. He was, in contrast to everything else around him, a surprisingly handsome man, except his face had long ago been distorted by anger and resentment against the world. His front door was little more than a sheet of corrugated iron, like the windows of his house, and when Sam knocked it made a dull 'clunk, clunk'.

Franz put one suspicious blue eye against the door, and saw Sam. 'Crap,' he muttered in German. 'Not you.'

'I'm pleased to see you too, Franz,' said Sam, breezing his way into the gloom of the house. Most of the furniture was overturned boxes, padded out with ravaged cushions that looked as though they'd been misused at some time by every creature from aardvark to zebra. The chair Sam sat down on was missing a leg, but a pile of trashy airport novels had been substituted to support it.

'Franz, I need your magic touch,' said Sam, tossing the letter and envelope at him. Franz read it, eyebrows raised. 'What do you want me to do with this?' he asked eventually.

'I want you to write me a new letter, in that hand.'

'What do you want me to say?'

'Something along the lines of "The Manager, Der Engelpalast etc., etc., the man delivering this letter is trustworthy. He has been employed to help track down Sebastian Teufel, tell him everything."'

'To help track down you?' asked Franz with a frown. 'Dare I ask?'

'Let's just say I'm going to bluff.'

Franz shrugged. 'I'll need paying.'

'I've no euros on me – I've just come straight through the Way of Hell.'

'You're a good customer. I'll take an IOU.'

'I'm not giving you a sample of my handwriting, Franz. I know you far too well.'

Franz grinned. 'Sebastian, how can you not trust me?'

'You'd be amazed. Shall we say two hundred euros to be paid in the near future?'

'Three hundred, Sebastian, three! You know you can afford it.'

'My account is being watched.'

'A pathetic excuse,' said Franz, waving a hand as though he could banish Sam's problems with a gesture. 'You can steal something.'

'Franz, not everyone is an anarchist. Just do it, okay? I'll pay soon.'

'All right, but only because you're a good customer.'
Franz sat down at a desk and switched on a very bright,
steady light. He peered over the letter. 'Does paper
matter?'

'I don't think so. Just try and get it as close as you
can.'

'It'll take time.'

'Do you have a street map?'

'Nah.'

'I'll be back in half an hour,' said Sam with a sigh.

He took the U-Bahn into the centre of town, where new
shining buildings were being thrown up as fast as could
be amid concrete apartment blocks, on which the tracery
of huge murals could still be seen, and oddments of
grand nineteenth-century architecture, much of it in
disarray. He walked down a broad avenue lined with
half-grown lime trees, past cafés and huge, ugly interna-
tional hotels that were the same in any country, past the
battered police station, past a chemist so new and bright
and clean it might have served as an even more hygienic
extension of the local hospital, and on to a small, anony-
mous building on the street corner. He pushed open the
door, which beeped with electronic boredom at the dull-
ness of its life.

Street maps covered the walls; so too maps of the sur-
rounding countryside and posters showing nearby places
of interest. Castles competed with new glass government
buildings in the heart of town, and pictures of carnivals
and traditional festivals. For some reason there was
even a picture of a white bunny with a bell around its
neck.

A young lady sat behind a desk, wearing the huge, patronising smile reserved for tourists. Sam matched her grin tooth for tooth. 'Er, hi,' he said in German, 'I need to find the Engelpalast, please.'

The girl's face fell at losing the chance to display her fluency in various languages. Sam was almost tempted to start stuttering in English.

'What is the Angel Palace, please?' she asked in German. 'A museum, a concert hall, a theatre . . .?'

'I was hoping you could help me find out. It has a manager, if that's any help.'

'Please wait.' Her smile was almost gone as the triviality of the task beckoned. She turned her attention to a computer screen, angled to be invisible to Sam's eyes. Probably she was playing solitaire on it. Sam waited while she tapped in her request.

'Der Engelpalast,' she said finally. 'It's a nightclub. Sixty-seven Engel Strasse.'

Beaming all over, he left the shop almost, but not quite, whistling.

'It's not exciting,' said Franz, handing over the newly forged letter. Indeed, he'd found it so uninteresting that he'd added an envelope, inscribed with the words 'by hand', just for something to do.

As Sam scanned the letter he said, 'Do you know where Engel Strasse is?'

'It's not far from here.'

Sam glanced up with doubt in his black eyes. 'This is the point where you acquire a sinister accent and go, "Ooooh, you don't want to go there, young sir, it isn't safe up in Engel Strasse."'

'Engel Strasse,' said Franz primly, 'is the new centre of the inner-city fashionable-yet-gritty business.'

'You mean where the rich and privileged go to convince themselves that they're down-to-earth and practical?'

'Essentially.'

'Anything else you might want to tell me?'

'Yes.'

'Will it make me happy?'

'No.'

Sam made an expansive gesture. 'Fire away.'

'Two days ago a man with red hair, a glare and a very large axe knocked on my door and asked if I'd seen you recently. I told him no. He said that if you did turn up I should phone him and he'd make it worth my while.'

'And what was your reaction to this?' Sam was suddenly tense, and conscious of his sword.

'I told him I'd consider what he said. But then he isn't established clientele, is he? Unlike you.'

'Did this mysterious stranger give a name?'

Franz watched Sam squirm, relishing the moment for all it was worth. 'Well,' he said coyly, 'if I didn't know better I'd say it was brother Thor.'

'But you know better?' said Sam hopefully.

'A figure of speech. It *was* Thor. He's looking for you.' Franz was really enjoying himself, and Sam couldn't resist saying as much.

Franz was unrepentant. 'I just get such a kick, watching the Children of Time go pale.'

'Only because you envy us,' declared Sam. 'Why did you wait before telling me about this?'

'I wasn't sure whether or not I wanted to sell you out.'

Sam sighed, and held out his hand. 'Franz, it's been a pleasure doing business with you, as always.'

'You still owe me three hundred.'

'I know, I know.' They shook hands. 'I'll deliver it as soon as things settle down.'

Departing, Sam grinned, waved, and felt slightly queasy. Of course, Franz might have thrown Thor's name into the conversation to try and scare him. But Sam was a good enough customer to merit Franz looking out for his survival. Therefore . . .

Is Thor trying to get his loutish hands on my hide? I really, really do hope not.

Engel Strasse was a long, wide road full of contradictions. What few houses survived had long ago been boarded up and sprayed with graffiti imploring the return of either fascists or communists. Grungy greengrocers competed for space with dark doors that led into who knew what basement, while cafés with pinball machines and snooker tables competed against newer, mass-market bars complete with dance floors and a stylised decor that was supposed to remind the drinker of summer and flowers. Between these were the dimly lit doorways of the night clubs. A bus stopped a few metres off and deposited an old lady, but other than that, the street was almost dead.

Der Engelpalast was just another entrance, if anything even darker than the rest, at the quieter end of the street. The door was open; from beyond it a purplish-blue light shone out. No one was about, so Sam went in.

There was a short corridor, barely illuminated, with pictures of famous people who'd never been to der

Engelpalast but had still felt the overwhelming urge to sign a picture to 'my good friends at the Angel Palace'. There was a small reception area, with no one manning it. Sam pushed open a double glass door and stepped into a large, square room whose low ceiling was strung with lights of every colour, most of them off. A long bar displayed more drinks, of more variety and maybe more toxicity, than Sam had ever seen. Behind it was a rather dumpy woman, wearing an apron and cleaning glasses.

There was a small bandstand, tucked away in the corner, and an empty stage. The floor was strewn with bits of paper – discarded telephone numbers, torn up beer mats, empty packets that could have contained any-thing from peanuts to ecstasy pills.

'We're shut.' A young man moved towards Sam with the determination of an avalanche. He wore a T-shirt and shorts and looked completely out of place.

'I'm looking for the manager.'

'He's out.'

'My name is Luke. I've come from London.' Sam pulled out his letter and showed the envelope, carefully inscribed in Tinkerbell's handwriting.

The young man frowned. 'Hunter sent you?'

Hunter? Tinkerbell's name is Hunter? Bloody hell . . . 'Yes.'

'This way, please.' Sam followed the man through a door he hadn't even noticed behind the bar, camouflaged by the paintwork. They went into a long, dark passage and up a flight of stairs to a plain, white, wooden door. The young man knocked.

'Uncle? A man from Hunter is here.'

The door opened almost immediately. Sam put on his brightest smile.

The manager was small, pudgy, and balding. He looked Sam up and down. 'From Hunter?'

Sam handed over the letter. The manager read it and shrugged. 'I suppose you'd better come in, then.'

Almost laughing with relief, Sam stepped inside the office. It was cramped and had no windows. On one side a large bank of screens was each linked to a camera to watch the club floor. A desk that dominated most of the room was strewn with papers and pens, and behind this the manager just about managed to squeeze himself, pressed between the desk and the wall like a fly.

He gestured for Sam to sit, but Sam said he preferred to stand. The chair he was supposed to sit on was already heaving with unopened mail, and there didn't seem anywhere else to put it.

'Fine. Where's Hunter's latest report?'

'I don't know.'

'Who are you?'

The manager certainly got to the point.

'Luke,' Sam said simply. 'Who are you?'

'Herr Hindsonn. What do you want from me? Why has Hunter sent you here?'

'I'm to assist Hunter with the matter of Sebastian Teufel.'

Herr Hindsonn's nod suggested that Sam had hit it right. Sam risked going on. 'I'm not sure who it is I'm working for, nor do I understand the situation we're currently in. I'm a bounty hunter, pure and simple. You want Sebastian Teufel protected, I can do it. You want Sebastian Teufel removed from the picture, I can do that too.

'But I work better when I understand what it is I'm

working for, why and what it is I'm up against. Hunter was going to explain, but Teufel scryed and Hunter was called away. He sent me to you instead for answers.'

'I wasn't informed that a bounty hunter had been employed.'

'I used to be of the order of Firedancers. One of the best.'

'Why did you leave the Firedancers?'

'I'd rather not say. Please tell me, Herr Hindsonn, why is Sebastian Teufel so dangerous?'

'He is a Son of Magic.'

'Yes, but even the Children of Magic have their weaknesses.'

'He is also the Bearer of Light.'

'This presents a problem?'

Herr Hindsonn shrugged 'Not for us.'

'Naturally. But that is another issue I wish to see cleared up. The Light, as I understand it, can destroy a Greater Power. How come you have nothing to fear from it?'

'Sebastian Teufel would have to engulf all life, in order to read us.'

'Why?'

Again, a shrug. Sam wondered whether he was going too fast.

'We are the Ashen'ia,' Herr Hindsonn said simply. 'Our souls, our minds, are bound in places he cannot touch with just a local discharge. And he is a coward. He dares not use a full discharge.'

'The Ashen'ia are protected from him?'

'Of course.'

'And wish to protect him from Seth?'

'Yes.'

'Yet the Ashen'ia's plans are such that, should he know too much, he becomes a threat, and must be dealt with.'

'That is why we employ you and Hunter.'

'At what point do you think he should be regarded as a threat?'

'Well, naturally if he discovers the Ashen'ia's aims, he will turn against us.'

'Why?'

Herr Hindsonn looked surprised by the question, then suspicious. 'You must have seen the files on Teufel.'

'The files are extensive. I'm still new to this job.'

'What are you being paid?'

'The contract is negotiable.'

'I don't like bounty hunters – they are mercenaries. They don't understand what it is that's being fought for.'

'Then enlighten me.'

Hindsonn grinned. 'Power, bounty hunter. We are fighting for power.'

'I understand power.'

'Not this kind of power. We are fighting for the power to make the Greater Powers bow before us.'

'And Sebastian Teufel is a part of this plan.' Sam made sure it didn't sound like a question. Statements, all the time statements. I'm just an innocent bounty hunter trying to get the facts clear in my head . . .

'Naturally. As Bearer of Light, he's essential to our plans.'

'May I ask – why let him roam, a loose cannon, potentially damaging to your plans? I mean, you yourself admit that he might turn against you. So why not just pull him in?'

'This is a balancing act, Luke. Sebastian Teufel is alone, he doesn't dare turn to anyone for fear of the Pandora spirits. We have to let him discover how alone he is, push him almost to destruction – then the master and mistress will approach him. When he's got nowhere left to run, when he's been shot, beaten, stabbed, chased and is terrified almost out of his wits, then they'll go to him. And they'll say, "Look, Sebastian, we are your friends." And he will join us of his own free will. With his help we can destroy Seth, Son of Night; his power will tip the balance.'

'You think he'll trust you?'

'He'll have no choice. He'll be in no position to resist the master and mistress. Not when he sees who they are.'

'You expect his reaction to them to be that extreme?'

'Of course. He'll understand that he's no longer alone, that it wasn't all for nothing.'

'Tell me. If a Pandora spirit appeared here, right now, what would you do?'

'Lock the door and wait for it to pass. What would you do?'

Sam was silent, mind racing. Finally he said, 'You know, I was talking with one who didn't know the identity of the master and mistress, and who wanted to find it out.'

This got a surprisingly strong reaction from Herr Hindsonn, who sat up straight in his chair, eyes aglow. 'What was this one's name?'

'Sam. Sam Newcastle. Is there a problem?'

'Ashen'ia do not ask the identities of the master and mistress! They merely accept that they are both Children of Heaven! To ask their identities is to risk destroying everything!'

Children of Heaven? There are Waywalkers in this organisation – the Ashen'ia? One of my brothers and one of my sisters . . . ? 'What's so dangerous about knowing?'

'If Seth found out . . .'

'If Seth found out their identities? This would be dangerous?' Sam leant forwards. '*You* don't even know their identities, do you? Who does? Who are the master and mistress?'

Herr Hindsonn was on his feet, surprise in his eyes. 'How dare you —?'

Sam's hand shot out, and caught Herr Hindsonn by the back of his collar. The silver dagger was instantly in his left hand. He pressed it against Hindsonn's flabby red neck and hissed, 'The Ashen'ia have a plan to use the Light for their own ends. What is it? And if your plan is so wonderful, why wait until Seth is on the verge of releasing Cronus? Who are the Waywalkers, your beloved master and mistress? *Who are they?*'

'I . . . don't know,' stuttered Hindsonn, composure failing him, his tears starting to flow like a baby's. 'I just deliver messages!'

'Who do you send Hunter's reports to, Hindsonn?'

Hindsonn closed his eyes. His lips shaped words. Sam half caught them. 'She who guards my soul, have pity on your servant, I call on thee—'

Sam shook him. 'Who do you pass your messages on to, Hindsonn? Who are the Ashen'ia?'

Hindsonn opened his eyes, and stared at him.

Sam had never seen such a look of inhumanity. The man's eyes had become covered with a translucent silver film, like a fish's, and seemed to glow from within.

Hindsonn grinned – a cruel, calculating grin – and

spoke in a voice that could have been playing through a very old speaker system, underwater. 'Little light and little fire seeks to play the bigger game?'

Sam hardly saw Hindsonn's hand, it moved so fast to lock around his wrist. He gave a yell of pain, dropping the knife and unable to resist as Hindsonn swivelled him backwards, with a strength surely far beyond his own species. He found himself slammed against the wall, his hand wrenched tightly behind his back, while that same cracked voice, that might have been many voices speaking in unison, whispered in his ear. 'The Ashen'ia serve me, Lucifer. And because you will soon serve me too, I will allow you to live.'

Sam kicked out. His foot hit something bony and bounced straight back off. But whatever it was that wore Hindsonn's shape was taken by surprise. For a second, the grip on his arm slackened. With agony screaming up his arm at the least movement, Sam kicked again.

Hindsonn staggered back, bumped against his desk and straightened, anger in his eyes. He lashed out with the flat of his hand, and Sam ducked to avoid the blow. The hand buried itself in the wall behind Sam, sending up a cloud of dust. 'Time above . . .' muttered Sam. Hindsonn leapt on to the desk in a single movement and gave a cry. It was loud, it was feral, it sounded like hyenas would if they were thirty foot tall and firing off machine guns. It made Sam's ears go pop, it made his skin crawl, his blood go icy, his stomach try to clamber up his throat, his throat try to crawl past his heart. It was, in short, the battle cry of a Son of War.

But Hindsonn wasn't a Son of War; he had about him no magical aura of any kind. He was about as human as they got. But something very warlike in persuasion had temporarily borrowed his body.

And whatever it was, it expected Sam to *serve* it?

Struggling not to faint from the sheer pressure of the noise in the room, Sam brought his hands up in front of his face, clenched his fingers tightly in front of his eyes and slammed the palms of his hands together. The noise died with an abrupt clicking sound as Hindsonn's jaws were forced back together by Sam's magic.

Hindsonn glowered at Sam, and leapt from the table with one leg thrust forwards, the other tucked under in a karate-style kick that would have made numerous Hong Kong film directors go wobbly with admiration. Instinctively Sam raised his hands, catching Hindsonn in mid-air with magic. Hindsonn hung there, an out-thrust foot an inch from Sam's face, a surprised expression on his own.

Sam grinned and pushed, sending Hindsonn flying back hard against a wall. He called his dagger back to his hand, and edged towards his sword in its hockey-stick case as Hindsonn staggered a few paces, looking dazed. Drawing his sword, he straightened, and slowly swung the blade a few times in the cramped space, driving Hindsonn back against the wall again.

'I don't know who you are,' Sam declared, 'but I really don't like you.'

'You fool,' muttered Hindsonn, reaching behind him. Sam saw the butt of the gun and was already there, slamming the pommel of his sword into Hindsonn's chin and lashing out at his gun hand with the dagger. Hindsonn seemed to expect this, however, and squirmed away at the last second, catching Sam a ringing blow across his shoulders as he did with the butt of the gun.

Sam staggered, slipped on a pile of papers, and sagged against the wall. He recovered his balance – and turned to see Hindsonn raising the gun, grinning. 'And to think that no one else will hear either.'

Sam squeezed his eyes shut, heard the click of the trigger, felt nothing, opened his eyes. Hindsonn was staring at the gun, with something like disgust.

Sam almost laughed. 'Always keep your weapons loaded,' he said cheerfully, advancing again, swinging the sword once more in easy arcs. 'Either that or have a trick up your sleeve.'

As Hindsonn backed off, he was reaching into his pocket.

Sam saw the gleam of a penknife. 'That?' he asked. 'You're going to spit a Son of Time with *that*?'

Hindsonn grinned, and shook his head.

Too late Sam saw him turn the knife towards himself, too late he thrust out his hand and tried to hold Hindsonn back with magic. The spell had only a partial effect. At the last moment Hindsonn's hand seemed to jerk and slow, the penknife already touching his ribs. Sam's hand, thrust out with magic at the fingertips, began to shake. Hindsonn was trying to force the penknife into himself with every incredible ounce of strength he had. Sam could feel the knife being pulled, millimetre by millimetre, further towards Hindsonn's heart – and could do nothing to stop it.

The door burst open.

The young man Sam had first met stared at the scene and yelled, 'Holy shit!'

Sam's concentration broke.

Hindsonn's hand completed its fatal journey, the penknife stabbing deep into his own flesh. Sam saw Hindsonn smile, heard the young man give another yell of dismay, saw Hindsonn crumple. He threw down his sword and leapt towards Hindsonn, to squat by his side.

The film was retreating from Hindsonn's eyes, leaving normal human features. As the eyes changed, so did the expression, from smug grin to terror.

'Time have mercy,' whispered Hindsonn hoarsely as the blood poured from his self-inflicted wound. 'The bitch killed me . . .'

'Who? Who killed you?'

Hindsonn looked up at Sam. His mouth opened and closed, he tried to speak. 'Come on,' yelled Sam. 'Who did this? Who – what – just possessed you, who killed you to stop you talking?'

Hindsonn raised a trembling hand, and pointed at something past Sam's head. Sam half turned, to stare at the picture on the wall. It showed a bright, sunny landscape, maybe in Italy, with a willow tree hanging over a river and a young lady in white standing alone looking wistful.

Sam turned back to Hindsonn. 'Tell me who did this!'

Hindsonn's head lolled. 'Jesus,' whispered the young man. 'Oh shit . . .'

'Get an ambulance!' yelled Sam, checking for a pulse, laying Hindsonn out flat. 'Get one now!'

'Shouldn't we take the knife out?'

'No, that'd let him bleed, get an ambulance!'

The young man ran. Blood was everywhere, soaking the papers, covering Sam's hands. Swearing, Sam tugged

his jacket off and wrapped it round the knife still sticking
into Hindsonn, pressing it down into the wound to
reduce the bleeding. 'Come on,' he muttered, 'you can
live, you know you can.'

Hindsonn didn't stir. Sam drew his bloody hands
back and looked deep within for his regenerative powers,
ready to give them to Hindsonn if it would save the
man's life. The nephew reappeared in the door along
with two other, large, men. 'Get him!' he shrieked, one
trembling finger thrust at Sam.

Sam sprang back as the men barrelled into the room.
He kicked the first man in the groin and hit the second
with a frost spell. The young man began to back away,
muttering, 'Holy shit, who the hell are you . . .?'

Sam hit the man's head with a disruptive spell, that
sent his eyes rolling an instant before he slumped on to
the stairs. Sheathing his dagger and brushing traces of
magic light off his fingers, Sam turned back to stare at
the picture on the wall.

Nothing. He had no idea what it meant. Had
Hindsonn been possessed by Earth? Air? Water? Love?
And even if he had been, Greater Powers couldn't
possess mortals unless the mortals actually gave them a
way in. So why might Hindsonn have done such a deal?

Again he looked at the picture, trying to fathom it out.
He saw the signature in the corner of the canvas. Keith
Ware, 1994.

He looked back at Hindsonn. 'You bloody fool,' he
muttered under his breath. 'You sold your soul to War.
Are you the only idiot involved, or have all these
Ashen'ia people done that?'

Crouching next to Hindsonn, he put his hands over

the man's injury. He knew he couldn't just say 'let it be healed' and it would be. His only real healing abilities lay in his regenerative gift, something all Children of Time possessed.

He closed his eyes, searched for it, felt it answer, raised it to his fingertips ready to give it to Hindsonn. Heard the door open one last time. Looked up, the rainbow light at his fingertips dying, regenerative gifts settling down inside once more.

The policemen had guns. They were, to Sam's disappointment, aimed at him, a stranger with bloody hands, crouching over a dying man.

'Erm . . .' he began.

They didn't seem to want to listen.

FIVE

Hospital

His sword was in the boot of the car. So was his bag. It had been searched, and the Molotov cocktails and Coke cans discovered. That had just about clinched it. His hands were cuffed behind his back. The two policemen in the front of the car didn't look the least sympathetic as they wove through the traffic towards the station. There'd been three cars and two ambulances outside the club when Sam was marched out of it at gunpoint. He'd wanted to explain that the ice spells and general disruption were nothing a good cup of coffee couldn't deal with, and that the only real casualty was Hindsonn. He'd have been more inclined to add that if Hindsonn died, he'd be really, really pissed off.

The policemen had searched him, but there'd been nothing a bit of illusion couldn't disguise. His dagger was still in his sleeve.

Sam shifted position slightly, so that the fingertips of

his right hand could touch the lock of the left cuff. Tendrils of force were sent out from his fingers' ends, restrained, slipped into the lock, pushed. The lock clicked, its sound muffled behind his back. He slowly pulled his hand free, pressed it against the other cuff and clicked that open as well.

So far the two policemen hadn't noticed anything.

Sam turned his attention to the doors. He leant forwards, keeping his hands behind his back, and peered through the grille that separated him from the front of the car and the controls to the central locking. Seeing a button with a picture of a car key on it, his eyes narrowed. The button depressed, the doors unlocked.

'What's that?' demanded a policeman as the doors whirred. The car slowed in front of lights. Sam waited until it stopped, then turned his attention to the front passenger door, pulling at the handle with his mind. It flipped back and he shoved the door open with all the mental muscle he could muster.

'Christ!' yelled one of the policemen as the door slammed back on to its own hinges. The car pulled over and both policemen got out.

With the driver's seat empty, Sam carefully opened one of the back doors. The policemen turned as he made a run for it. One just had time to yell, before Sam, several paces away, tugged his feet from under him with a gesture. Seeing the other fumble for his gun, Sam held out a hand. The gun leapt out of the man's holster and flew towards Sam instead.

Feeling the weight of the gun in his hand, Sam beamed at the policeman. 'I'm really not a bad person,' he explained. 'And under different circumstances I'd stop to explain. Now get in the car. And drive me to wherever Hindsonn was taken.'

The policeman didn't move. Sam sighed. 'Once you're dead, what use can you be to anyone?'

'You're the kind of sick bastard who'd kill just for kicks,' hissed the copper.

That was the trouble with good people in a bad situation. They simply acted heroic.

'I could say I'm out to save the world, but it wouldn't help, would it?' He turned the gun on the policeman's fallen comrade and held it trained on the man with a nonchalance that took more acting than actual skill with a gun. 'Now will you drive?'

Sam cuffed the policeman he'd knocked over, touched his hand and plunged him into a shallow trance. Shallow, because the man might have to be woken quickly if Sam needed a hostage. He motioned to them both to get in the car, where the other man drove, aware that behind him sat, for want of a better description, a madman with a gun.

'And no funny business,' said Sam brightly. 'Because for all you know I might be a psychopathic killer.'

'In which case we're dead anyway,' said the man at the wheel.

'If I really were bad, to prevent any escapes I'd have broken at least one bone in each of you. I'd like you to take that into account.'

'You seem very relaxed.'

Sam knew what the policeman was trying to do: talk him round, find flaws in his armour, and by indirect means persuade him to be nice and reasonable. But having just been under attack from a madman possessed by War herself, two mortal policemen were hardly a priority. The threatened end of the universe, then the Berlin constabulary.

'You wouldn't believe what I've been through recently,' Sam said.

'Why? You hurt?'

'Nope.'

'You going to finish off Hindsonn?'

'No. And while we're on the subject he stabbed himself.'

'The sword?'

'Family heirloom. I was trying to sell it to Hindsonn.'

'Why did he stab himself?' asked the policeman, failing to hide his disbelief.

'Would you believe me if I said he was possessed by ghosts?'

'Do you think I should?'

Sam sighed. 'You concentrate on driving.'

The policeman said nothing. But Sam knew that several of the things he'd just seen were worrying him, and probably would until the day he died. He was half tempted to explain it, shatter the man's world view and drive profoundest doubt into his soul. Of course it would eventually cause a family crisis, and divorce from his wife, which in turn would lead to drink, a dishonourable dismissal from the police, separation from his children and his eventual spiral through debt into madness and—

The car turned a corner and into a hospital car park in front of broad canopy over an entrance identified as 'Accident and Emergency'. There were a couple of ambulances outside, lights flashing. Sam pulled off his jumper, goosebumps crawling along his cold arms. He wrapped the jumper a few times around his hand and said, 'Okay, out.'

The policeman glanced back at his unconscious colleague. 'What did you do to him?' he asked as Sam marched him round the back of the car.

'Nothing that wouldn't sound corny and unconvincing,' said Sam. 'Open the boot.'

The policeman didn't move. Sam sighed. 'Look, there are plenty of innocent people in the hospital for me to shoot at. Please don't assume you can make trouble.'

Reluctantly the man opened the boot. Sam's belongings were all there. Once he'd taken possession of them once more, he closed the boot and beamed at the man he was holding at gunpoint. 'What's your name – first name?'

'Marc.'

Probably a lie, but who knew? 'Well, Marc, because I don't trust you one inch, I'd like you to accompany me through the hospital. Please don't do anything silly, because I get nervous very easily.'

They marched in through the double doors and up to reception, Sam keeping the jumper low, where only someone who looked would see. 'We're looking for Hindsonn, just brought in.'

'A moment please.' The receptionist seemed hassled. She took in Marc's uniform and turned to check a computer screen, scanning down it just as the phone rang. Muttering under her breath, she said into the receiver, 'He what? No. No. No, he isn't here. Look, give me the number, okay? I'll pass it on.'

When she put down the phone Sam was still standing patiently, a smile on his face. 'Well?'

'Oh, yes. Hindsonn . . . Hindsonn – stabbing. He's gone into surgery.'

'How is he?'

The woman frowned. 'Are you a relation?'

'Friend. I work with him.'

'Your name?'

Sam could see Marc looking hungry at this potential information. 'Luke. Luke Satise.' An unusual name, but too late to change it now.

'Well, Herr . . . Satise . . . your friend was critical, but the doctors say there's a good chance. He won't be out of surgery, though, for several hours . . . yes, of course you can wait.'

He had to get Marc away from the crowded reception area. He guided the man downstairs towards the basement, right into the bowels of the building. Bright lights getting dimmer, scrubbed floors getting dirtier, white paint getting greyer. Sam pushed open a shabby green door and peered down a flight of concrete steps at a room full of boilers. Reluctantly Marc was made to walk ahead, down the short flight of stairs into the boiler room, stepping through a puddle from a dripping pipe. Sam closed the door behind them, found a bolt and kicked that shut.

Marc looked defiantly back up the steps, but Sam could sense the fear coming off him.

'What now?'

'We wait,' replied Sam, sitting down.

'For what?'

'For Hindsonn to leave surgery.'

'They'll notice I'm gone. They'll soon find the car.'

'And no doubt they'll search the hospital and look through footage from the security cameras, and sometime in the next three hours they might realise we never left the hospital. And maybe in four hours' time someone will stumble on this place, but by then Hindsonn should be out of surgery and I can ask him some questions.'

'What questions are those?'

Sam gave Marc a weary look. 'Time above, you don't give up, do you? Listen,' he said as politely as he could, 'there are things out there so big that humans can't even begin to contemplate them. There are Powers moving through space that can destroy worlds on whim, and those that can create them. There's always a war to control the universe, there are always wars for power. But not little power, not the power to make the sergeant the lieutenant and the lieutenant the captain. These are wars for the power to make suns live and die, wars for power over the stars.

'This' – vaguely gesturing with the gun – 'is just a tiny, tiny dot on a tiny dot on a tiny dot on a tiny dot in the huge, endless battle between the Powers. And it is my unfortunate fate to be another tiny dot, but possessing the final and unique screw that makes the whole machine fit together. It doesn't matter that the machine itself is a gigantic cannon with a tendency to backfire. All anyone ever wants is the screw, so that they can at least possess the cannon, even if they don't know what to do with it. And this cannon – this cannon can engulf worlds, make the Powers themselves feel fear. So you see, the fact that the tiny dot is holding a gun on another tiny dot isn't very relevant. It's the missing screw in the dot's coat pocket that gets people fussed.'

Marc was thinking, trying – or pretending – to turn confused words of other worlds and other things into logical Berliner sense. 'Which matters more? The tiny dot that holds the screw, or the screw itself?'

'In my own opinion, the tiny dot is infinitely more valuable than the screw. Unfortunately, not everyone sees it that way.'

'You seem confused. There must be a reason why you're risking so much to keep me alive.'

'And you seem like a patronising bastard,' sighed Sam, leaning against the wall. 'And as for why I'm keeping you alive, the answer is twofold. One, if I'm caught it would be useful to have a hostage, especially one who can flash ID to get me access if necessary.'

There was silence. Then Marc said, 'And the second reason?'

Sam seemed to have forgotten about it. He looked slightly surprised. 'I don't like loud noises, that's all. Now sit down and wait. We could be here a long time.'

Marc evidently thought at length that it was safe to make his move. Sam, head leaned against the wall, eyes half closed, could hear his breathing and the creak of the leather in his shoes as Marc edged up the stairs towards him.

'Don't,' said Sam, adjusting the position of the gun.

'I thought you were asleep.'

'That's no excuse.' Sam stretched and glanced at his watch. He was tired, he was overworked, and he was still uncertain what he could do to change anything.

It was two thirty. With luck, Hindsonn should be out of surgery. Sighing, he got to his feet. 'If someone says we're not allowed through, show them your ID and tell them it's official police work. Let's move.'

In reception Sam asked politely if Herr Hindsonn was out of surgery yet.

'He's in intensive care . . . Yes, he's stable.'

'Stable' in Sam's mind was a worrying term. Death was 'stable'. 'We'd like to see him.'

'I'm sorry, that won't be possible.'

Sam nudged Marc in the small of the back. Marc, slow and reluctant, pulled out his police badge. 'Ma'am, this is official business.'

'He's unconscious.'

'We'd still like to see him,' said Sam quickly, filling the silence before Marc could. 'We won't wake him.'

The receptionist shrugged, clearly uncertain but not sure what she could do about it. 'Down that way, first left, first right.'

They headed down a long corridor, Marc's shoes squeaking on the plastic tiles, Sam blinking from fatigue under the bright white lights. Sometimes very sensitive eyes had their downside. A doctor exited a room ahead of them but after a glance at the two men she quickly looked away. A policeman and a plain clothes detective were no real surprise on the ward. Sam felt cold in just his shirt and trousers, his gun hand sticky with sweat under the tightly wrapped jumper. The place stank of disinfectant. Someone in the distance was coughing, someone else was crying.

They stopped outside a door with a glass panel. A nurse was leaning over a bed on which lay the pale figure

of Herr Hindsonn, his eyes closed, tubes leading into his
arms, mouth, nose. Machines beeped all around, impressive but to Sam's eyes meaning nothing. He pushed the
door open. The nurse looked up. 'I'm sorry, you can't—'

Marc waved his ID without being told, his face sullen.

'Please leave,' said Sam. 'We'll call if we need you.'

'But I—'

'Thank you,' he said firmly, holding the door open.

'I'll come back in five minutes.'

The door closed behind her, and Sam looked down at
Hindsonn, then up at Marc.

'Cuffs,' he said.

'What?'

'Don't be obtuse, please. Give me the cuffs.'

Marc tossed them over, worry showing on his for-
merly empty face. Sam cuffed him to the radiator and
said, 'Look, I'm not going to hurt anyone, okay?'

'I wish I could believe it.'

'Have I hit anyone, have I killed anyone? Give me a
chance, copper.'

Sam edged away from Marc, aware of the policeman's eyes on him, and lay the gun in the jumper on the
floor at Hindsonn's bedside. He leant over the sleeping
figure and carefully put his hands over the man's
face, fingers spread to get as much physical contact
as he could. Closing his eyes, he let his mind sink into
Hindsonn's.

He'd been tempted to try and heal, but that ran the
risk not only of draining him to the core but of the woken
Hindsonn calling on War again. Sam knew better than
fighting that fight once more, only minus his own regenerative powers. So he chose the more subtle solution.

By degrees he could feel Hindsonn's sleeping mind. Gently he eased his own thoughts into it, saw as Hindsonn saw, felt as he felt, heard . . .

The sound of wind over an empty landscape. Sam looked around. Never had he seen such desolation. Huge craters full of mist and trapped pools of yellow gas, trees blown to pieces, barbed wire hanging limp around deserted trenches, shattered guns pointing skywards, sandbags blasted open, spilling their contents in a sodden landscape of torn-up mud.

Sam turned, searching through this landscape for Hindsonn. Heard a sound, other than the wind. A man in a helmet and army uniform was peering at him from the edge of a trench. He held a gun, aimed at Sam. Sam stared at him, refusing to feel fear. This wasn't real, it was just part of Hindsonn's mind.

'Hindsonn,' he said quietly, 'none of this is real, none of this is you, you do know that, don't you?' The hands holding the gun were shaking, terror was on the man's face.

'You've sold yourself to War. I don't know why, but it's been done before. You feed your blood to a Greater Power, and receive some of their strength. Unfortunately they also gain a certain control over you. If the Powers fought directly, their battles would probably tear worlds apart. So if they can fight through mortal agents it's more convenient, wouldn't you agree?'

'She . . . she . . . she . . .'

'She killed you. Well, tried. You called on her to protect you, and she possessed you, and so that you wouldn't tell me anything, she killed you.'

'I . . . I . . .'

'You'll live. This' – Sam waved a hand at the ruined landscape – 'is just a part of her power in you, the power of War. But Greater Powers can't actively possess mortals for long, it leaves them exposed, weakened. So she's probably not coming back for a while.' He edged closer to Hindsonn, but the gun went up again, pointing straight at Sam's face. Sam slowed, letting Hindsonn see his empty hands. 'You're in an intensive care unit. There's nothing to fear.'

'You . . . you attacked . . .'

'Do you know me?'

Hindsonn shook his head.

'I'm the man who tried to stop War from killing you. But War was strong, I couldn't keep her back. You'll never be free of her, Hindsonn. If you wake up and I'm here, she'll kill you rather than let you talk. And if she discovers that I'm talking to you here, in your dreams, she'll try to kill you again.

'But the thing is, I'm not going to leave you alone. Not ever. So you can either tell me now, while there's very little chance of War possessing and destroying you. Or you can wait until both you and she are strong enough to get up and fight, and we can go through the entire sword-knife-gun business and I'll win, and you'll get stabbed again but this time I don't think you'll live.

'So save yourself from yourself, and tell me what I want to know. Who's the link? Who do you report to?'

'There's . . . a phone box. Grunfrau Strasse . . . at five thirty.'

'The Ashen'ia – have they all sold their souls to War, or are you the only one?'

'No, no, they . . . they give to everyone. Fire, Water, War, Chaos . . . but not Time, never Time, we're too scared of Time.'

'Why do you want the Bearer of Light?'

He looked up at Sam with a frown on his face. 'Because . . . he can destroy any one of them at will. He can hold the universe to hostage.'

It sounded so obvious, so simple.

Sam stood there, rigid. *He can hold the universe to hostage.* 'Why now?' he asked quietly. 'Why move on him now?'

'He's alone, he's exposed. Before he had an army. Now, thanks to Seth, he has nothing. Soon he'll have to stop running. Soon we'll have him, and it'll all be over, it'll all be ours . . .'

Tinkerbell is instructed to keep me alive. But if I learn too much, such as, say, what the Ashen'ia are and what they're planning, he's instructed to 'bring me in'. The Bearer of Light can hold the universe to hostage . . .

'Who are the master and mistress?'

Hindsonn opened his mouth to answer, but nothing came out except a high-pitched scream that seemed to go on for ever.

In the real world, Sam opened his eyes. The scream was still there, but it wasn't coming from Hindsonn's tranquil face. It came from behind him.

Sam pulled his hands away from Hindsonn's cold skin and turned. The nurse had opened the door, seen him with Hindsonn, seen Marc handcuffed to the radiator, and screamed and screamed and screamed.

Sam scooped up his gun for all to see.

'No!' yelled Marc, as Sam pointed it at the nurse, who went on screaming. Sam glanced at him, and saw the realisation spread across Marc's face. The policeman knew Sam wasn't going to pull the trigger.

Hissing annoyance, Sam scooped up his things, turned and ran, knocking the nurse out of his way as he sprinted down the corridor. First left, first right, don't stop running . . .

Coming in sight of the exit, Sam slowed. There were four security guards on the door, looking very large and very imposing. He turned and fled, the way he'd come; they followed, breaking into a run. Reaching some stairs, he took them two at a time.

Behind, people were yelling for him to stop, to little effect. That syllable had never been a great word of power. Sam reached the first floor and ran down a corridor at random. There was a sash window at the far end, and the light beyond looked so wonderfully bright, and the window itself just so open, that he saw no choice but to head that way. He pelted down the corridor, knocking into a janitor. The man's mop and bucket went flying, spilling soapy grey water everywhere. Behind him Sam heard someone yell that they'd shoot. He got one leg out of the window as the bullet shattered the glass above his head. Jagged shards rained down all around him, tearing through his shirt and skin. He looked down, judged the drop to be about ten feet on to grass, and jumped.

As he landed he rolled, cushioning the fall with magic. The impact still sent stars spinning through his head, and pain through his side. He'd landed badly, one leg bent under the other. Staggering up, he struggled to limp away at a run, blood singing in his ears, body screaming for a regenerative trance. His hands stung, from leaving muddy skid marks on the grass.

Sam's eyes fell on an ambulance. The driver was sitting in the front, but Sam had had enough of mortals. He clambered up to the man, surprised him with a punch in the stomach and, as he crumpled, dragged him bodily from the ambulance and on to the tarmac. The keys were in the ignition. Sam climbed into the driving seat, slammed the door, turned the keys and put his foot down, feeling his skinned hands burn on touching the cold steering wheel.

The ambulance swerved out of the hospital car park and into the nearby traffic. Sam looked around until he found a promising-looking switch, and turned on the ambulance siren and lights. Traffic scattered to get out of his way as he careened at high speed down the main road, and away.

Things, he decided, could have gone a lot worse.

Grunfrau Strasse was a leafy byway off a small park in east Berlin. Its houses had once been grand. Large abodes with trees in front and gardens behind that had housed one family and its half-dozen servants now sheltered at least four or five families. Their ornate rooflines were dominated by a nearby industrial centre with a cluster line of dull metal chimneys pumping out invisible and highly toxic gases. The gardens were full of litter and disused kitchen appliances; at the kerbside the cars were small and many of them looked like they hadn't been used in months. On the corner a pleasant little church had been replaced by a large concrete warehouse that no one used any more, in whose

dark recesses bored kids experimented with illegal
substances.

Sam locked the ambulance doors, and lay on the
stretcher in the back. His arms had been quite seriously
hacked by the shattered glass, his ankle throbbed, his
body ached all over. He let his eyes close, and drifted in
the warmth of a regenerative trance, giving way to dull,
voiceless thoughts.

There had once been a Waywalker who'd sold his soul
to a Greater Power. It had been before Sam's time, when
Balder was still alive. But Sam knew about it nonetheless. He'd asked questions.

He'd asked Freya.

He couldn't remember how they'd got on to the
subject. It was in South Africa, in 1944. They were
sitting on the veranda of a small house in the middle of
nowhere, watching the sun go down on a seemingly
endless horizon. Drinking inventive cocktails, as far
away as they could get from the wars in Heaven, Earth
and Hell.

Prohibited love. Freya could never love Sam, it was
forbidden. He was the bastard Son of Magic, and an
exile who more often than not had fought his own
Heavenly brothers. She was a Daughter of Love and
dutiful servant of the House of Valhalla. To love each
other was unforgivable.

That evening, both were prepared to forget such a
thing. Sam especially was ready to shrug off any guilt.
Guilt that he had defied Heaven, guilt that because of his
defiance he and Freya could never love properly. His
fault, not hers. Always his fault.

'Did you ever meet Loki?' Sam had asked.

She slurped her cocktail. 'Yes.'

'What was he like?'

'Before or after he gave blood to Cronus, sold his soul?'

'Both.'

She sighed, and put her glass down. 'Before, he was nice.'

'Nice?'

'Well, a joker. A prankster, but devoted to the House of Valhalla. He always had a dark sense of humour, but he could also be the perfect gentleman.'

'What happened?'

She shrugged. 'He had views that . . . the House disagreed with. He said that Time was a harsh king, that any Prince of Heaven could step into Time's shoes, become King of Heaven and redefine the universe. No more death, no more suffering, no more pain. We all thought he was joking, even his wife.'

'Was he a good husband?'

'And a loving father. But his sons, they spent a lot of time in Earth and Hell, and often he went with them. He saw things, I think, that upset him. He wanted to know why Time didn't put a stop to it all, why he let the bad things happen. Time replied that if Loki just waited another ten thousand years, he'd understand it all. Loki said people never changed. That some things were timeless, things like hate and anger and jealousy – that's why they'd last for ever, and Time would have no power to destroy them. He grew angrier the more he saw, and as he grew more reactionary the House pulled further away from him. And that just made him more angry. He thought the House was too cowardly to try and change things. He remained a gentleman to the last, though. Passionate, but never violent, never rude, just very, very stubborn.'

'He thought Cronus was a way out.'

'Yes. He gave his blood to Cronus; he thought Cronus would give him power against Time, the power to fight back. He thought that if he let Cronus out, Cronus and Time would destroy each other and the universe would be free for him to step in and create his paradise.'

'He was wrong, I take it?'

'Yes. Cronus was afraid of Balder; he thought Time had persuaded Balder to use the Light against him.'

'Had he? Was Balder really prepared to die for Time?'

'I think so. At first he'd refused to use the Light on any terms – said it was an evil weapon. Then, when he realised exactly what Cronus was, he said he might use it if Cronus was ever freed. And Cronus heard these words, and he feared them. If he was going to be freed, he wanted to be sure the Bearer of Light wouldn't be a threat.'

'What was Loki like, after he'd sold out to Cronus?'

'We didn't know what he'd done.'

'But you must have noticed changes.'

'He was . . . arrogant. Also he was stronger, so much so that he didn't notice what he did. He'd open a door and end up pulling the thing off its hinges. And he suddenly began to hate. He'd never hated in the past, but now when he looked at the Children of Time he did it with fire in his eyes. And when he saw suffering and pain he would yell, "This is not necessary, why do we let this happen?", but no one really listened. Time summoned him once, told him he had the taint of Cronus inside his soul. But Loki just laughed and said, "Then destroy me!"'

'And Time didn't. Why?'

'Some say Time *wanted* Loki to free Cronus. He'd looked into the future and seen a thousand destinies in which Loki opened the doors to Cronus, and Cronus, believing himself freed by an ally, escaped into the universe – only to be destroyed by the Bearer of Light. There were few futures, few indeed, where Loki actually killed Balder.'

'But one of those futures came to pass.'

'Yes. Loki didn't start by freeing Cronus, as Time had expected. Instead, Loki killed the Bearer of Light. Time must have been terrified, as future after future faded and died, possibility after possibility shutting down around him. Leaving just Balder's death everywhere he looked, filling his eyes. It's said that Balder was the only child Time ever truly loved.

'When people found out what Loki had done they hunted him down. They didn't want Cronus to be freed if the Bearer of Light was dead. There were whispers that Time had been weak, that he'd let his love for Balder blind him to the fact that his own son wasn't strong enough to use the Light against Loki. When they found Loki, they locked him away.

'He's locked up to this day, the taint of Cronus still on him. But Time won't let Loki die. He wants him to suffer for what he did. And, rumour is, one day he might want to use him again.'

'For what?'

Freya shrugged, not meeting his eyes. 'Perhaps Time has another plan to destroy Cronus. Perhaps he thinks another Bearer of Light might stand more chance than Balder did, and this time Cronus *will* be destroyed.'

Sam stared at her, his mouth dry. She glanced in his direction, saw the horror in his eyes and grinned nervously. 'Or perhaps not. Who knows?'

'Time knows,' said Sam.

'Yes,' she replied thoughtfully. 'I suppose he does.'

SIX

Phone Call

Later that afternoon, Sam woke from his trance. He sat up in the ambulance, blinked to clear his head and tenderly felt his ankle. Not a twinge. Nonetheless he took his time in getting up.

Under one of the seats he found a jacket with luminescent stripes and the ambulance service badge of the serpent and staff. It was heavy, and a bit big for him, but he pulled it on, slipping the gun into a pocket.

Outside, the local call box was just a phone under a tiny glass shelter next to a large green recycling bin. Sam leant up against it, trying to look casual, and watched the road as if the phone box was nothing to do with him.

At exactly five thirty, the phone rang. Sam waited a few rings, then picked it up. A voice said in French, 'I heard the first bluebird of spring.'

Damn. Bloody word games. The idea of code words had

seemed so silly, he'd not considered it. He snapped in German, 'Hindsonn is in hospital, he was knifed.'

Silence. Then someone said, also in German, 'Who is this?' A woman's voice, accented with a language Sam couldn't recognise, and impatient, suspicious. Its snap of authority made him picture the German equivalent of the world of wellington boots, hunting and a lot of talk about cricket.

'My name is . . . Marc. I work with Hindsonn. He's in intensive care.'

'What are you doing on this phone?'

'Hindsonn told me to come here. He said he had a message to be delivered urgently. A matter of death, he said —'

'Who attacked him?'

'A large man. Red hair, looked like a ton of bricks.' *Name of Thor, surely. Let's see if I can get my brother into trouble . . .*

'What's the message?'

'I don't know. He gave me a floppy disk, told me not to open it, just pick up this phone. Look, if this is something to do with Hindsonn's attacker . . .'

'Leave the disk by the phone and go.'

'But I —'

The line went dead. Sam put down the receiver and tried to think, very fast.

The answer was in his bag. The notebook he'd bought in London was backed with cardboard, and Sam made quick work with his dagger of cutting out a more or less square shape that might pass, momentarily, for a disk. He stuffed it into the envelope Franz had made for him and shoved it into the gap behind the phone.

In the ambulance he waited.

After two hours it was getting dark, the sky grey-blue, going on black. The yellow streetlights were flickering on and off as if undecided which way to go. Sam began to doubt if anyone would come.

When the car pulled up he didn't even notice. He only saw the man reaching behind the phone for the envelope because at almost that moment the little white light in the booth flicked on.

It illuminated a grey hood over a hidden face. The man was stockily built, and wore outsize leather gloves, as if to hide as much skin as he could. There was a glimpse of red hair under the hood before the man hastened back to the car. Sam jotted down the number plate and watched as the car pulled out. He didn't want to crowd the man. Only when the car was about fifty yards away did he start the ambulance engine and follow.

They swung out into thick traffic, and for ten minutes or so they edged round a maze of one-way systems and traffic lights. Eventually the traffic picked up speed, but Sam was careful to keep at least two vehicles between him and the car in front. As the evening darkened, the road became a bypass, sweeping east into a hinterland of railway sidings, disused factories and lifeless housing estates.

On a minor road now, the city became just a blur of light in the driving mirror. Trees grew all around, creating a tunnel over the small spot of Sam's headlights. He felt terribly exposed, his vehicle the only other one on the road, and all the more noticeable as an ambulance in this remote place.

Sam slammed on the brakes as the road turned a corner. There was the car, parked by a wide metal gate into a field. Of the driver there was no sign. Sam parked the ambulance on the side of the road where it would be obscured by a line of trees. He got out slowly, wary of a trap. The darkness was total: no moon, not a light, not a star to illuminate the fields around. There seemed no distinguishing feature in this empty landscape, not a building, not a—

His internal radar gave a little beep. He frowned, and concentrated. Yes. There was a building, a shape in the darkness, no lights on inside it, and just behind it . . . a Portal.

He climbed over a fence, keeping clear of its barbed wire topping as his eyes adjusted to the darkness and took on reflectivity, like those of a cat. Moving slowly, feet crunching on the recently harrowed earth, Sam edged towards the house. When he was about fifty feet away, a light went on inside. He froze, then ran the last few metres to the window and peered in.

The hooded figure was standing at a kitchen table. Sam saw him open the envelope, saw him start at the sight of the cardboard disk. Saw him turn towards the window. Saw the patches of red scale on pale skin, the bright red hair sticking out from under the hood.

A demon. A demon from the hot part of Hell, a demon in Berlin . . .

The demon walked up to the window and for a moment Sam feared he'd been caught. Then he realised the demon was using a phone next to the window itself. He pressed his back against the wall and wished he could hear. After a while the demon moved away from the phone and began to pace up and down, hands clasped in front of him, looking nervous.

After half an hour, Sam saw the beam of headlights moving towards the house. They belonged to a blue Volkswagen of an unbearably boring variety, evidently registered in Berlin. Three figures got out of the car, and headed into the house. A few moments later, Sam made out more demons, two of them, in the kitchen. There was also a woman in a long fur coat who had heavy red lipstick and immaculately permed hair, dyed blond. She wore an expression that said, 'Children, please'.

Several times the hooded demon gestured at Sam's cardboard 'disk'. At one point the woman made a phone call; then another. Sam was getting increasingly impatient with this. Another car pulled up, possibly in response to one of the calls. Sam watched a lone figure get out, enter the house. He peered in – and found it hard not to jump and yell.

The new arrival had short red hair, green eyes, and an attitude to rival the lady in the fur coat. She stood glaring round the room at the demons, who cowered.

Gabriel.

The archangel Gabriel, or Gail, depending on who she was with, stood in the kitchen, talking to people who, Sam assumed, were Ashen'ia to the core. Gabriel, neither dead nor imprisoned, after all. The same Gabriel who'd helped Freya in her battle against Seth, who'd fled from a small farm in Mexico as the Pandora spirits poured down around her to try and drive hate into her heart. The same Gabriel he'd raced across half the world to protect, not quite knowing what he did.

Gabriel, here, and talking to Ashen'ia . . .

He remembered his scry. *Who do you serve? I serve you. I have always served you, master. Will the Bearer of Light come? Yes, he will come. He cannot help it, he seeks you even now.*

And now he thought about it some more. Minds, stirrings, memories. Gabriel's voice in his head, briefly connected through the scry . . .

<Sam?>

<Gail, I'm here . . .>

<Where are you?>

<Earth.>

<You're in danger.>

<I know.>

<People seek you.>

<I know that too.>

<Some would help you.>

<Who?>

The same story. People would help him: the Ashen'ia. People would seek him: the Ashen'ia.

Gabriel had run from Mexico straight to the Ashen'ia. How long had she been working for them? Had she known all along that the Ashen'ia wanted Sam, wanted the Bearer of Light to hold the universe hostage with his power? Had she lured him across the world because the Ashen'ia ordered it? Or because she genuinely feared Cronus?

Sam wondered what the hell he should do now. He could feel his list of allies diminishing. Was the entire world either Ashen'ia or serving Seth? For the first time in centuries, Sam was vulnerable. And the Ashen'ia had seen this and were exploiting it, determined to get at him for their own purpose.

On the other hand he didn't think the Ashen'ia would

take keenly to the idea of Cronus being unleashed on the universe. And if they wanted to threaten the Greater Powers with destruction they'd need a universe of free will in which to do so. Which again meant stopping Cronus. They'd also need Sam, alive.

So, even alone, Sam had some bargaining power. That still didn't mean he knew what course of action to take.

After much consideration, he came up with a plan. It wasn't brilliant, but it would have to do.

He headed for Gabriel's car.

Tyres, he discovered, were surprismgly hard to puncture. He had to use a lot of force before his dagger would damage any of them. Finally he gashed a front tyre and, to make sure, one at the back as well. He then punctured two tyres on the Volkswagen and ran through the darkness across the field. There, he used a touch of his mind to trigger open the padlock on the gate before driving the ambulance into the field and parking it about quarter of a mile from the house, where not even an archangel's vision would penetrate.

Back in the house they were *still* there, arguing – about him, he hoped. It would be satisfaction of a sort to cause that much dismay.

They argued. They kept on arguing, as if this was the only thing they did well. Sam sat underneath the window and drummed his fingers on his knees, feeling cold even through the ambulance driver's coat. He got out his notebook, and doodled. For something to do he drew a cartoon cat with a cigar, a dog with a top hat, a horse with an idiot smile and finally a large dragon eating a cheeseburger. He began to shiver as the wind picked up.

At last a door opened. There were footsteps, and
someone opened a car door. Sam heard the engine firing;
then the car backed up a few metres, and stopped. He
heard the door open again, heard voices raised in dismay,
bit back on a laugh that welled up inside his gut and
begged for freedom.

'The tyres are bloody blown!' said someone. There
was a hurried conference. Soon they'd realise that four
tyres on two separate cars just didn't blow themselves.
Before then he'd have to move.

Sam reached into his bag and pulled out a Molotov
cocktail. He rose to his feet, peering through the
window. It was empty, everyone outside. He slipped his
dagger through the join between the windowpanes, slid
it along until he encountered resistance, then pushed.
The latch clicked back, and he pushed the window
open. Carefully re-sheathing his blade, he touched a
finger to the petrol-soaked rag, ignited it and threw the
bottle as hard as he could into the kitchen.

It exploded, flames spreading across the old wooden
floor as the petrol poured outwards. Within a minute the
kitchen was engulfed. Sam pulled the window shut
again and crept into the darkness, to lie about twenty
yards from the house, watching, waiting.

They took all of three minutes to notice the fire, by
which time it was eating at the floor above. 'Holy Hells!'
someone cried. 'Get a fire engine, call the police . . .'

No one really noticed the hasty arrival of Sam's ambulance; it was just another emergency vehicle. A police car
pulled up, but Sam wasn't too concerned. The odds of

being recognised from the hospital were slim, especially this far out of Berlin.

The woman in the fur coat was talking urgently to a couple of policemen. Gabriel was looking at the burning house with a huge frown as though trying to figure something out. Someone had given her a cup of coffee and sat her down by a fire engine.

When the lady in the fur coat was finished with the policemen, they went up to Gabriel and began talking to her, leaving the woman alone. Sam pulled out a first aid box and a blanket. He advanced on the woman and said in German, 'Are you all right?'

She peered at him through the orange gloom, frowning, as though uncertain if she might have seen him before. 'Just . . . a bit shocked,' she replied.

'That's understandable. Do you have somewhere to go?'

She shrugged helplessly. 'My car is broken down.'

'I'm going back to Berlin if you want a lift?'

She glanced back at Gabriel. 'The police . . .'

'I'm sure if you give them your phone number they'll let you go,' he said, kindness to the core.

Sam waited while she talked to a policeman, who turned and gave him a thumbs up. Then, as she headed towards Gabriel, he quickly squatted down to do up a shoelace, bending so that his hair fell forwards, hiding his face. When he glanced back up, Gabriel was turning away from the woman with a nod and giving her hand a reassuring squeeze.

Trying not to move too fast, Sam helped the woman climb into the front seat, and gave her the blanket against the chill of the night. Once he'd started the engine, however, he was relieved to get away as fast as he could.

'This is very kind of you,' said the woman, who introduced herself as Ursula.

'It's my job. What happened back there, you any idea?'

'Probably kids.' Sam knew she was lying. 'Lonely house in the middle of nowhere, you know how it is.'

Sam said yes, he had a vague idea. 'What do you do?' he asked. 'For a living?'

'I'm in business.'

'What kind of business?'

'Oh, you know. I give advice to companies. It's really not interesting.'

Don't ask, in other words. 'Married?'

'No.'

'A pity. An attractive lady like yourself should be married.' He sensed her darting a look at him, running him up and down with her eyes.

'You married?'

'I had a girlfriend, but she buggered off. Last week, in fact . . . Do you have a boyfriend?'

'Uh-uh.'

Sam smiled. 'Is there a story here?'

She grinned in reply. 'I'll swap you mine for yours.'

'Not much to tell. I was always working silly hours, she met another guy, an advertiser, who went to the gym, self-satisfied bastard if I ever saw one, and took off to live with him in Frankfurt. You?'

'Do you miss her?'

'Yes. But come on, I want to hear your story?'

'Oh.' She arranged her face into a little grimace. 'Young, handsome, got freaked.'

'By what?'

'By me.'

'Why?' asked Sam, trying to sound surprised and indignant all at once.

'Because I'm a witch, of course,' she said with a laugh that sounded far too rehearsed. Sam laughed with her, forcing the sound out through vocal cords that had suddenly decided to have a sense-of-humour failure.

When the laughter had subsided, Sam tried again to steer the conversation. 'What was that place that burnt down?'

'Oh, my friend's house. We were having a drink. She must be upset.'

You aren't half bad at lying.

Heading into Berlin, Sam followed the signs to the centre of town, hoping that Ursula wouldn't notice what a stranger he was to the area. 'You look tired,' she commented.

'It's been a bad week. Hell, the entire month hasn't been good.'

'Girlfriends,' she agreed with a sigh.

'Witches,' he added with a laugh. She laughed too, suddenly uncomfortable at his tone of voice.

'Do you believe in magic?' he asked, confident that this strategy was the one. Go in hard, go in fast, don't let her catch her breath . . .

'What a strange question.'

'Do you?'

'Sometimes, yes,' she admitted. 'You?'

'I know it sounds crazy, but – yes – I do really believe in magic. Sometimes I feel things, think things, and I can't understand them. But they make so much sense.'

'I know the feeling,' said Ursula, just a bit too fast. Eager to please, her voice saying one thing, her hungry eyes saying something else.

'Whereabouts in Berlin are you headed?' asked Sam. Give her a taste, steer it away again, keep her on edge, let it haunt her . . .

'I can take the U-bahn.'

'No, it's all right. I might as well take you to your door,' he replied, eyes flicking between the road and the mirror. He felt terribly tired. When had he last slept? Proper sleep, not a regenerative trance; real, peaceful sleep . . .

They turned to discussing politics, movies, music, books, Sam all the time struggling to hide his ignorance of recent German culture. Finally Ursula changed the subject, to give directions. Left, right, here, there. Street lamps turned the inside of the ambulance yellow and orange for brief seconds, then black again as they drove past.

Following directions, Sam finally drove into a walled-off courtyard of balconied flats built over garages and ranged around a tall sycamore tree. It was late, and few lights were on. Ursula clambered out, thanking Sam all the way. He climbed out into the darkness with her, saying it was nothing, playing the nice guy.

Reaching a flight of stairs, Ursula turned, as he'd known she would, to look him over again. Then she said the words he'd been waiting for, the purpose of the exercise. 'Do you want to come up for a coffee?'

He made a show of thinking about it, staring for a moment at a point past her head. 'That'd be great.'

He followed her upstairs, thinking of the gun in his

jacket pocket and the dagger up his sleeve. Coming to a front door no different from any other, she opened it and showed him inside, turning on lights as she went.

'Sitting room is through there,' she said, breezing through a bead curtain into what was evidently the kitchen. Sam stepped into a room full of cushions, crystals dangling from the ceiling, candles, not lit, on every surface, long silk tapestries hanging on the walls, and mirrors in every place to reflect light back at each other in a thousand directions. When Ursula entered after a few minutes, she ignored the two cups of coffee she put down on the table. Instead she sat next to him on the sofa and looked him up and down.

'You've got potential,' she said finally. Her voice was soft, and almost menacing. She smiled and held up her hand.

In it a tiny bead of fire sprang up, grew into a small ball about the size of a tennis ball, hung there. She let him stare at it for a long time, a smile tugging at her lips, before closing her fingers around it, letting it wink out.

He turned to her, careful to show amazement in his eyes. 'How did you do that?'

'You'd like to learn?'

He nodded dumbly, conscious that words might reveal him as the magician he was. A fireball wasn't a particularly impressive achievement, not by his standards, but for a mortal it was probably a remarkable trick.

Ursula, still smiling, brushed one hand along his cheek, and held it at his chin, tilting his face this way and that to get a good look, as though sizing up a choice cut for the oven. 'Yes,' she said finally, 'you'll do.'

He gently caught her hand, smelling the perfume on it. 'What must I do?'

'You can be my apprentice.'

'How? Tell me.'

But she seemed not to want that. What she did seem to want was to kiss him. Sam stood up and backed away. She rose too, looking disappointed. 'I don't bite, you know. I'll teach you everything, honestly.'

'What are you?'

She pouted, a coy expression too young for her. In the bright light, he could see lines beneath the thick make-up. 'Ashen'ia.'

'What's Ashen'ia?'

She looked impatient, but told him anyway. 'And soon the Powers will bow to us. They'll bow to you too, if you join us,' she finished.

'Which Power do you serve?'

'Fire.' She caught him round the waist and pulled him towards her. He was taller than she was, and she had to bend her neck to look up at him. 'Give your blood to Fire, and he will make you great.'

'Do the Ashen'ia serve anyone else?' he asked softly.

'The master and the mistress, but they keep themselves to themselves, they won't bother us . . .'

'Who are the master and the mistress?'

She sighed. 'Questions, questions.'

'I'd like to know.'

'No one knows, that's the point. No one except Gail.'

'Who's Gail?'

'A friend.' She was tugging at his shirt. He reached round behind him and caught her hands, holding them gently but firmly.

She looked up at him with a pitiful, puppy-like expression, trying to pretend at being hurt. 'What are you doing?'

'Where is Gail?'

'She moves around. But what does she matter?'

'I'd like to meet her.'

'Why?'

He tightened his grip on her hands. 'I want to know who it is I'm expected to serve.'

'I'll take you to see her tomorrow.'

'Can't we see her now?'

'What's the rush?' Pulling back from him now, dismayed.

'You have her address?'

'Yes, but why—'

Sam smiled, shook his head. 'Bring it to me.'

Ursula had finally found the good sense to get worried. 'Give me a reason.'

'Please. Hunter sent me. Gabriel has turned to the enemy. I was sent to determine whether you have too.'

'Hunter . . . Gail . . .' Her mouth worked up and down several times. Then she managed to stutter, "You're . . . Ashen'ia? Who do you serve?'

'War. Hunter sent me, from London. Gabriel has betrayed the Ashen'ia; she's working with the enemy. I'm sorry I lied to you but I needed to know whether you'd turned with Gail. Now bring me the address book, please.'

She looked paralysed.

'Bring it now!' he snapped.

The sound of command in his voice seemed to jerk her awake and she hurried into another room, returning a few seconds later rummaging through her handbag. She thrust a piece of paper at Sam which bore an address and telephone number. She was shaking with shock.

Sam patted her on the shoulder. 'Just sit still, everything's going to be fine.' He headed for the door. But before he got there the phone rang.

'Answer it,' he said quietly. 'Don't tell anyone I'm here.'

She nodded and picked it up. Sam looked round for another extension, and grabbed one from behind a door into the kitchen, pulling the wire taut so that he could watch Ursula while keeping his ear to the phone.

A familiar voice said, 'Ursula, love, you there?' Tinkerbell. Hunter. Call him what you would.

'Yes. I'm here.'

'Are you all right?'

'Fine.'

'Look, I've phoned to warn you. We think Sebastian has come to town.' Ursula's eyes flew to Sam.

'What . . . what gave you that idea?'

'We think he might have found the address for der Engelpalast. If he has, then chances are he was the one who stabbed Hindsonn – and took your phone call. And if *that's* so then he might have followed you home.'

Silence. Then Ursula in a weak voice said, 'I . . . was given a lift home.'

'Who by?' Silence. 'Ursula, who gave you a lift?'

Ursula's eyes were locked on Sam. He slid one hand into his coat pocket, felt the gun. She followed his hand all the way.

Tinkerbell's voice was now urgent. 'Ursula! Ursula, who gave you a lift home?' Sam pulled out the gun, slow, leisured, letting her see that he meant business.

'A . . . a man in an ambulance. He's gone now.'

'Look, love, don't move. I'm coming over.'

'Fine,' she said quietly.

Sam gestured with the gun for her to put the phone down. She obeyed. They stood staring at each other.

Sam said, 'Okay, I know this seems nasty, but there is purpose to it. And the Ashen'ia are mad if they think anything they did would make me discharge the Light against a Greater Power. Tell them that. The Ashen'ia are right, I am alone, and you people may be my only potential ally. But you'd have to help, rather than hinder me. And how long have you people been waiting for me to become weak enough so you can risk using me? Because you've screwed up big time.'

'You will share in our glory.'

'Lady, if you could see as many flaws in the scheme as I can, you'd never say that.'

She gave no answer. Sam smiled wanly. 'Anyway I did like your company, kinda. A bit off-key for my tastes, but that's forgivable. So sorry about this.'

She was already trying to move, but not fast enough. The air distorted around him as Sam swept his hand up and pushed, sending a disturbance that smashed into Ursula, picked her off her feet and sent her flying backwards, smacking hard against a bookcase. Briefly she slumped, head on one side. Sam pocketed the gun, looked down at the address in his hand and went in search of Gabriel.

SEVEN

Coming Together

Close to Gabriel's Berlin flat, while navigating a tricky roundabout, Sam felt someone scry for him. Dizziness washed through his mind and images flickered in front of his eyes. He hastily pulled over and put his head in his hands, leaning on the steering wheel and trying to focus on the source of the scry.

He sent his mind out, and felt . . .

<Hi, Jehovah.>

<Sam. Just seeing how you are.>

<Oh, I'm fine. How's the end of the world going?>

<All right, thank you.>

He could feel Jehovah hammering away at his shields, trying to pinpoint Sam's exact location. And behind Jehovah, another mind. Sam reached out for it, felt anger and strength combined into a particularly lumpy combination. <Hi, Thor,> he added.

Thor didn't answer. A sudden stab of pain as Jehovah

tried to worm his way into Sam's eyes, see as Sam was seeing, and Sam recoiled, lashing out with tendrils of wild magic, burning across Jehovah's senses. The scry abruptly winked out, leaving Sam shaking.

He gripped the steering wheel and tried to breathe steadily, wondering how much Jehovah and Thor had gleaned. It was a worrisome reminder that there were other things out there, more powerful and potentially more dangerous than the Ashen'ia.

But what to do about them without the Ashen'ias' help?

He drove on.

In a tiny courtyard of high red-brick buildings, dripping black iron pipes and slippery black iron steps, lived Gabriel. Sam could see the light on in her flat. He could also tell where she was, from feeling her archangel's power. He jogged up the stairs to her front door, and knocked, leaning away from the spy hole on the door. Gabriel's feet sounded in the hall, and, after a pause, the door opened.

Sam waited until she stepped out on to the metal stairs in front of her door. He looked to see that her hands were empty, and stepped forward, meeting her eyes squarely. She froze, fear bleaching her skin.

'I gather,' he said into the ringing silence that followed, 'that I've been playing the puppet to your clown.'

Gabriel made no response. He gestured at the door. 'Shall we?'

She moved like a robot, knowing that even though his hands held no weapon at any moment he might hit her with all the anger of a Son of Magic.

The flat, Sam thought, looked like something Gabriel *would* use. Artful dabs of paint in red frames hung on the walls, a collection of small potted plants, well tended, sat on the radiator casing by the window, the table was swept clear of all but a few neatly folded newspapers, the carpets were clean and matched the wallpaper, the wallpaper matched the sofas, the immaculate kitchen, just another section of the main living room, was all stainless steel. Sam sat down on a giant sofa and smiled thinly at Gabriel, who stood looking at nothing.

'So,' he said, 'you're Ashen'ia. But you're also an archangel. Admittedly a traitor, like myself, who refused to countenance Jehovah's orders when you found out about the Pandora spirits and Cronus, but still an archangel. Shouldn't you know better than to think I'd play your little game of let's-threaten-the-Powers-with-the-Light-and-see-what-happens?'

Gabriel shrugged and met his eyes. 'We need the Ashen'ia, Sebastian, if we're to stop Seth from freeing Cronus. When we've finished using them we can still just walk away.'

'Who's "we"? You, and the elusive master and mistress?'

'Sebastian,' she said reproachfully. 'Remember when we had to get out of Mexico because of the Pandora spirits? As I fled, I was met by the Ashen'ia.

'They'd been watching you. They said that with the Bearer of Light threatening the Greater Powers with destruction, the Powers would have no choice but to give the Ashen'ia magics beyond what anyone, mortal or immortal, has dreamt of. All I had to do was help them catch you.'

Sam's face said nothing, but his eyes spoke freely enough. 'Who did you sell your soul to, Gail?' he asked bitterly.

She looked down. 'It hardly matters.'

'Did it make you happy?'

Her eyes flashed. 'Sebastian, listen to me. I told the Ashen'ia that if we moved too fast on you, you'd fight us to the last. I told them that the longer you'd have to operate against Seth, the more you'd realise you needed us!'

'Yet you didn't want me finding you.'

'I knew there was no way you'd agree to help the Ashen'ia.'

Sam's voice was low and dangerous. 'If you knew I wouldn't help, why bother trying?'

'The Ashen'ia are going to fight Seth, even though they'll almost certainly destroy themselves. But they'll severely weaken Seth in the process. Possibly so that you, the Bearer of Light, can finish the job.'

Sam stood up and turned towards the window, staring into the darkness. 'This could just be an elaborate trick.'

She shrugged. 'Where will you go if it isn't? You know that alone you can't win. And you know that only the Ashen'ia can resist the power of the Pandora spirits, because the spirits target souls, and our souls are split, hidden in places they can't find.'

'If the Ashen'ia are so powerful, let them deal with Seth. I can tuck myself away in a quiet corner of Hell and let this pass me by.'

Her laugh sent a chill through him, made his hand twitch near the gun. She said, 'The Ashen'ia won't move without the Light. Somehow they'd drag you back in.

Assuming, of course, that Thor didn't find you first.'

He looked at her, saw the expression on her face, and turned back to the window. 'I can deal with Thor,' he said quietly. He added, 'Who's the master and who's the mistress?' His voice had a low, insistent edge.

The smile in her eyes died, and something hard passed over her face. 'They are Waywalkers who have given their souls.'

'To whom, Gail?'

She didn't say.

He looked sadly down at her. 'When you served Freya I thought so much of you. You had abandoned Jehovah, your master for a thousand and more years because he was freeing the Pandora spirits, you had put your life on the line for others, risked everything, become an outcast from Heaven. What happened to the archangel I knew?'

'Cronus will be freed, Sebastian. Not-living, not-dying, not-changing. This puts the steel in anyone's soul.'

Sam sagged wretchedly against the window, eyes fixed on a distant point. 'You know I have nowhere else to go.' Time have mercy, he was tired. 'You know I've no choice.'

'You never did have a choice, Sebastian,' she replied. 'From birth to death your single purpose has been this – stop Seth from freeing Cronus. That's why they called you the necessary child.'

Sam didn't say anything, he was watching her with a look of half-recognition, half-disgust on his face. Disgust at what? At her? He didn't think so.

Gabriel ignored his look. 'Of course, you couldn't be

legitimate. That's common sense. The more you're alien-
ated, the more you're pushed into being alone, the less
dependent on others you are. You're sharpened against
betrayal, cynical, suspicious, a fighter. Everything that
Balder wasn't.'

'Time loved Balder,' said Sam bleakly, wanting to close
his eyes, forget about everything, sleep . . .

'And his beloved child died. How much easier, therefore, to risk losing a child that he doesn't love?'

Sam smiled faintly. 'You've learnt to play nasty, Gail.
I should have expected that.'

'Why bother to fight, Sebastian?'

'I don't know,' he said with a half shrug. 'Pride?
Perversity?'

There came a knock on the door. Then a hammering.
Sam sighed. 'That'll be Tinkerbell. Does he know you
plan to destroy the Ashen'ia?'

'No,' said Gabriel, heading to the door. 'I don't think
he's in it for the power. But involved he is, whatever his
reason, and I'm not going to test his loyalty to the
Ashen'ia.'

She pulled the door open a few inches. A large, red fist
caught her squarely across the jaw, then picked her up
and threw her backwards across the floor. A long red
arm followed the fist, one large sleeve rolled up over
bunching muscles. A red nose, a square red face, red
hair. Thor himself stepped through the door, turned,
looked at Sam, smiled.

'Little light, little fire,' he whispered. In a strange voice
that reminded Sam of . . . Hindsonn?

Sam sighed and pulled the gun out of his pocket. 'It's
been a really bad month, have I mentioned this?'

Thor looked at the gun with a frown on his huge butcher-slab face, as if trying to work out what it was.

'You pull the trigger and it kills people,' Sam explained wearily when Thor didn't move. 'I'll demonstrate.' He raised the gun and pumped four shots into Thor, with perfect accuracy.

Trouble was, Thor had moved.

And Sam had never seen anyone shift so fast. Not even a Son of War should be able to move that quickly! There were four holes in the wall behind Thor – and a loud ringing in Sam's ears – and Thor was straightening up, axe raised in one giant's paw, a grin on his big, idiot, bearded face.

His eyes had a translucent film over them, like a fish . . .

'Hell, you really have sold out to Cronus, haven't you?' muttered Sam, disbelief temporarily drowning out the fear. He dropped the gun back in his pocket and fumbled for his sword. Thor caught Sam's wrist as he tried to yank the sword from its bag, picked Sam up bodily and slammed him against a wall. The ringing in Sam's ears grew. Thor's face was an inch from his. His breath stank like a misused chemistry set.

Thor dropped his axe and closed his fingers round Sam's other wrist, which went up above his head to join its partner, pinning him helplessly against the wall. Seen this close, the grey film over Thor's eyes was resolved into a whirlwind of strange colours and patterns. He grinned, and spoke in the strange, distorted voice Sam recognised from Hindsonn when possessed by War. 'Little light, little fire,' he said again. 'That's what they called you in Heaven, wasn't it?'

Sam brought a knee up into Thor's groin. Thor's eyes widened, he made a little *whump* sound, and staggered, head rebounding against Sam's, but his grip on Sam's wrists hardly faltered. Slowly, catching his breath back, Thor raised his head again and grinned. His teeth were yellow and uneven: clearly this was one Son of Time who hadn't appreciated the dental revolution.

'Little light and little fire needs to grow up,' he said softly. Bones grated together in Sam's wrists, taking a lot of nerves with them.

'You're imprisoned, Cronus,' Sam managed through gritted teeth. 'You're possessing a Son of Time in the universe of Time. And I guess Daddy won't be happy about that, so bugger off before the cavalry comes!'

'I'm coming back, little light, little fire. I'm coming back – and then see what your "Daddy" can do to protect you.'

'Clearly you're worried.' Sam gasped as the pain in his arms shot down to his elbows and up to his fingers, turning them numb. 'That's why you're so interested in killing me: you're afraid. Cowardy Cronus, doesn't dare come out of his prison for fear of a little light, a little fire . . .'

Thor, or the creature possessing Thor, growled, shook Sam like a doll. Sam forced out an agonised laugh, which acted like sandpaper down his throat. 'Thor, you always were a great one for wit. I see Cronus takes after you.'

Cronus/Thor gave a snarl of rage and pulled a hand free of Sam's wrists, hitting him hard across the face. Sam fell to the ground and tried to crawl away, but the possessed Waywalker still moved fast. A boot connected with his side, then hands grabbed him and pushed him back against the wall, his legs sprawled in front of him, hands limp at his side, eyes dazed.

Thor's face swam in front of his vision. 'Little light, little fire dies as easily as the first one,' he growled.

'First one?' echoed Sam dully. 'Oh, Balder. Only you see, Time loved Balder.'

The dagger was out, Sam's hand shot forwards, drove into Thor's thigh. A faint sigh, a whimper escaped Thor's lips as Sam pushed harder with all his might, driving the blade in.

'That's something you can't say about me,' muttered Sam, worming his way out from Thor's grasp. Thor staggered to his feet, stared in horror at the dagger embedded in his thigh. The weapon of a Son of Time would create a wound that couldn't be easily regenerated, it would take time to heal, real time . . .

As Sam watched, he saw Thor grit his teeth, reach down and pull the dagger out. The merest act of touching Sam's blade seemed to cause him more pain, and Sam wasn't about to waste a weapon in another's hands when it was specially tuned to him. He called to it, whispering of fire and lava, and the blade began to glow red hot in Thor's bloody hands.

Thor yelled, dropping the blade, backing away. As he did, the door opened again, and Sam saw Tinkerbell, a crossbow held in either hand. Thor swung on Tinkerbell, and raised his hands with a roar, sending ripples through the air that threw the other man off his feet. He called his axe across the room to his hand, and turned towards Sam, a huddled figure in the corner.

But instead of delivering the expected blow, he smiled – a weak smile, which faded into a look of pain as

the eyes cleared. Thor staggered a few paces to the
doorway and paused; and Sam saw on the old Waywalker's face a look of such longing and torment that he
almost, but not quite, felt guilt. Thor's mouth moved, with
a dry sound that might have been Thor's ordinary voice
coming from Thor's ordinary mind as he whispered, 'For
Freya', before he turned and limped away.

Sam sat there, dazed and in pain. His gun was still in
his pocket, his bloody dagger lay on the floor. He called
the dagger back to his hand, wiped it clean on his
already filthy shirt, re-sheathed it and staggered to his
feet. Dragging himself to the kitchen sink, he turned on
the cold tap and stuck his head under the flow. The chilly
water was shocking, but welcome. Behind him he heard
a sound. He spun, gun coming out of his pocket, fearing
that Thor had returned.

Tinkerbell was leaning against the wall, both crossbows now pointed at Sam. More people were coming
through the door, men in dark clothes who Sam half
recognised from the flat in Southwark. Gabriel was
climbing to her feet. All eyes were on Sam and the gun
he held two-handed, steady, in front of him.

Sam thought. He looked from Gabriel to Tinkerbell to
the men in the doorway, and a tiny voice inside whispered, *No choice. Gail was right about that at least.*

He smiled a feeble, unfelt smile, and let the gun hang at
his side. Tinkerbell edged towards him. Submissiveness,
Sam guessed, wasn't on Tinkerbell's file.

'Hiya, Sebastian.'

'Hello there. Give me a reason why I shouldn't go
ballistic as only a Son of Magic can. Apart from the
crossbows, I mean.'

Tinkerbell considered. 'Perhaps . . . because we've only ever been trying to look out for you.'

'This is protection, huh?'

'You're one man, Sebastian. A powerful guy, but still very much alone. You must know that we – the Ashen'ia – are the only ones who can keep you safe.'

'Where's the catch? The part where you use me as Bearer of Light to hold the universe hostage?'

Tinkerbell smiled an easy smile too good to be true. 'Consider it the lesser of two evils. You can wander around alone and get killed by Thor, Odin, Seth or Jehovah. Or you become part of the Ashen'ia and end up as one of the most powerful men in the universe.'

Sam sighed, rubbing one hand across his eyes. 'I hope you have a long spoon,' he muttered. 'And don't think this means I agree with you. But . . . like you said, I appear to have run out of options. I assume these gentlemen are here for the "taking" instead of the "offering" part of the deal?'

Tinkerbell's smile turned strained. 'You help us, we help you. You want to stop Cronus – so do we. So join us. Dare I say, sell your soul to the Devil?'

Sam raised his hand and spoke in a slow, deliberate voice. 'You want a truce, right? Not a treaty.'

'Of course.'

'This,' he declared with a sigh, 'is very unoriginal. But sometimes you've just gotta say these things. Take me to your leaders.'

EIGHT

Trusts and Truths

They had a white van. Sam had always imagined that
demons would drive white vans, vehicles that
implied a certain attitude towards the road. They took
the gun, his dagger and sword. He let them. There didn't
seem any alternative. *No choices.*

Once, he remembered, he'd been shown a computer
game by a friend. And no matter what you did, whether
you talked or fought or stole your way through the nar-
rative on the screen, the story adjusted itself around
what you did. So if you were a good enough bluffer you
could discover where to find the socks of power or
whatever the game was about. If you were a thief you
could steal a letter describing what you needed to
know. If you were a murderer you could kill the guy
and then conveniently discover in some drawer a
spell that would bring him back to life, under your
command, whereupon he'd tell you everything. Thus,

no matter how hard you tried, it was impossible to cock up the story.

If only he could try out variants of his own life, reloading situations again and again to see whether thieving, murdering or lying was the best way out. Meanwhile he was in the back of a darkened van, with demons sitting on either side of him and Ashen'ia of the suspicious I'm-watching-you variety in front. Sam felt cold. He felt tired. The ambulance driver's coat was too large. He just wanted to sleep.

Against expectation, lulled by the motion of the van, he did.

A long time ago, when Sam was still young, in Heaven, and thus with access to the Eden Portals, he'd studied the wards on the Way of Eden. He'd heard rumours of Eden, the beauty of it, the majesty that made Heaven look drab by comparison. Some of the oldest Waywalkers could even remember it from when they'd journeyed into Eden in the good times. It was these older ones who hungered for the Way of Eden to be reopened after Light sealed it, fleeing from the reality of her son, Balder's, murder and closing the Way behind her.

When Sam had been approached to try and unseal the wards, at first he'd been optimistic. He'd gone down to the nearest Eden Portal and sat for hours on end before the shimmering white doorway suspended on nothing, eyes closed, probing with his magically attuned senses at the wards that covered the Way. The wards were strong, far beyond the capacity of even combined Waywalkers to dislodge, but that was to be expected. They'd been written by a Greater Power, after all. Their weakness was that they were so obviously written by a Greater Power, they were all Light and nothing but. If you could summon Darkness, that elusive Greater Power, never acknowledged in Heaven or indeed in any other world, a Power shunned by all the others, then the wards could be breached.

It was summoning Darkness that had got Sam worried. As he had sat, cross-legged, face serene and mind far away, he had wondered. Darkness was shunned for a reason. She existed to sow discord, she hated everything, but at the same time she possessed a seduction and a power that alarmed her sisters in the pantheon of Greater Powers. If she were given the excuse that she'd been summoned by the Children of Time, she'd come to Heaven to wreak as much havoc as possible on these same Children, in revenge against her sisters.

Sam had said as much to Odin. Though to Sam's mind Odin seemed far too serious about everything, he was an elder Son of Time, and Sam admired his dedication to the House of Valhalla. He appeared the kind who could do no wrong and who would listen to Sam's worries with a fatherly ear.

Yet Odin had responded like the others, with an arrogance only a Son of Time could show. We can contain her, he'd said. Darkness is an old Greater Power, she can be commanded, controlled. It's nothing for you to worry about.

It was that last, almost patronising sentiment that had resolved Sam not only to worry, but to get downright angry. Especially when he'd fared no better with Jehovah.

'I would be happy to see the Way of Eden reopened,'

Sam had told his brother, 'since I think Light would not stop us passing through it. What I object to is your method of opening it.

'But what you propose is calling up the Power of Darkness. To breach the wards written by a *Greater Power*. The effects will be disastrous if you attempt to channel that much of Dark's essence against Light. By forcing so much power against opposite-aligned wards, you might disrupt the Ways themselves. We might lose the Eden Portals for ever. What then? What will you do, when the Portals collapse in on themselves and the darkness pours across the land and eats your souls?'

Jehovah had managed to make his stony features look sad. 'So you won't help us.'

'You guessed, huh?'

'You can't stop us. The Way of Eden will be opened, no matter what.'

'Light put those wards there; you cannot displace them.'

'*You* can. You're the Bearer of Light. If you target wards with their opposite power, they'll fracture, they'll die, no backlash, no overspill, no—'

'You know as well as I that if I used my power against Light, it would almost certainly get out of hand and I'd have destroyed a Greater Power!'

Jehovah had shrugged. 'It's a pity that you won't. But the Way of Eden will be opened; nothing you can do will prevent it.'

And Sam had left, not just angry but humiliated. The worst thing was knowing what his brothers planned – that and being almost certain there was nothing he could do . . .

Somewhere in a small white van, surrounded by demons, memories blurring into fears, Sam dreamed on.

The Room of Clocks, Time's throne room. It was hard to not recognise it, even when dreaming. Clocks of every kind covered the walls, floor and ceiling, and they all beat exactly in time, a huge roar of a click sounding every second. And at the far end of the room, past the simple stone throne, another clock, hands moving so fast that you couldn't see them. This clock measured the heartbeat of the universe not in seconds, but in the wavelengths of visible light.

Sam walked towards the throne, curious, peering at the clock, trying to distinguish numbers. He heard a sound behind him and turned. For a second he thought he saw a shadow move. A dark figure in black, with black eyes and black hair, flickered and was gone. He frowned and peered closer. Flicker, vanish, in a different part of the room. The room itself was darkening also. Sam thought he heard a voice, speaking indignantly, but it quickly faded. He heard another sound and turned, to stare himself in the face.

Not quite himself, he realised, but a younger version, animated, saying something.

He could hear snatches of words drifting out of the empty air, just on the edge of hearing. *Eden* ... *Darkness* ... *arrogance* ... The figure faded, then reappeared seconds later a few metres away, pacing, hands moving up and down in anger, face contorted in a scowl of dismay. More words, clearer this time. *Help me, Father. They'll summon Darkness, and she'll lay waste the Way of Eden, destroy as much as she can, destroy them, possibly contaminate*

the Ways just for something to do. You must be able to stop this.
Silence. Figure winking in and out, reappearing, words.
Why don't you care any more? You cannot let this happen! In,
out, coming, going.

Sam turned through an increasingly dark room,
peering, trying to find himself again, recognising his own
words coming at him from the past. Several of him now,
in the shadows, speaking with one voice. *You'll let them
destroy themselves with Darkness? They are your children, they
are my brothers and my sisters!*

More of him appearing, filling the hall, dark shapes in
the darkness, thickening, drawing all light to them,
black eyes looking at him everywhere, flashing with the
same anger, filling up everywhere, driving Sam back
pace by pace, words becoming audible, a gentle murmur
rising to a flood. 'Do you care about anything, Father?
Stop them. Stop them or I will. Stop them, Father. Stop
them, stop them, stop, stop, stop—'

Sam stumbled back against something. Figures from
the past, his past, pressing down on him from every side,
voices roaring in his ears, dark eyes glaring accusingly.
He felt what he'd stumbled against – the stone throne –
and fell into it, covering his ears to keep out the deafening roar. 'What are you planning, Father, why do you let
it happen, why don't you stop it, why don't you care . . .?'

Sam heard Freya's voice in the throng, louder than all
the others. She was speaking of Loki, Balder's murderer,
amid voices growing so loud . . . *He wanted to know why
Time didn't put a stop to it, why he let all the bad things happen.*
'Why don't you care any more, Father, why don't you
stop them, stop, stop, stop, stop—?'

'Go away!' he screamed. Silence, abrupt and louder

than the noise that had gone before. He opened his eyes. A thousand Sams stared back at him. They didn't say a word, just kept on staring. He cowered against the back of the throne, cold and afraid. 'Who are you?' he asked. 'What do you want?'

And they spoke as one, not shouting, but still a deafening sound. 'We are the intention and the act, the strength and the weakness, the light and the dark, the individual and the whole. We are you. You are we. The One is the Many.'

'Delighted to meet you, leave me alone,' he gasped, shaking all over.

The crowd parted. A woman stepped towards him, smiled coyly. 'Remember me?'

'Of course, you're . . .' His voice trailed off. The other Sams stared stonily at him. 'I never met you,' he murmured, looking round the hall again.

'Remember me?' asked another voice.

'And me?'

'And me?'

'And me?'

'And me?'

He turned to look at each face in turn as they pushed their way out of the crowd, Sams parting all around to let them through. 'I . . . I never met any of you.'

'But you know me.'

'And me.'

'And me.'

'And me.'

'And me.'

'Just like we know you.'

'We are the intention and the act,' said one.

'The strength and the weakness.'

'The light and the dark.'

'The individual and the whole.'

'Keep away,' hissed Sam. 'Leave me alone!'

'You can't be alone. You're the Bearer of Light,' said someone, as if it were obvious. The Sams around the hall were thinning out, more and more faces replacing them, leaving just one of him in a sea of strangers. Strangers that he knew so well . . .

'We are One.'

'The One is part of the Many.'

'The Many are united.'

'Is this a trick?'

'This is a nightmare,' explained a voice in his ear. He turned. Freya smiled at him. 'You're slipping, Sebastian. You're drowning in the voices.'

'Who sent me this nightmare?'

'You're doing it to yourself.'

'No. This is too real, I have too much control.' He reached up and tweaked her nose. She recoiled, surprised. 'See?' he asked. 'Control. Someone's filling my head . . .'

'Me,' whispered someone.

'And me.'

'And me.'

'And me.'

'And—'

'Shut up!' he yelled. 'Get out of my head! Leave me alone!'

Darkness. Kneeling before the empty throne, the clocks roaring around him. Thor staring sadly down at him, fish-eyes and all. 'You'd die for this, little light, little fire?' he asked.

Sam raised his head, opened his mouth to say something rude, and the floor opened up beneath him.

Falling. Drowning, water in his lungs, burning in his chest, voices in his ears, always the voices, so many voices, and him speaking with them but he couldn't hear his own voice, all he knew was that to not say the words was to explode, and that somewhere, someone that might once have been a tiny spark in a sea of sparks was whispering with a billion others. *We are the intention and the act, the strength and the weakness, the magic and . . . and—*

Leave me alone, get out of my head.

You're slipping, Sebastian. Drowning in the voices.

The light and the dark, the magic . . . the magic and . . . and—

For Freya.

One is Many, Many is One, Thor loved Freya too . . .

No more loneliness! Maybe not together, but not alone either! But then everyone loved Freya.

Leave me alone! Go away, leave me alone, go away, go away, go away!

He started awake, cold, afraid. Gabriel moved her hand from his arm, as though embarrassed to have touched him. The van had stopped. Sam had no idea where.

'Come on,' she said quietly. The doors at the back of the van had been opened, and Sam squinted at the light shining through. They had been driving for hours. Tinkerbell smiled as Sam got out of the van, but whether it was a smile of triumph or of reassurance Sam couldn't tell. Whatever it was, he didn't feel inclined to return it.

There was a house. It was small, painted white and sat in the middle of nowhere as if thrown there by a careless passing tourist. A cat lounged on the front porch looking bored, and gave the party only a sceptical glance, as if there were things far more interesting to look at than mere two-leggers. The kitchen contained a large iron stove in one corner, blackened by age and not enough cleaning, the cupboards held little more than a few tins, mostly of cat food, and underneath the sink someone had found a dead rat, brought in by the cat as a rare gift for its keepers. The floors were splintery old boards pocked with holes, and the creaky wooden stairs looked as though they were about to collapse. At the stove an old lady with an ugly gap in her front teeth that seemed to draw all eyes to it stirred what might have been anything from an elixir of immortality to tinned tomato soup.

Tinkerbell, no doubt wondering what had inspired Sam's change of heart, led the way upstairs to a room that rumbled ominously in time with the boiler next to it, and tossed Sam's bag on the bed. Inside the bag were the crown, clothes, the phone card and the chocolate bar that Sam still hadn't got around to eating, but the Molotov cocktails had been removed. They hadn't, Sam noticed with a faint smile, removed either the surgical spirit or the Coke cans. Clearly, in the darkness of Soho Square, not even Tinkerbell had seen what a useful weapon the Coke can might be.

The room itself was small, and looked like spare bed-rooms everywhere. There were the dusty old books that no one wanted to read, the clock that had stopped three years ago, the tape machine that didn't work, and the cross above the bed with Christ impaled upon it, a symbol that had always struck Sam as a disturbing thing to worship. The bed was covered with blankets and a flowery duvet cover with frilly bits around the edges. He kicked his shoes off and crawled under the blankets, head languishing on the smelly pillow printed with yet more flowers. There was a spring loose in the mattress that pressed against his ribs, so that he was forced to contort himself into a corner in order to lie comfortably. Above the door was a spider's web, its occupant waiting patiently for the next meal to fly in.

He closed his eyes, and touched the mind of the spider. The creature was practically blind, completely deaf to the sound of human voices and no use as a spy.

But it was extremely sensitive to even the slightest movement within its web. Sam whispered to it, sent it scuttling under the door and into the corridor outside, sent it crawling its way down the stairs, scampering back and forth, its world shifting up and down, up and down as it hit the verticals on the stairs and ran straight down them as if they weren't there. Guided by Sam's mind, his brief impressions of the house, the spider bumped against a banister and crawled up it. There it began to weave another web. When it was completed, Sam withdrew his mind and dozed.

The spider's web was trembling. Sam could feel it shaking the entire spider's body as its delicate threads hummed back and forth. Someone was coming up the stairs, and that vibration had disturbed the spider's silk, which disturbed the spider, which disturbed him and jarred him to full wakefulness.

The door opened. Tinkerbell stood there, smiling down at Sam. 'Want to come and chat?'

He followed Tinkerbell downstairs into the kitchen. A

couple of dozen people, some of them demonic, sat arguing around a long table on which a scratch meal had been laid out: bread rolls, an heroically smelly kind of cheese, and sausages that looked like they could hold a conversation in their own right. As Sam came in, everyone looked at him with a mixture of suspicion and awe.

'Is that for me?' Sam asked brightly, sitting down. 'I haven't eaten for ages.' He started tearing into the bread with satisfaction.

At the head of the table sat Gail, a queen holding court. 'You all know why we're assembled—'

Sam raised a hand and said through a mouthful of bread, 'Uh, no. But I'd be interested in finding out, since it seems I'm vital to your plans.'

There was a muttering from a pair of demons in the corner. 'Hi,' Sam said cheerfully. 'Is there a problem?'

'We are here,' said Gail, cutting in with a show of determination, 'to discuss the problem at hand. Seth. And Cronus.'

'Why is *he* here?' hissed someone, ignoring her.

'Sebastian is here because he knows more about Cronus and Seth than any other. Because he is a Waywalker. And because he is Bearer of Light.'

'And a charming guy on his own terms,' murmured Tinkerbell, half to himself.

'Well said, that man,' called out Sam. 'I'm here, from what I gather, because you cannot "hold the universe to hostage" without the Bearer of Light. And because I suspect that without the Ashen'ia I can't prevent Cronus from being freed. However unfortunate this situation – and, believe me, I dislike it intensely – we do need each other. For the moment.'

His eyes met Gail's, and he saw something in them like . . . fear?

'Quite,' she said against a swell of murmuring. 'The situation is . . . a compromise. For both parties.'

'On the contrary,' said someone loudly in a heavy Hadean accent. 'Now that the bastard child has got himself so exposed, we can take what we want.'

Sam gave a faint, dangerous smile. 'If you're under the impression that you can stop Cronus without my co-operation, think again. On the off-chance that Cronus is freed – and to this end Seth has a large army at his disposal – you'll need a Bearer of Light who's very sympathetic indeed to your cause.'

'It will never come to that,' Gail insisted. 'No one here – no one at all – intends seeing Cronus freed. What we do mean to achieve is simple. You' – doggedly meeting Sam's gaze – 'will remain with the Ashen'ia until Seth is defeated. In that way we shall ensure the power that we desire.'

'Power? Gail, you've changed. What happened?' He looked sharply at her, searching her face and again saw . . . something.

What's your game? The Gail I knew was not interested in power. Her interests began and ended with preservation of that which she believed in – which was life, pure and simple. Why is she joined with the Ashen'ia? And why does this all seem so wrong?

'He *is* dangerous,' snarled someone.

'Shut up,' retorted another.

'Fire-brains, if you could see as I could see—'

'Don't you speak ill of Fire; my master is just as power-ful as yours!'

'Water will always extinguish Fire. You should have thought of that before you gave your allegiance to such an unstable Power!'

At this, uproar broke out, several people yelling abuse seemingly at random. Sam, who felt already that he had the measure of this company, carried on eating with a faint smile on his face and his eyes focused far, far away.

It was some time before even Gail could break through the noise. 'Gentlemen!' she yelled. 'Gentlemen! Enough of this! I asked you here as representatives from each Power. But we are here to discuss the future, not argue about the nature of our organisation!'

'And what might that be?' murmured Sam, more to himself than anyone else. A little more loudly he said, 'So why isn't Time involved? Why hasn't the All-Father got his dirty fingers into you, if you hold so many cards?' He looked at Gail, frowning as he studied her face for answers that weren't there. 'Why doesn't *he* seem actively involved?'

'He is,' someone spat. 'Through you! His *necessary* child.'

'Is he? I suppose he is, in a way. But from Time's point of view it just doesn't seem enough.' Sam's brows drew tighter together as his eyes moved past Gail to where Tinkerbell lurked. Truly nothing here seemed as if it might work.

'We Ashen'ia,' said Gail firmly, taking advantage of a moment's silence, 'have waited centuries for an opportunity like this. Let no one here think that, at a time like this, anything will stand in our way.'

Sam swivelled to look at her, eyes bright with concern. 'You speak like Time himself – nothing stands in his way.

Yet the Ashen'ia are surely arrogant to think they can threaten a Greater Power, even with the Bearer of Light.'

'And you are arrogant to think you're anything but our prisoner!' yelled someone.

Silence fell. Sam half turned to look at the man who'd spoken and said, in a low voice, 'That's one way of seeing it. But only a fool would say so out loud.'

Placing his hands palms up on the table he calmly studied them as if trying to read his own future. In a level voice he said, 'All right. We have no reason to trust each other, but we cannot afford to fall out. I cannot say that I believe in your scheme against the Greater Powers, especially since I've no intention of letting my head be fried in destroying any one of them. But you shall have your reward.'

'The only reward we want—'

'Shut up. If you have nothing useful to say then say nothing at all,' snarled Tinkerbell from the corner, the first time most people there had noticed him.

Several pairs of eyes turned to him. Someone sneered, 'Don't you lecture us, night-spawn. You may think that, because of your blood, you are greater than us. But you're even less than *he* is.' A finger stabbed at Sam. 'At least his blood was first-generation.'

'I know the nature of my blood. Do you know the whore who mothered you in Hell?'

Gail slammed a hand on the table. 'We're not here to argue!'

'But isn't that inevitable?' murmured Sam. 'With so many Powers represented here? Including rivals such as Order and Chaos, for Time's sake! Gail, I marvel that you're part of this.'

Gail's eyes locked on to Sam's gaze. 'You fail to comprehend the nature of the Ashen'ia,' she said in a low voice. 'I think it best, Sebastian, that you leave this meeting.'

Sam watched her face for a long time, then rose to his feet. Tinkerbell drew himself out of the shadows and together they left the room.

Tinkerbell followed Sam up to the bedroom. In the doorway Sam stopped, frowning faintly. 'Night-spawn?' he asked.

'Ignorant demons,' Tinkerbell replied with a shrug.

'No. There's more to you than meets the eye, Tinkerbell. Isn't there?'

'Naw,' he said, wagging a finger reprovingly at Sam. 'You're the star, not me.'

'But why are you a part of this? If the Ashen'ia don't tear themselves apart, they'll be destroyed by the Powers they sold their souls to. Why are you involved with these crackpots?'

'And why do you ask questions that won't get answered? You need the Ashen'ia. So do I. Let's leave it at that.' Tinkerbell gently pushed Sam back into the room, and pulled the door shut. Sam hammered on it.

'What about Time?' he shouted. 'Doesn't he need the Ashen'ia now? Where's Time, then?'

No one answered.

Sometime later, he felt the spider tremble. Sam closed his eyes, afraid. *What have I got myself into?*

He lay on the bed, feigning sleep, and listened. He couldn't even hear the footfall, and was grateful to the spider for its senses, giving him advance warning of intruders. The door creaked. Sam kept utterly still, though his eyelids begged to be open, to see who was there. Very carefully he extended his mind, and encountered a shield of such perfect formation and craft that no mortal could possibly have woven it. An immortal was standing in his doorway, looking down at him.

He heard a man ask in Elysian, 'Is he all right?' The voice seemed familiar, but Sam couldn't place it.

'He's fine. Tired.' Gabriel's pragmatic voice, easily recognised.

'Thor is looking for him. He isn't safe here.'

'We'll move him as soon as you want.'

'Does *she* know he's here?'

'No.'

'Well, it hardly matters. How does he seem?'

'Exhausted, both in and out. He's been through a lot.'

'Will he discharge the Light?'

'Possibly. He doesn't have much left to live for, after all. When push comes to shove, I think he'll do it. But if he knows in advance, he'll fight us. And he's still a tough fighter, however much he's been through. He might still be able to stop us.'

'We'll guarantee he can't, have no fear. When did he last eat?'

'He had some bread earlier, but I don't think he's had a proper meal for ages. I doubt if he's slept properly either. He's been regenerating, sure, but that's not the same.'

Voices retreating, vibrations on the stair. 'Does he suspect?'

'I don't think so.'

'We must keep him safe. If he finds out, and goes wandering off by himself, Thor or Seth or even Odin will easily be able to pick him off . . .'

Silence. Sam opened his eyes. Now he knew the voice. Hell, he even knew the mind, that stony wall of blankness that defied all probes but the most powerful. Scrambling out of bed, he rushed to the window, dragging half the bedding with him. He saw a man, tall, slim, hooded like most of the damned Ashen'ia, getting into a red sports car that looked far too young for the clothes he wore. White robes, almost like something out of a biblical drawing. Now the man was leaning out of the window and talking to Gabriel, his hand slowly gesturing as though trying to assert that really the end of the world was something to be relaxed and rational about.

Holy bloody shit, they sold me out . . .

Sam struggled to raise the window. It was locked. He looked up at the sky and at the road as the car began to reverse, then down at the car again. His eyes narrowed on a back tyre. He bit his lip, squinted at the tyre and tried to get a good enough focus on it to make it burn.

Come on, come on . . .

Sensation, contact, push against the hubcap for all you're worth, heat it up as fast as you can, think fires, think lava, think heart of the sun, think rosy red glow, come on, come on . . .

The car was reversing, making his target even harder to hit. He concentrated until his eyes hurt – and heard a bang. The tyre had burst, black rubber smacking up and down on the ground, pathetic as a fish flapping on dry land. The car skidded, sparks flying from the smoking hub as it cooled rapidly in the breeze, and bashed into a stretch of wooden fencing, lifting it off the ground and carrying straight on as if it wasn't there into a field of wheat. There the car stopped, trapped on a bump, front wheels suspended slightly above the ground. It scarcely looked like a sports car now; more like a comic-book disaster.

Sam grinned and rubbed his eyes. The driver's door opened and the robed figure got out. From the way his hands were bunched into fists, and the rapid rising and falling of his chest, this was not one happy bunny. He turned to the house, and Sam lurched away from the window, pressing his back against the wall and looking idiotically cheerful. There was something very satisfying about trashing the car of a mysterious stranger, if he was the mysterious stranger you thought he was.

Think, Sam. Think. What is he doing here, why haven't they just killed me already if he's *here?*

Time to get out, perhaps. Whatever his gratitude to the Ashen'ia for their hospitality, now might be a good moment to say thanks . . .

Sam ran for his bag, found the surgical spirit, pulled it out. He splashed it across the floor in front of the door, sending up a vile stench, soaking the wood. Surgical spirit, while not as useful as petrol and whisky for sheer explosive force, was a brilliant catalyst of coldfire, as he'd discovered when he'd tried to use it along with a coldfire sterilisation spell on a particularly nasty blister. It might not burn as well as real fire, but it was a terrific way of causing heavy damage that little could prevent, short of a major magical effort.

Sam heard footsteps on the stairs, even as the little spider curled away from the vibrations of all those feet. He kept pouring, watching the clear liquid spill out under the

door and into the corridor beyond. There was a squelch-
ing sound, and a voice asked, 'What's that smell?'

'Surgical spirit,' said Tinkerbell's voice. Then, louder,
meant for Sam's ears, 'That's very impressive, but it
doesn't make things easier for anyone.'

'Tell me, Tinkerbell, are you possibly standing in the
stuff?' Long silence, that Sam took to be a yes. 'Only it
goes up brilliantly when you apply a coldfire spark to it.'

More silence. Then, 'Why are you doing this,
Sebastian? I thought you were on our side.'

'I am. But it seems you want to turn me over to the
enemy, so I've kinda rethought my position.'

A silence even longer than before. Sam let it last,
counting under his breath. The guys outside were very,
very uncomfortable if they couldn't think of anything to
say for over fifteen agonising seconds. 'What makes you
think we're doing that?' asked Tinkerbell finally.

'Well, let me see. Could it be the fact that a guy
bearing a remarkable resemblance to Jehovah in voice,
mind and abominable fashion sense has just attempted to
leave this house?'

'So you blew the tyre, huh?'

'You can tell, can't you?' asked Sam, slinging his bag
over his shoulder and edging up to the window. He
placed one hand over the locking mechanism, pushing
his mind into it. It was warded.

'Look, this isn't what it seems —'

'Nah. It's just a litre of coldfire catalyst, a man who's
working towards the release of Cronus even as we speak
and who has sworn my destruction several times chatting
nicely with Gail, and a rather disappointed Bearer of
Light: nothing is ever as it seems, is it?'

The locking mechanism was the only thing warded, however, which Sam thought ruined the point. This was the trouble with magicians. They often thought of what they'd do if locked in a bedroom in the middle of nowhere, but rarely considered the alternative methods of escape. He picked up the holy cross hanging above the bed, wrapped the corner of the duvet cover around his hand and swung the cross against the glass. The window exploded outwards.

'Sebastian? What are you doing?'

'I don't fancy dying this young, that's all,' he replied gaily. Having bashed out the rest of the glass, Sam manoeuvred himself until he was sitting in the empty frame, legs dangling out of the window, just as the door opened. A demon stood there, and looked at him.

Sam beamed, waved, and threw a fat blue spark into the pool of surgical spirit at the demon's feet. As the spark touched, and ignited in bright blue flames, he swung himself around and caught a drainpipe, swinging his weight on to it. The pipe creaked pitifully, but held. He began to lower himself hand over hand, bag bouncing against his back, bare feet wrapped like a monkey's around the cold metal, keeping his elbows into his sides and trying not to look down.

After what felt like an eternity his feet touched ground. He could see light, an unnatural blue tinged with white, flickering out from his window, casting its glow across the ground. He ran.

Behind him a door opened. Sam half turned to see a demon raising a crossbow. He grabbed a Coke bottle and threw it, breaking the ignition ward as it went. There was a dull explosion behind him; not loud, but with the reassuring sound of jagged metal flying everywhere, not to mention boiling hot Coke. *If only the manufacturers knew*, he thought, running past the empty red sports car with no real sense of direction. He felt terribly exposed, fearing the pain at any moment of something hitting him in the back, then the regenerative trance pulling him down. Or worse, no trance at all. Just death, sitting there with a big grin and maybe worse dress sense than Jehovah.

He tried to focus. A Portal, that's what he needed to find. A nice Hell Portal somewhere, a place to run, now that he knew for sure that the Ashen'ia were under no man's control except his enemy's . . .

There was a road beside the field, cut off from the rest of the world by high hedges. He turned into it, the tarmac hard and unyielding on his bare feet after the grass, his soles aching in protest.

Ran round a shallow corner. Slowed, stopped. There he was. Leaning calmly on his staff, almost like an old man. His brown beard was neatly trimmed, his steady eyes shone with that intensity that had always annoyed Sam. Even when young, Jehovah had had a gleam of old age in his eyes. Sam imagined him standing every night in front of a mirror trying to out-stare himself. The bastard was even wearing his crown of thorns, which it was said cut everyone except him. Just as Sam's crown, when put on by anyone else, would drive the wearer mad.

Sam refused to let himself be unnerved. Of all his siblings, Jehovah had been the most open in his dislike. It was something to do, Sam guessed, with the discovery that Sam, one of his dedicated servants, was a Waywalker in his own right. But to discover that the Waywalker was not only a bastard son but the Bearer of Light too – that had been almost more than Jehovah could take.

He had loathed Sam ever since, with more or less show of politeness. He was being polite now. Much in the style of an iceberg facing down an ocean liner.

Sam pulled out a Coke can and held it ready in his right hand, with little optimism. Jehovah smiled faintly, and shook his head. Again, playing the father figure. At that, Sam felt a spark of anger stir inside him, grabbed at it. Anger was what he needed at that moment; anger gave strength, even if it did reduce your capacity for defence. He knew he was fairly defenceless anyway. Attack was the key.

'It's not what it seems, you know,' said Jehovah.

NINE

Jehovah

'Truly it's not what it seems.'

'That's nice,' Sam told Jehovah.

'Now you know who I am, you must understand that you're double the threat.'

'No. Enlighten me, as Buddha would say.'

'Because,' said Jehovah, lightly swinging his staff back and forth, 'if Seth and Odin discover that I've betrayed them for the Ashen'ia, they'll kill me. And the Ashen'ia will lose their inside man. I can understand you trying to run. You know that I was originally one of those who freed the Pandora spirits, and the situation between us,' – a faint smile – 'is hardly fraternal. You're scared. I understand this.'

Sam inwardly counted the seconds while his mind raced. 'You're sure you're not a treble agent? Betraying everyone except yourself?'

Jehovah shrugged. 'There is more to everything than meets the eye.'

'Surprise me. One of the Big Three traitors turns out to be playing a double game. For how long?'

'Not as long as you think. At first I was genuinely determined to get power through the Pandora spirits. Since then my attitude has changed somewhat.'

'You killed Freya?'

'No.'

Sam gave a little laugh of disdain. 'Sure. You freed Suspicion?'

'That I admit.'

'Why'd you do it?'

'As I said. Power in Heaven. I wanted to be King.'

'And you don't any more?'

'No. I see that it is impossible.'

'So you've had a miraculous change of attitude?'

'You could say that. But I also realised that in order to stop Seth it might be useful to have a power base within his army. So I went on playing his game.'

'And quietly sold out to the Ashen'ia. How admirable.'

'You'd rather have me as foe than friend?'

'Actually, yes. It'd make it more satisfying when chopping you up in bits and serving you to Thor as cat food. And if you have things so obviously under control, you hardly need me, do you?'

'You're the Bearer of Light.'

'Actually, I'm not. It's all been an elaborate hoax. I've been on a secret mission for thousands of years from Time himself to cover up for the real Bearer of Light, help keep his identity a secret.'

Jehovah sighed and gave Sam a mournful look, as if disappointed in him.

Sam shrugged. 'Okay, so maybe not. But I had you worried for a second, right?'

'The odds we fight against are still huge. Seth is served by Odin, and by Thor who himself has—'

'I know, sold his soul to Cronus; we met and talked about it.'

Jehovah's face, never animated, seemed to twitch. He never liked to be interrupted, Sam remembered, and inwardly vowed to butt in as much as possible.

'There's still a chance that Seth will free Cronus. In which eventuality, we need you alive.'

'So I can die destroying Cronus,' said Sam bitterly.

'Essentially, yes. Or you could live, by a miracle. You are the miracle-maker, after all.'

'You're just seeking to use me. Little light, little fire, that's what they call me. Little Lucifer, the poor bastard Son of Time who never had the guts to use his full power for fear of all those minds inside his mind, all those voices. You'll send me against Cronus and let me die.

'And at the end of the battle you'll stand up, with no enemies left to challenge you. You'll walk the fields of the living and say, "Look, for I have defeated these evil people, the bastard Son of Time who closed the Way of Eden for ever, the evil Sons of War and the Son of Night; and Cronus himself is dead at my hands. Worship me, peoples of the worlds; if you don't, I'll destroy you." And it'll take a miracle to stop you, won't it?'

'But you can't make miracles when you're dead,' said Jehovah with a faint smile that seemed almost to touch on pity.

'No,' Sam agreed, looking small and rather sad, a figure with torn clothes, no shoes, a battered old bag and a Coke can as a weapon. 'I can't, can I? And you, like Gail, are lying.'

Jehovah raised his eyebrows. 'How so?'

That was possibly the most annoying thing about Jehovah. You could tell him he had a face like a mouldy turnip that had been through the digestive system of an elephant, and he wouldn't even blink. Sam resisted the urge to hit him.

'If you had no ulterior motive in preventing Seth from freeing Cronus, you would have come directly to me. Instead, how did it feel, *brother*, watching our sisters and brothers cower in terror of you when you marched into Heaven with the Pandora spirits at your command? I imagine you liked that, went round telling everyone it was for their own good, no doubt. As for those who disagreed with you, who tried to stop you, you sighed and patted their heads and said, "Don't worry, a dungeon will cure your heresy." You must have been having a ball, dear *brother*.'

'Whereas you have enjoyed a peaceful regime of getting shot, stabbed, chased and captured, not necessarily at different times!' snapped Jehovah.

Sam was surprised. Pleased, but mainly surprised. His brother had actually shown anger. He lowered his voice. 'Why hasn't Father stopped you? Naughty boy is playing a little game of his own. And the only reason he hasn't been fried is because Time likes Jehovah doing his footwork for him, and disposing not only of the Ashen'ia, but of Seth too.'

'I don't do Time's dirty work, you do,' said Jehovah,

voice controlled again, but that angry gleam still in his eyes. 'You were the necessary child. You were the one created to die.'

'And you ask why I fight?' demanded Sam with a disbelieving snort. 'I've known for thousands of years that I was created with a purpose. I understand that my own father had me born in order to die for him! But that doesn't mean I'm going to accept it! I'll stop Seth without you!' Sam's free fist was opening and closing at his side as he flung the words at Jehovah. 'I'll do it without you, without the Ashen'ia. Cronus will remain imprisoned, and the Ashen'ia will never catch me. And you'll remain what you always were – a messiah with a press-ganged congregation.'

Jehovah didn't say a thing: he didn't lunge at Sam screaming, he didn't spit defiance. He simply swung the staff, a sweeping gesture that bathed the road and much of the hedges around in fire. Sam covered his head with his hands, seeing it coming and wincing at the brightness of the flames as they struck his shielding and poured off like running water. The fire died and Sam raised his head.

Jehovah's staff caught him squarely in the belly. He flopped forwards, breath wheezing in his throat, tears in his eyes. Standing over him where he lay curled up on the ground, Jehovah seized the back of Sam's shirt and hissed, 'Up. Get up!' Sam struggled to his feet and half turned, ramming the Coke can into Jehovah's belly.

Jehovah grinned in surprise, snatching the can from Sam and pushing him back. 'This?' he asked, looking scornfully at the can. 'This is your great weapon?'

Sam staggered back from Jehovah, waiting for the

world to steady. 'Watch,' he croaked, triggering the ward.

The can exploded in Jehovah's grasp. Sam heard his brother's scream, and looked down to see him kneeling on the ground, clutching one bloody hand. Jehovah looked up with murder in his eyes. 'Bloody idiot . . .' he hissed. But which of them he meant, Sam wasn't sure.

Sam grabbed his bag and fled, bare feet slapping on the tarmac road as he ran and ran and ran, breath hissing through clenched teeth. There was no sound of pursuit. In the distance he could hear church bells, and sensed from roughly the same direction the pull of a Hell Portal. He kept on running. Hedges fell away; there were open fields, the occasional coppice of trees. The air was fresh and cold, the clouds low. Was he on high ground? There were hills all around, and on the horizon a high range of rock faces that had to be mountains.

A village ahead. He slowed, looking it over. A church with a bulbous spire, a post office, a few run-down East German cars. One or two cats in the street, a chained dog behind an iron fence with an electronic buzz box. Small, neat houses with well-tended flowers, no doubt maintained by people who took a deep pride in their neighbourhood. It was almost a fairytale village, but for an old woman with a limp and thin white hair who swore at him as he passed. He did look like a beggar, he realised. His stomach rumbled; he felt like one too.

There was a small bakery, just opening. A young woman was helping load up a tiny delivery van, more of a box on a motorbike. She stopped as he approached, and where the old woman had sworn she gave him a look almost of pity. He summoned the illusion of two euros and asked for bread. She not only gave him bread, she took him into the bakery and gave him a glass of water.

So it was then, sitting in the window of the bakery on an empty wooden box, tearing into a loaf of bread paid for with illusionary money and gulping water from an ancient glass turned almost white with use, he heard it.

You don't trust anyone, do you, little light, little fire? We come, we are the powers you people created, you mortal minds, we come now to wreak our revenge, grow strong by making you hear nothing but our voices, feed on the harm you do each other, we come, and you cannot hide . . .

Music, filled with words, the chanting of a Pandora spirit. *You don't trust anyone, do you?* Suspicion was coming, sent by Jehovah. Suspicion was going to hunt Sam down and there was nothing Sam could do to stop it.

Except discharge the Light.

We come, little one, we come to reclaim the minds of men, you cannot hide . . .

My mind is Many minds. I am what you cannot target, I am Many minds with all their contradictions. You cannot target too much at once. So leave.

The song filled his ears, the Pandora spirit danced through the air around him, laughing. *You cannot fight the power of Suspicion.*

I can. I am more than you are, for you are just one timeless entity. I am Many. I am the Bearer of Light.

And what is the Bearer of Light? A weakling fool with voices in his head?

It's what the voices say that's important. I am the intention and the act, the light and the dark. I am Many things, you are but one, a part of me. Just another concept created by life. Life is in me, you are in me, but I am greater than you are because I am more than just one concept Incarnate. I have seen the minds of the world, and in a small way they are all part of me, as I am a small part of them. You cannot touch me.

No? Perhaps not. But – even more potent – we can touch others.

Silence. In vain Sam got to his feet and searched around desperately for the voice of Suspicion. But the song was still there, filling his ears.

Then he heard a different voice, slightly indignant. 'Did you pay for that?'

'What?' He looked at the woman from the bakery, slightly irritated to be broken out of his own darker, more pressing thoughts.

'Did you pay?'

'Yes. I gave you two euros.'

'Where are they?'

'I gave them to you.' *Admittedly, I dropped the illusion immediately after.*

'I can't find them.'

'Look, I'll give you more . . .'

'Who are you, anyway? How did you end up this way?' asked the woman, suddenly not interested in his money. The boy who drove the motorbike-van was pressing his nose against the window, curious.

Sam suddenly felt very cold and knew exactly what Suspicion had done. He said, 'Look, I've really got to go,' and backed to the door.

The woman followed. 'Just who are you? Claus, stop him!' This to the boy. The boy didn't stop him though, but danced round Sam as he went down the street yelling, 'Thief, thief, thief!'

Doors opened as Sam toiled briskly up the small hill

towards the church, feet and face burning alike. Other
faces peered out as the woman and boy circled around
and around him, shouting, 'Stop the thief, stop him!'

More people entered the street, even some wearing
dressing gowns and slippers, and began following them.
More cries took up the chant. 'Thief, thief, thief, thief!'

And then the inevitable. A policeman headed towards
them, stopped in front of Sam and held up his hand. Sam
stopped too, and the crowd with him. The policeman
didn't say a word, but slowly looked Sam up and down.
Then, very quietly, he whispered, 'Thief.'

The crowd took it up, whispering quietly the same
over and over again. 'Thief, thief, thief, thief . . .'

Sam looked round at the faces. Narrowed eyes,
clenched fingers, flushed faces, sweaty despite the cold.
He looked back at the policeman and ran. He reached
the end of the street with the entire crowd behind him,
screaming their chant. 'Thief, thief, thief . . .!'

He turned. More people. People ahead, another mini-
mob. People behind, closing in, chanting the same thing
over and over again. Thief, thief, thief, thief.

Wildly he raised his hands, ready to summon magic.
Women, men, grannies, grandfathers, grandchildren,
everyone in the village seemed to have turned out.
Hands grabbed him, hit him, spun him round and round.

'I didn't do anything!' he yelled as hands scratched at
his arms and face. He tried to push his way through the
throng; immediately more arms grabbed him, and held
him in place no matter how hard he struggled. The
voices roared in his ears, the song of Suspicion filled his
head. *All those minds . . . you're too much of a coward, that's
your weakness . . .*

Even more potent.
Little light, little fire.
All those minds.
You're slipping, Sebastian.
Thor loved Freya too.

'Please, I didn't do it!' Hands all around, pulling, pushing, tearing, clutching, voices yelling, screaming, chanting, singing. 'Believe me!' he screamed.

A bright white light around his fingertips. He stared at it in horror and trembled. *Oh, Time, no* . . .

Growing, cascading through his mind, fire lighting more fires, burning, brighter, brighter, expanding outwards. Silence falling as the people saw the burning white light, brighter than the moon, fill Sam's cupped hands. Sam's black eyes themselves gradually turned white, and as the crowd around him began to back away he rose uncertainly to his feet, hands clutched in front of him as though trying physically to hold back the Light. He staggered a few paces like a blind man, and opened his hands.

In total silence the Light rushed out from him in every direction, a white blanket spreading across the land, growing thin as it stretched to cover the fields and forests around.

He tried to hold it back, even as it roared through his head. Finally he caught it and held on, teetering close to total collapse as the Light strained at the edge of his control, begging to be let out to touch all those waiting minds, each mind representing power, more power, more and more, so many minds to drown in, so much power . . .

He clutched it desperately, and for a moment the Light

hung across the land within a mile radius of Sam, hovering there, not moving. He heard the song of Suspicion, and turned the Light on it.

Please, believe me. Trust me.

Every mind within the radius of the Light was touchable. He felt the Light riffling through them, under no control of his, bringing out trust. Some minds trusted instinctively, like the woman in the bakery; some had little trust to give, such as the old lady on the road. But still the Light worked on, isolating this one feeling and enhancing it. Trust in the tattered, weary man in black, trust in your husband, wife, neighbour, child, aunt, uncle, postman, dog, cat . . .

He turned to Suspicion. It was scared, he realised. Even though, from just these few minds, he hadn't nearly enough power to destroy it, Suspicion was frightened of him. As the voices rose up through his head, he raised his hands at the sky and opened them. The Light snapped back towards him across the land, thickening and growing brighter as it retreated from the countryside. Struck him. He seemed to rock physically with the impact of the Light coming back into him, but otherwise didn't move. For a long moment, nothing happened.

You're slipping, Sebastian.

Even more potent.

I am Many. You cannot touch me.

Go away, leave me alone . . .

He felt it move inside him. The Light found its target, focused, fired. From his open fingertips a beam of white light, too bright to look at, shot skywards. It struck something that hung over the village and for a second inside the white beam something vaguely human shaped, but twisted out of all proportion, a huge head on a tiny body, clawed finger- and toenails, writhed in agony.

It was locked there for a second, then the Light winked out and the grisly image vanished too. Far below, on a street full of people, a tiny black figure staggered and shrank in on himself. He stood there for a long moment, then raised his agonised face again. Putting his hands over his ears and squeezing his eyes shut against the flame of every living thing in the vicinity, so bright with life that they threatened to blind him, he tried to shut out the roar of all those minds . . .

What happened?

Why am I here?

Why am I up?

Does he know?

Did she see?

Is it here?

Are we there?

What are we doing here?

Is this me?

Who is that?

Why does he cover his ears?

What was the light?

Why does he close his eyes?

Which voice is mine?

Go away, leave me alone, go away, leave me alone . . .

A hand touched his arm. He opened his eyes. A man stood there, dark, faceless, dark as ebony, and the mind—

Sam put his hand to his mouth to avoid crying out, and bit hard on the place between thumb and wrist. Dark as ebony, not burning with life like everyone else.

And when he listened to the mind he heard the endless tick of the universe, a roar of clocks, ticking away the time to doomsday, *which could be any time now*. A mind whose occupant had moved over to let another take command, another who hadn't been touched by the discharge of the Light . . .

Sam staggered and almost fell. A hand caught his elbow, steadied him. 'Careful, my son,' whispered the distorted, crackled voice of Time, speaking through Jehovah. 'Don't want to hurt yourself.'

'Father, please . . .'

Jehovah helped him walk to a nearby car. It was full of equally empty people, lives and minds taken over by Greater Powers. *Jehovah had sold his soul to Time.*

They laid him on the back seat of the car and drove. The voices grew fainter as they grew more distant, but still the world burned in Sam's eyes. He curled up, buried his head in his hands and trembled, with Jehovah's hands, or possibly Time's hands, depending on how you looked at it, on his shoulders. He felt movement near him and looked up through burning white eyes to see Jehovah flick a hypodermic needle. 'What is it?' he asked hoarsely.

'It'll help.'

'Please . . .'

'It's all right. Everything's all right. There's a plan, you know.' He saw the needle, but didn't have the stomach to watch it enter his arm, and shortly after felt nothing.

TEN

Tinkerbell

He woke on a warm bed in a warm room, in a pool of orange light. For a long time he didn't move but listened to his own head. No voices roared in his ears, but when he strained there were the faint, faint whispers of a thousand minds gradually fading down to nothing.

And me.

And me.

And me.

Which voice is mine?

And me . . .

He couldn't sense anyone in the room, so sat up slowly and looked around. It was more of a shallow cave, carved in the rock. The rock itself was yellow, unevenly hacked and chipped at so that the bed only touched the wall at a few points and balanced uneasily on a cratered floor. It was a strange sort of bed: the blankets harsh and itchy, the mattress smelling of . . . he

wasn't sure what. Some kind of animal, and not a
hygienic one at that.

At the end of the bed someone had laid out fresh
clothes. They were black silk, and looked like they'd
been designed to make him appear devilish. On the other
hand they were better than the near-rags he was
wearing, so he picked them up. At one side of the cave
was a small archway that he had to duck to get through.
Beyond it someone had draped a curtain. He pushed the
curtain aside and looked round at the gloom of a small
stone bathroom, complete with a standing pool of tepid
water.

It looked clear enough so he stuck his head in it,
washed, changed and, by the time he emerged from the
miniature bathroom, felt much better. There was even,
he noticed with faint smile, a pair of trainers by the bed,
his size. They didn't really match the black silk that hung
limply around his slim frame, but they were comfortable,
which was what mattered. He headed to the plain
wooden door, little more than large planks of wood
nailed together, and tugged at the handle. It was locked.

Change of tactic. He walked to the other end of the
room, where the wide cave mouth opened up on to a
small ledge overlooking a drop of more than a hundred
feet. It had no rail or wall to prevent you falling off, but
Sam could smell the magic in the air. He flicked his
fingers at the empty air and wasn't even slightly surprised when a fat green spark flashed off the wards that
encompassed the ledge. He looked beyond the ledge, and
the sheer drop of yellow stone below, to exhibit B. It was
big, it was bright, it was yellow-orange, and it seemed to
go on an awfully long way.

There wasn't evidence of a living thing in that desert, and the cliff wall in which his cave was set had been smoothed by the hammering from thousands of years of sandstorms. He didn't like to guess how anything, snake, beetle or bug, could survive out there. The rarely setting sun of Hell hung on the horizon looking big, mean and bright. It didn't care if you were thirsty and wanted a place to rest in the shade. It was more than its job was worth, gov'nor, to slip below the horizon for more than a few days each year.

Sam turned away from the ledge. It would take time to pick through those heavy wards and probably cause more attention than it was worth. Besides, where would he go?

He knocked on the door, and yelled, 'Hey!' No response. He paced up and down, waiting for an answer. Still nothing. This was discouraging, because 'hey' was one of those multilingual words that seemed to mean the same in every language, even to people who'd never heard it before. After a while he went back to the door, knocked on it again and yelled, in Elysian, at the top of his voice, 'It's coming through the walls, it's coming through the walls, oh, gods, we're gonna die!', and gave a little gurgling sound.

The door opened. A demon stood there, sword drawn. Sam beamed. 'Thank you for coming so promptly. I've just got a few questions –'

The guard, having ascertained that nothing really was coming through the walls, slammed the door. Sam sighed and fell back to pacing. After a few minutes the door opened again and a female demon entered the room, carrying a tray. She deposited it on the floor next to Sam's bed and turned to go. 'Wait!' he said, darting towards her. She turned and, saying nothing, produced from somewhere inside her dress a small but sharp-looking knife.

She had a no-nonsense face, so Sam stopped. 'I only want to talk,' he said, shrugging. 'Where is this?'

Without a word she turned and left, closing the door behind her. Sam headed over to the tray and sat cross-legged beside it. He lifted a pottery cover and peered underneath. It was, alas, gourmet Hell cuisine, but food was food. It tasted a bit like his mattress smelled – but then everything in Hell was made out of the same three animals, be it bedding or breakfast. He didn't dare speculate about where the strange red sauce came from that seemed to suck all moisture out of his already dry mouth. It was vaguely like a tomato would taste were it soaked in chlorine for a month, and the black bits looked worryingly fleshy. He ate anyway, and lay on his bed wondering what had happened to the sun cream he liked to carry around for these kind of excursions. Had he used it all up? Probably not. Most likely at some point on his journey it had been incinerated, soaked, squashed or blasted into a thousand fragments.

The door opened again. He turned his head with a carefully disinterested look on his face. Tinkerbell grinned at him, closing the door as he stepped into the room.

'If you've come to be mysteriously silent, then bugger off and do it somewhere else,' said Sam.

'That's hardly a nice way to greet your guardian angel.'

Sam sat up slowly on his elbow. 'You know, you're

absolutely right. Have some of my lunch. Traditional Hell cookery.'

'No, thanks. I've got a pizza waiting.'

'I knew it,' Sam said sourly. 'Pizza Hut has extended the franchise to the Hellish desert. Now I know the universe is doomed.'

'Actually, I Waywalked for it,' said Tinkerbell. He sat down on the side of the bed with his back to Sam, and began to pick at a loose thread in the mattress.

Sam raised his eyebrows. 'You're not a Waywalker,' he said finally, looking the giant man up and down, scanning him with every sense.

'Third generation. My grandfather was Eshu.'

Sam searched his memory. 'Son of Chaos, only ever went to Earth for sex, drugs and the Glastonbury Festival. I met him once.'

'I never did. What was he like?'

'In all honesty, I didn't take to him. Sons of Chaos can be temperamental. He tried to teach me to dance, and when he discovered that I wasn't the dancing type he got mad and tried to show me how people's innards could be blown out with the pure force of chaos. So I demonstrated how to shield against chaos with magic, and he showed me how to lacerate an order-based shield by sheer perseverance, and I showed him how to punch someone hard enough to break their nose, and he did a very good impression of an unconscious git on the ground, and I went away.'

'Sounds like a whirlwind romance.'

'It was. I hope we can still be friends, though. If you're a Son of Chaos, why "night-spawn"?'

Tinkerbell sighed. Rose to his feet. Paced. He seemed

agitated. 'Do you know where you are?' he asked abruptly, not answering Sam's question.

'Tell me.'

'You're in the Ashen'ias' stronghold, sixty miles east of Pandemonium.'

'Delighted to hear it.'

'Of course, I use the term "stronghold" loosely. James Bond would spit at it.'

'Is the master here?'

'Yes.'

'And the mistress?'

'Yes.'

'And where is Seth?'

'Out there,' he said, waving a hand at the desert. 'Somewhere.'

'Tinkerbell,' said Sam severely, 'Seth is my enemy, not the Ashen'ia.'

'You ran from the master,' said Tinkerbell. 'Were you afraid of him? Or was it something else? I know he's a Waywalker, a first-generation Son of Time. Which Waywalker could make you run, make you fight?'

'We could be allies,' said Sam cautiously, sitting up further. 'Tell me what you want, and I'll tell you what I want.'

'I *know* what you want,' said Tinkerbell. 'Your aims are simple. You want to survive, to be free, to live happy ever after. Ideally you want a pair of slippers and peace.'

Sam gave a shrug. 'For the moment, yes. And you? What do you want?'

Tinkerbell smiled, a long, slow smile that took time enough to read Sam's face and calculate its square and cube root too. 'Me? I'm a third-generation Son of Time.

I stumble through the Ways, half deaf, half blind. I'm not accepted in any world, Heaven, Earth or Hell. In such a situation, what wouldn't you want?'

'Perhaps I should have refined the question. What do you want that could possibly involve the Ashen'ia? Or me,' added Sam, a dark undertone to his voice.

For a moment, he thought Tinkerbell was genuinely going to answer. Then the man grinned, shook his head and said, 'You don't give up easily, do you?'

'So save yourself the annoyance and answer the question.'

'I . . . want revenge.'

'For what, against whom, and how? In that order, for preference, with diagrams if necessary.'

Only the flicker of a smile passed across Tinkerbell's face, which before had been wide open. It made Sam wonder how judicious Tinkerbell was with his smiles. 'For betrayal of my family, I won't say, and . . . with a sharp blade.'

'This betrayer – angel, human, faerie, demon, Waywalker or other?'

'Waywalker.'

'Anyone I should know about concerning this coming conflict?'

'No.'

'So not Jehovah, Seth, Odin —'

'No,' he said, cutting in sharply.

'"No" not one of them or "no" you won't say?'

'Once Cronus is defeated, then I can think of revenge. It has no part in these current battles.'

'Is this like the Ashen'ias' plans? Once the end of the world has been prevented, you want to use me too?'

'Yes.'

'And . . . I'd guess you're wanting to use the Ashen'ia too.'

'What gives you that idea?'

'You don't strike me as the kind of man to sell his soul for anything small and simple.'

Tinkerbell's eyes narrowed ever so slightly but the smile remained fixed. 'I always found it ironic that people were supposed to sell their souls to Satan. What use would he have for them?'

'Besides,' agreed Sam with a sigh, 'only vampirism can steal a soul. Or failing that, a Greater Power. And I'm neither. So when all this is over, you might decide to come after me?'

'If things turn out as I suspect, I may not need your aid.'

'What do you suspect, Tinkerbell?'

The big man cocked his head to one side, in an oddly childlike gesture of regret. At length he said, 'This will get us nowhere . . . That it?'

'Almost. What's your real name?'

In the door, Tinkerbell grinned. 'Brian Hunter.'

Sam thought about this, his features expressive as he worked the name round and round. Seven foot nothing great-grandson of Time with an axe. Called Brian, enjoys pizza. Sometimes there was no telling.

'Pleased to meet you. You know my name, I guess.'

''Fraid so. Though I never thought you deserved such a bad press.' In the doorway he paused. 'Think about it, Lucifer.'

ELEVEN

Ashen'ia

He expected them to come at night, but in Hell that was difficult. Instead, they came with the storm.

The Whirlpool Ocean, spanning the distance between the part of Hell that hardly ever saw night and the part that drowned in darkness, day or night, had convectional currents to make geographers weep with awe. As a result, it could engender storms of gigantic proportions.

When he first heard the thunder he thought, *This is it. Seth's freed Cronus and we're all gonna die*. When death didn't come he rolled over on the bed and looked out at the desert, just in time to see a shadow pass across it. He repeated his earlier thought, but with more cursing. And when the clouds rolled in like something from BBC nature footage, speeded up to give the impression of days taking hours, he practically got down on his knees and confessed to the deity he knew wasn't there and asked to be absolved of his sins. *Please sir, the Devil made me do it*.

The failure of the end of the world to come was made no less dramatic by the drop of temperature, by the roaring winds that sent sparks flying off the shield on the ledge outside the cave, and the lightning that stabbed down at the desert as though hating every grain of sand and every critter that had dared to believe it could survive in such conditions.

Then, when the black cloud had spilled across every inch of the sky and the winds were screaming for blood, when the man backstage was raising thunder with the entire cast to cheer him on and when the lighting engineer in his small box overlooking the theatre had been told to let rip – then there came the rain. Sam sidled out on to the ledge, not quite sure he believed his eyes. It struck the shield with so much force that soon the entire globe of magic around the ledge was lit with green flame that sparked and hissed and flashed as each drop struck. The wind tore over the shield, nails across sandpaper, the rain shot pins into it, and above the desert the lightning continued to dance, a mob-handed chorus line trying to upstage the lead. The thunder made a brave retaliation, but against the darkness, and the wind, and the rain, and the lightning, it stood no chance.

Sam heard someone laughing. It was him. He tried to hold it in – then laughed again and again, and went on laughing. If the end of the universe had come he might as well go down with a grin and a flourish.

The door opened, but he ignored it. He stood with his hands in his pockets and watched the storm, feeling better about the universe than he had for a long time. It was exhilarating to see all that power, and know that it was none of his concern.

'Sam,' said Jehovah behind him, 'don't be offended by this. It's just a precaution.'

'Brother mine, it'd take a lot to offend me right now.'

'Good,' said Jehovah, as they pulled the blindfold over his eyes, shutting out the storm and plunging him into darkness.

Walking through corridors. He wished he was one of those practical, assured people who could count fifty paces, left turn, ten paces, right, up a flight of three stairs, right – but he couldn't even keep the route in his head, let alone play it backwards.

Even here, with the Ashen'ia dug into cliffs and caves, he could feel the thunder through his feet. He could feel other things too, just on the edge of his senses. The demons were afraid; they were terrified of the storm. Fear spilled over the usual confines of the brain and infected the entire place with a tang of dread that anyone could register, immortal or not, even without a sixth sense. With every strike of lightning the demons quaked, with every roll of thunder.

They stopped, the hands that had guided him pulling the blindfold clear of his eyes. Sam blinked, his vision fuzzy as his eyes adjusted to the light. He heard a door closing behind him and turned.

Jehovah was watching him with an unreadable smile, the only other person there. Sam turned again and examined the room. This one looked as if it had been properly carved out by somebody determined to make a good job of it – smooth, circular walls, where at one end a mirror had been inset.

There seemed no particular purpose to the mirror; it

just sat there. Square and silver and smooth. He tapped it, felt round it. It seemed ordinary, which got him worried. In Hell, last he checked, there were no such things as 'ordinary' mirrors. There was bronze and on rare occasions tarnished silver, but a mirror this large —

'Sam?'

He turned, smile already armed. 'Jehovah. There's purpose to all this, right? This the bit where you threaten me with news of a piranha tank, ravenous man-eating penguins and chanting monks with sickles?'

Jehovah gave a sigh, pointedly looking down at the floor. Sam looked too, to see what was so interesting.

It was a warding circle, that much was clear. Inside it was something drawn out in blue and red paint that seemed to pull the eye in and in and in, finding complexities at every turn. He turned his head this way and glimpsed a sword, turned it that way and saw a dove, turned it another and saw a clock, then a square, then a storm, a lightning bolt, a volcano, a tidal wave, a forest . . .

'Sam.' Jehovah was holding out a knife. It was small and dull and looked like the kind of thing someone very dedicated had spent a lot of time sharpening before wrapping it in silk and murmuring incomprehensibly at it. Sam took the knife, glancing worriedly over his shoulder at the mirror.

Then he looked back at the circle on the floor, suspicion mingling with dread. 'It's a summoning circle,' he said flatly. 'What do you want summoned?'

'A Greater Power.'

'Which one?'

'Time.'

Sam looked up quickly. *They give to everyone . . . but not Time, never Time. We're all too scared of Time.*

No one dares sell their soul to him. He sees too much, he knows too much.

'Tell me about Seth,' he countered. Buying time with a currency he wasn't sure he wanted to deal in. 'Where is he headed?'

Jehovah said nothing. 'Look,' said Sam, as reasonably as he could manage, 'you're the spy in Seth's midst, right? You must have some idea where he's going. Where Cronus's key is hidden.'

'I know where the door to Cronus's prison is.'

'So do I, so does every Waywalker. What's important is the key. Where is it?'

'There is a city.' Jehovah stopped.

'Yes?' prompted Sam. 'And?'

'Long before the Children of Time were ever spawned, this city tried to revolt against Time. Through their magic they tried to create a weapon similar to the Light and discharge it against Time. Naturally they failed – there is no substitute for the Light itself.

'Time punished them. He sent armies of angels, demons, valkyries and avatars against this city and for their crimes bound the souls of the slaughtered citizens to their city for ever.'

'How quaint,' Sam said, face and voice as cold as each other.

'Anyone entering the city who doesn't bear the mark of a Greater Power will be destroyed by the spirits that guard it.'

'Can these spirits be destroyed?'

'If you can destroy the homes they're bound to – yes, then they die.'

'But I'm guessing you'd need an army to do it?'

A pause. Then, in an almost embarrassed voice, 'Yes.'

'Which is why bastard Seth decided he'd like to pinch my army?'

A longer silence, Jehovah doing his best to look majestic and wise but not quite pulling it off in the face of Sam's stubborn stoniness. 'Yes,' he said finally.

'Thank you for clearing that up. Where is this city? What's it called?'

'Tartarus.'

Sam considered. 'As in the sauce? Tastes nice with fish?'

'I knew you'd say that, brother. I saw you open your mouth and I thought, He's about to say something irrelevant and glib, just as he always does when he's panicked.'

'I'm not panicked. A little alarmed, yes. But I've been alarmed for well over a century now, and I've got used to it. Are you seriously telling me that whatever genius power, Dad I'm thinking of you, created this universe, he decided to hide the key to Cronus's prison right next to the doorway?'

'The Ashen'ia are not aware that I know the location of the key.'

Sam stopped. He glanced over his shoulder at the mirror, looked down at the knife in his hand. His eyes drifted up to the door beyond and finally slid across to Jehovah. 'Why?'

'They want power. Think how much power they'd have if they could take the key and say to Time, "See, we

can free your enemy unless you bow before us."
Therefore I haven't told them where the key is hidden.'

Sam thought about this. 'No,' he said. 'You're lying.
Partially, at least; I'm not sure about the details. But
there's two ways of looking at it. Either the Ashen'ia
really don't know where the key is. Or they do know, but
are too afraid of Cronus to use it. Hence their need for
the Bearer of Light, not only to hold the Greater Powers
to hostage but as insurance against Cronus being freed.'

Jehovah raised his eyes, and they burned. There was
a darkness on his face that sent a shiver down Sam's
spine, but he met Jehovah's eyes stare for stare.
Suddenly, with no apparent cause, Jehovah smiled.
'You're close. Worryingly so, but I don't think it presents
a problem yet.'

He began to walk round the edge of the circle,
towards Sam. There was no menace on his face, no
threat in his stride, but Sam instinctively backed off,
talking fast as he did. 'So you're using the Ashen'ia, fine.
With me as bait. I understand, no problem. You need
something big to bait an army like the one the Ashen'ia
presents, and the Bearer of Light is a convenient weapon
to this aim, fine, okay. But I can't believe that you, being
in possession of a Pandora spirit, being a Prince of
Heaven and a Son of Time, ruthless to the extreme,
would let Seth get to Cronus's key so easily. So if you
know where it is, why haven't you moved it?'

Jehovah darted forwards unexpectedly. Sam stifled
his gasp of alarm as Jehovah snatched his free hand and
held it up, turning it this way and that. Not violently, but
with a firm, irresistible force.

Jehovah smiled at Sam. 'I'll tell you everything, when

I have my guarantees.' He caught Sam's other hand, pulling it up with the knife still held there, pressing the blade lightly against the palm of Sam's empty hand. Not hard enough to draw blood, but the meaning was clear. When he was sure he had Sam's full attention, he gave him a gentle push, and Sam staggered into the centre of the summoning circle.

'Summon Time. Call him.'

'The Ashen'ia fear Time,' said Sam quietly. 'He's the only Greater Power they do not wish to call.'

'No Ashen'ia serves Time.'

'You do,' said Sam. 'I felt the heartbeat of the universe when I heard your mind. The Light showed me your soul, and it's only yours by a thread. The strings that pull you are controlled by Time, you can barely command which finger you move, let alone which song you dance to. Yet you would have me summon Time. The Ashen'ia would probably take hard to that. To their illustrious master being a servant of Time.'

Jehovah smiled and nodded slowly. 'Perhaps the Ashen'ia are not just my pawns, perhaps they're Time's too. You see, Father saw centuries ago that Seth would revolt against him. And he also saw centuries ago that the Ashen'ia would be a factor in Seth's downfall. That's why he let them endure. But it always pays to make sure, doesn't it?'

Sam felt realisation creep through him like frost over stone. 'You're his insurance. How long have you been serving Time?'

Jehovah looked uncomfortable. 'I . . . gave him my undivided loyalty before the Pandora spirits were freed. I originally agreed to help Seth and Odin with all my heart. But I was quickly persuaded that their intents were far different from mine.

'Father told me I would be destroyed if I didn't accept his power. So I let him in, and under his counsel I went to the Ashen'ia. It was easy to take command. They were weak and scattered, and in awe of a Waywalker. I hid my identity, because I feared that if an Ashen'ia were captured he might reveal to Seth or Odin who I was.

'Then, when the Pandora spirits were freed, I caught Gabriel trying to escape them. Not only did she join the Ashen'ia; she also sold her soul to Time.'

'Did you kill Freya?'

'No, I said I didn't!'

'You lying bastard!' Sam leapt at Jehovah, not caring about the consequences, and saw the look of fear pass across his brother's face. He hit him on the mouth with one flailing fist and brought the knife up. Jehovah's hand closed around his wrist and caught it, centimetres from his throat. Sam's eye was a few inches from Jehovah's; he could see his own reflection in the iris. 'Bastard,' he hissed, struggling to drive the knife forward. 'Murdering, manipulative bastard . . .?'

Jehovah struck back at him, but Sam hardly noticed. He was feeling inside for the magic. They'd never known the true extent of his power, his brothers and his sisters. But they'd always feared him, as a Son of Magic, because they never understood how potent that element could be. The Children of Magic were the ones who, at the last moment, would turn a battle the other way, would heal the dying king, catch the fleeing assassin, save the sinking ship, calm the roaring volcano, purge the plague. They lived in those rare, fleeting futures which had next to no chance of coming about. They would, with their magic, make all Time's carefully planned out futures collapse and fail, at the very last second, and Time would be powerless to prevent the impossible, and frequently unwanted, conclusion coming to pass . . .

Fire flashed at Sam's fingers, grew up around him, covered his arms, his shoulders, his head, his waist, his legs, all in the same bright yellow flame. Jehovah opened his mouth and screamed like an animal as the fire spread from Sam to himself. But where with Sam it hadn't burned, on Jehovah it caught the sleeves of his robe and set them alight.

With a shove Jehovah pushed Sam away, to sprawl in the centre of the summoning circle, blazing with magic. Sam staggered to his feet and pushed his arms out to the side, forcing the fire to expand and expand, filling the air and spreading to every corner of the room.

Through the blaze his black eyes caught the space where the mirror had been. He had enough time to wonder at the doorway that now stood there before something heavy and burning with living flame came out of the inferno and hit him. He staggered and fell forwards, fires winking out. Jehovah was clutching one hand – the same hand that had been cut by the exploding Coke can, and was bleeding anew. As Sam raised his head he wondered who it was that had hit him. Whoever it was didn't let up the pressure, and hit him again. And again. And just to make sure, they hit him again.

He lay in the centre of the summoning circle, cheek pressed to the ground, and wondered whether the universe was worth saving after all.

Jehovah made his way across the floor and with one

bloody hand caught Sam's face and pulled it up towards his own, spitting words at him through his teeth.

'Freya was the one who convinced me to join Time!' he hissed. 'She was already serving him, she was Balder's lover! She gave her soul to Time when Balder died; she gave it hundreds of years ago. The only reason she ever went to you was because Time commanded her to watch you, watch the Bearer of Light.

'She never loved you! She was using you like the rest of us, she's been using you for years, and it was she who made me sell my soul to Time, no one else! She's the one who really controls the Ashen'ia, she's the one who has the plans. How do you think she found out what Seth was planning? She knew years before Seth did what he was going to do!'

Sam said nothing, refusing to believe, trying to shut the words out. *Lies. He's a Son of Belief, he lies . . .*

Jehovah sat back, letting Sam's head fall to the ground, and nursed his bleeding hand. 'She made you love her. Then she let Seth realise that she knew about his plans. So that Seth would send assassins. She *let* herself be betrayed. So that you would get involved, try to revenge her death. She had to get you involved, don't you see? You're the Bearer of Light.'

'She's dead,' whispered Sam, not moving. 'You murdered her.'

'No. I didn't.'

'You lie. You're all lying. You've been lying for centuries.' He closed his eyes, trying to shut out something more than the words. His other senses were picking up another mind in the room, someone standing behind him, the watching figure beyond the mirror. He strove not to sense it, tried in vain not to recognise the mind that stood behind him. 'You want me to sell my soul to Time like you did. You're lying. It won't work.'

'Why deceive yourself, Sam?'

'Following a trend.'

And she spoke. He'd known she would, he'd known when he saw the mirror draw back and the dark shape emerge from it, shielding against the fires.

He'd known, and wished he hadn't.

'I'm sorry, Sebastian.'

Sam said nothing. He didn't know what he could say. He lay there, a small figure in black on a floor of swirling colours and buried his head in his hands.

Another hand touched his shoulder, warm. Just like hers.

'I'm so sorry.'

He lifted his head and stared ahead of him at the room as though he'd never seen it before.

'I founded the Ashen'ia,' she said in his ear, a statement of fact, not trying to excuse. 'I promised them they'd have you. More to the point, your power. I knew Seth would send someone to kill me. Jehovah helped me fake my own death, so I could disappear. I had to get out of Seth's sights, don't you see?

'Also I had to drag you in. We needed you to delay Seth until we were ready. We also needed you to have a cause to fight for. And I knew the only thing you'd be guaranteed to fight for was me.'

'Go away.'

'Sebastian—'

'Go away. Leave me alone.' *Leave me alone, get out of my head.*

You're slipping, Sebastian. Drowning in the voices . . .

She spoke so factually, so coldly, like a spy reporting to her master, but still her warm hand brushed his hair from his face and her voice tickled his ear as though they'd never stopped being lovers. But for the words she said, he could almost believe they'd never parted.

'I was sent to make you love me.'

You're slipping, Sebastian.

The light and the dark, the magic . . . the magic and . . . and . . .

'Go away. Please go away.'

For Freya.

'I . . . do love you.'

So many minds, filling my soul, drowning out my voice, no escape.

'It's a trick.'

'I wasn't meant to love you, Sebastian. I couldn't help it.'

Not even the magic can hold me up, lost in a sea of thought.

'Go away!'

He'd yelled it, felt her hand recoil sharply from his face as though stung. Saw Jehovah take Freya by the hand and pull her away from him. He brought his knees up to his chin and buried his face against them, wrapping his arms around his shins to protect himself.

He felt them move away, felt Freya's eyes on him every step, heard the door close. When he was sure they were gone, he raised his head, face burning, tears stinging his eyes, and put his hands to his ears.

You're slipping, Sebastian, not even the magic can hold me up, but then everyone loved Freya, go away, leave me alone, go away, and me, and me, and me, lost in a sea of thought, go away, no more alone, go away, go away, for Freya, leave me alone, leave me alone . . .

His mouth opened in a scream that refused to come. Hunched within the summoning circle the Bearer of Light held on to his head as though it were about to explode. A thousand voices roared Freya's name in his mind, and not one of them his own. *Go away, leave me alone, go away, go away, go away . . .*

Alone, the Bearer of Light fell to the ground and wept like a baby.

TWELVE

A Question of Loyalty

He warded the door, sealing himself in, and explored the cubbyhole behind the open mirror. It was just a dark space, but the mirror was two-way, letting in light from the torches burning in the small room beyond.

Sam sat on the edge of the summoning circle, cross-legged, and watched the knife in the middle of it. Finally he said to the empty air, 'It's a silly ritual anyway. You are everywhere, so why should I have to shed blood to summon you? That's just the painful part of a spell, put in to make foolish men feel better about their weak magics. But I know. You're everywhere. You'll always be everywhere, there's no way to escape Time, is there? So appear. Talk to me.'

And where there hadn't been a man, there was a man. Or possibly he'd been there all along. He wore a silver crown, the twin of Sam's, and in one hand he carried a short silver sword, also identical to Sam's. But his hair

was blond and his clothes were white, and unlike Sam he
carried the dagger in his belt, rather than hidden away
where none might suspect it.

Sam recognised him from the paintings in Heaven,
and Balder knew that he did, for he smiled. Or it wasn't
Balder, but someone borrowing Balder's shape, for Sam
knew also that Balder was dead and buried.

'Well?' he said finally, when Sam didn't speak. His
voice was light and innocent. 'You've called me here.
What do you want?'

'You know.'

'I know what most probably you want. I can see billions of billions of futures where you want answers and
truths, and very few universes indeed where you desire
anything else. But to make these futures happen, you
must ask.'

'You sent her.'

'Yes,' he said simply, not a qualm.

'How long have you been planning this?'

'Thousands and thousands of years. I had thought it
would be Balder who would fight this battle, but he is
dead and you are not. So the Light is yours, the duty is
yours.'

'All so I can stop Seth?'

Balder raised his eyebrows, looking at Sam with a
faint smile on his lips. Then he laughed. 'Whatever gave
you the idea that I wanted you to do that?'

Sam had opened his mouth to speak, before Balder's
words smote their way into his brain. He looked up at
Balder with horror in his eyes. 'You've . . . let Seth get
this far because you *want* him to free Cronus?'

Balder shrugged, walking up and down within the

summoning circle as though he hadn't a care and was mildly amused to see a mere immortal puzzling it out.

'So that I will have to discharge against Cronus,' added Sam. Another shrug, a casual little matter, not worthy of great attention. 'Ridding yourself of your great enemy.'

'Uhuh.'

'And your son?'

Another shrug. 'Casualty of war.'

Sam followed his pacing and spoke in a soft, low voice. 'You bastard. You've been behind this all the time . . . But why not free Cronus yourself?'

'Wouldn't come out. Cronus has a limited sphere of influence, but he can sense if someone genuinely wants him free. Seth does. So it is necessary that Seth opens the door to Cronus.'

'You knew this was going to happen. You sent Freya to ensure I was involved. You knew Jehovah would then turn to you, sell his soul. You knew that I would end up with the Ashen'ia. That's why you made sure Jehovah had me watched and protected, to ensure I didn't die. You must have known more, though. You must have known that I'd stab Adam when a Pandora spirit possessed him, that all these things would come to pass, that I'd love Freya! You knew!'

'Of course,' said Balder. 'But you changed one of those things, didn't you? In nearly all the futures I saw, you killed your friend Adam. But you didn't, did you? You're the miracle maker, you just have to defy destiny. I saw futures span out from that one event I hadn't seen before.' He didn't raise his voice, didn't even look in Sam's direction, just wandered round the room with the distracted interest of a busy tourist who'd been expecting something more.

Sam was shaking with anger. 'All this? Just so you could destroy Cronus once and for all?'

'You seem surprised. I thought more of you, son.'

'You've let worlds be torn apart so you can be rid of a helpless enemy!' yelled Sam. 'You've turned Hell upside down, Hades razed to the ground, thousands and thousands of demons marching to die against the Ashen'ia who all the time are nothing more than pawns in your grand scheme! On Earth you expected Adam, my friend, to die under the influence of the Pandora spirits, along with who knows how many others! In Heaven, Jehovah has turned Suspicion loose and now all of your Children cower in fear! All so that Cronus can be destroyed?'

Balder sighed, as though annoyed by a persistent fly. 'You cannot see the future. More good things will come out of this than you know.'

Sam gave a strange, twisted laugh. 'Or ever will know, Father. For I'll be dead or mad or a wandering ghost, mind shattered to a hundred billion other minds, be they ant, angel, human or horse. That's your grand plan, isn't it? Convince Seth that he's freeing Cronus through his own intelligence and power, so that Cronus will see a loyal servant of his unlocking the gates. And Cronus will rush forth, and your little son, little light and little fire, will stand before him, a dwarf faced with a giant. And I'll discharge the Light, and both of us will die.

'Congratulations, Father, you've freed the world of two devils with one stroke. Hurrah for the new world order, come join the plots of Time. For nothing can he fear while little light and little fire is betrayed and beaten by all he loved.'

Sam paused for breath, anger bubbling like boiling oil, fingers opening and closing at his sides, wishing he had a suitable weapon. *But you have a weapon, little light, little fire,* whispered the voices in his mind. *We are your weapon. We are the intention and the act, the strength and the weakness, the —*

Shut up.

There is a part of Us that can destroy Time. For Time is but a One, and we are Many.

Shut up.

You're slipping, Sebastian . . .

'Finished?' asked Balder, seeing Sam stand wretched before him, shifting from foot to foot as though not quite comfortable inside his own body.

'No,' he snapped. 'How much of my life have you planned?'

'All,' said Balder mercilessly, driving the word at Sam like a jousting knight. 'From birth to the present day, always am I around you. I am Time. I am Destiny. I am Fate. You cannot escape me.'

'Never once?' asked Sam, seeming to shrink in on himself. 'Have I never once defied and won?'

Balder seemed to hesitate, just for a moment. Then he sighed and looked away. 'Once. I did not mean for you to be exiled over the Way of Eden. I wanted you distanced from Heaven, not banished by your own actions.'

'You must have seen I'd close the Way of Eden.'

'I saw it. But I thought it was beyond you.' He turned back to Sam, and there was something in his face that Sam couldn't read. It wasn't anger, it wasn't hate, though it came near both. Something else tempered his borrowed features – lowered the eyebrows, twisted the mouth and made the skin pale.

'Truly you're the miracle-maker, to have closed the Way of Eden as you did. I didn't think you had the courage, the strength, or the understanding. I was wrong on every count.'

'I can't make miracles when I'm dead,' said Sam.

'No,' replied Balder with a faint, almost sad smile. 'But while you live, perhaps?'

'If by a miracle I can stop you in your aims, I'll do so. I won't let you overturn worlds because of a feud millions of years old that has no need to destroy so much.'

'"Won't let?"' echoed Balder, the smile turning to something cruel and amused. 'How so?'

'I'm the miracle-maker, I'll find a way. You've underestimated me before, haven't you, Father? Why should I not be able to destroy your plans now?'

Balder spoke quietly, his blue eyes boring into Sam's. 'You're right, of course. I made you almost too good at what you do. But you're still not capable of challenging a Greater Power.'

'Yet you'd make me destroy Cronus.'

'Cronus is challenging you, not the other way round. Conflict with him is something you cannot avoid.'

'Watch me.' Sam drew magic inside him, framed his thoughts, his target. *Seth. Tell Seth what's happening, warn him off.*

'If you try to touch Seth's mind,' said Balder, his voice so gentle it was hardly audible, 'I'll kill Freya.' He advanced towards Sam, menacing, graceful as a cat; but Sam didn't doubt he had sharp claws too. 'You're already slipping,' Balder whispered.

There is a part of Us that can destroy Time. For Time is but a One, and we are Many.

'Not even the magic can hold you up any more, can it?'

We are the intention and the act, the strength and the weakness.

'You've used the Light too much, son.' Time reached out and gently clasped Sam's head in his two hands, as though he knew about the voices that buzzed away in Sam's skull, making him feel as if he were about to burst.

. . . the light and the dark, the individual and the whole . . .

'All those voices are becoming one in your mind, aren't they? So many voices, you can no longer tell them apart. And as they lose individuality and speak with one voice, so your thoughts begin to speak with them. You're already remembering things that don't come from your own mind.'

. . . slipping from the One into the Many . . .

'They say . . . I can destroy you,' said Sam, surprised at the weakness of his own voice and the racing of his heart. 'They speak as one. They say they are life, for life is many things, and you are just another part of being. They say there is much that is timeless in this universe; you are not necessarily required.'

'They're just memories. Figments of other lives, ingrained on your mind.'

'No,' Sam whispered, clasping his father's wrists in his hands, holding on to them as though he feared the hands on his head might slip and the voices would pour out, fill the world, drown him in their chant. 'When I use the Light a part of my mind is written on to the minds of those I touch. So parts of their minds are written on to mine. So many minds, all connected by the Light, and through the Light they speak as One. Many become One, yet there is only One of the Many, so many minds inside my own, and they never go away, they stay there for ever, and the more minds you have inside your own the louder they grow until you can hardly hear yourself think!'

. . . so much in so little, so much in me . . .

Balder smiled faintly. 'When put like that,' he said, 'what is to be feared from dying?'

'I'm afraid,' Sam whispered.

'I know.' Balder pulled Sam closer, wrapped his long arms around him and held him. 'I know. Who isn't afraid of the unknown?'

'Seth isn't. Cronus isn't the end of the universe, Father. He's the end of the universe as we know it. There's a big difference. Cronus might be nice.'

'Do you believe that?'

'No. But I have never seen any proof. I have never seen proof that man landed on the moon, or that Odin's crown is little more than painted tinfoil. Yet I believe these things. Why can't I then believe that Cronus would bring happiness?'

'Because of the Light,' replied Balder, leaning his cheek against Sam's hair and rubbing his limp arms. 'The Light touches all those minds, and between them they carry every aspect of life, trust, hate, suspicion, greed, love, jealousy, anger, peace, contentment, resentment – it's all there. And though it will drive you mad, you have learned to like life, and fear its ending.

'That's also why you instinctively fight me. Because I

am also, eventually, death, and that too is inescapable. And in touching all the minds of the universe, you have, in a brief, small way, touched mine. So you know I'll kill her.'

'I need . . .' A faint smile crossed Sam's lips at the irony. 'Time.'

'You have three days until Seth reaches Tartarus. Unless, that is, he's prevented by a miracle. But I don't think he will be, do you?'

'Don't leave me alone,' whispered Sam, squeezing his eyes shut against the burning tears that were beginning anew.

'You're never alone. You're the Bearer of Light. I will give you your time, but in three days be ready.'

And Sam was facing empty air. Or perhaps that was all there'd been anyway. He sunk to the ground and lay back, staring at the ceiling with wide open eyes, while in his mind a thousand voices whispered to him, and he was entirely alone.

THIRTEEN

Remission

S am found Jehovah sitting on a ledge, alone, smoking. He sat down next to him. 'I didn't know you smoked.'

'It's a new and bad habit. It means that every twenty or so years I contract lung cancer and end up in a regenerative trance.'

'How often have you had lung cancer so far?'

'Three times. But though it means spending several weeks in a trance I find the the habit' – he twisted the cigarette through his fingers – 'strangely appealing.'

'I want to leave.'

'I know. Father told me.'

'He moves fast.'

'Of course. He demands that you take protection. So do I.'

'I'm not going seeking danger, if that's what you think. I just need time to work a few things out.'

'What deal have you made with him? Your soul? As first he wanted?'

'Is that what he was after?' Sam gave a little snort of laughter. 'No, I haven't. He didn't even ask. I think he realises there are other ways to get to me.'

'So what is the deal?'

'Two lives for one.'

'Whose lives?'

'Mine is one. Another is Cronus's, if he can be said to live.'

'And the third?'

Sam didn't answer.

Jehovah looked away and said in a slightly pained voice, 'Ah.'

'Where is she?'

'Around.'

'Did Gabriel know?'

Jehovah looked back at him, eyebrows raised. Sam smiled uneasily, raising his hands in a gesture of defeat. 'She served Freya, when she left you. Did Freya tell her the scheme?'

'I did, after I joined the Ashen'ia. It was quite embarrassing, to follow in a servant's footsteps. Gabriel had left me for my sins, and when I realised what those sins were, I had no choice but to ask her forgiveness.'

'What about the rest? Michael, Uriel, what happened to them? Michael shot me, but only with lead, where he could have killed me with silver. Did they know whose side you were really on?'

'Michael spared your life under my orders. But I haven't told them why. I think it best that as few people as possible know the truth. You are one. Gabriel another. Freya the last.'

'You must have hated having to admit Gabriel was right.'

He smiled and shook his head. 'No worse than having to admit you were right about Christianity.'

'You never admitted anything of the kind.'

'I admitted it to myself.'

'When?'

'At the time of the crusades. I tried to build something Heavenly on Earth. I tried to make a religion that would inspire mortals to do great deeds, to love each other and live by good rules. You told me it would go wrong.'

Sam stared across the desert, swinging his legs where he sat on the rim of the ledge. The storm had passed, and the desert was a sea of dark brown mud, every feature destroyed that he'd noted before from his room. In the distance he could hear the rumble of thunder and see black anvil-shaped clouds, but nearby all was quiet. 'Where you went wrong was in allowing the Crucifixion. A religion born of blood will die in blood; you should have known that.'

'I admit it. Christianity could have been beautiful. But mortals twist everything, and I am not the miracle-maker.'

'And I am. Which is why, though you admit I was right, you'll never forgive me.'

Jehovah's voice was calm and matter of fact as he replied. 'Yes.'

Sam went on watching his own feet swing back and forth over the huge drop below. At the foot of the cliff the muddy sand was pocked with raindrops, to make the impression of a galaxy of tiny stars in a brown void. 'Because the right kind of miracle might have prevented

all those holy wars, all those prejudices, all that blood.
But your grand design didn't receive that miracle, did it?
Because I was banished and you had helped banish me.'

'It was entirely your own fault that the Way of Eden
was closed,' said Jehovah, stabbing the cigarette butt in
Sam's direction accusingly. 'No one asked you to do it.
You disapproved of our methods and decided to take it
all in hand yourself. Typically, I might add.'

'Well, it's done and can't be undone, so there's no point
biting your nails over it.'

'Where will you go?' asked Jehovah.

'I don't know.'

'You could go to Heaven,' he said, watching for Sam's
reaction. 'I control Heaven, you see. And I certainly
won't harm you. Not now.'

'You'll keep Seth and Odin away?'

'They're entirely focused on Hell.'

'What about Thor? He must still be seeking me.'

'That's why you're taking protection, isn't it?'

'Oh, yes, Tinkerbell – I mean Brian Hunter. Eshu's
grandson.'

Jehovah's face was a mask of incomprehension.
'Hunter isn't Eshu's descendant. His grandfather was a
Son of Night. His grandmother was a sorceress, but she
never told her children who their father was. Hunter
sold his soul to Night, and Night is in his blood. At no
point is he a relative of Eshu's.'

'Why did he lie to me?'

'I don't know.'

'He said he wants revenge against a Waywalker.'

'Did he give an indication who that might be?'

'No. He said I'd approve, though.'

'Be careful of him . He has a large following within the Ashen'ia. In seniority he's barely under Gabriel.'

'I didn't know that.'

They watched the desert. The sun, in all defiance of probability, refused to go down. 'I hate waiting,' said Jehovah finally. 'I've been waiting for so long, now that the end seems to be drawing near it seems slightly pointless.'

'You think you have a problem?'

Jehovah gave him a look out of the corner of his eye, a half-smile twisting his face as though not sure what it wanted to be. 'I have done you wrong.'

'Really.'

'And I have, in my time, plotted against my brothers and sisters. I helped free a Pandora spirit, I put my name down to an enterprise that I knew at the time would lead to conflict within Heaven. I have not been punished for any of these yet.'

'You repented. You gave your soul to Time.'

'Yes, but I doubt if it will end with Tartarus.'

'I know for a fact that it will for me unless a miracle happens.'

'You can't make miracles when you're dead, brother.'

'You neither,' he pointed out mildly.

'I never could.'

'But I'll bet you tried.'

'Yes. I expect everyone does.'

'Including Freya?'

'I don't doubt it. Go on and find out, Sam.'

Sam looked warily at Jehovah, and more or less smiled. 'Maybe another time soon. While there is time, that is.'

❋

There was a Portal in the desert, Tinkerbell assured him.

'Going on a trip, are we?'

'Uhuh.'

'Any idea where?'

'I'm seeing what takes my fancy.'

'Sure, no problem,' Tinkerbell replied, swinging his crossbow into a more comfortable position. 'Oh, and I was told to give you this.' He tossed Sam's bag at him. Inside was the sword, dagger and crown, along with what remained of his explosive arsenal. 'I gather you've made a deal with the powers that be.'

'You wouldn't believe,' Sam replied, slipping the dagger into its sheath on his arm.

'I'm your protection for this little jaunt.'

'Somehow I imagined you would be.'

Tinkerbell led the way down rough-cut stone steps, through natural caverns and bored-out corridors of red stone, and down a wooden ladder through a claustrophobic tunnel that ended with a squelch under Sam's boots. He looked at what he'd trodden in. Hell's equivalent of bats had a wingspan of five feet or more, and hugely bloated necks to store precious water seeping down through the rock, and they liked to use giant natural caves as toilets.

'Ugh,' said Sam. The smell was something extraordinary, but Tinkerbell didn't seem to mind. 'I spent a lot of time near this biogas factory in India. You don't know anything until you've seen what goes into that,' he said cheerfully, picking his way across the slippery floor towards a patch of light in the distance. Sam half expected to see cave paintings of giant stalagmites; but even here the sand had blasted everything clean.

They stepped from the cave mouth on to sand already dry in the blazing sunlight. Tinkerbell squinted across the endless yellow sea and pulled on a pair of sunglasses that seemed to match everything about him; they made him look like the hero of a particularly gory American thriller with a garage soundtrack.

Sam cast his mind about, and sensed the Portal nearby.

He also sensed something else, standing just beyond the next dune. 'Uh, Tinkerbell?'

'You want something, Hook?'

'A few minutes with someone.'

Tinkerbell frowned and squinted across the desert, and Sam could sense him casting about. Then he shrugged. 'Hell, your senses are better than mine. I can't feel a thing.'

'She's shielding. It's kind of an instinct in a Waywalker.'

'You want me back in five minutes?'

'Please.'

Sam picked his way up the nearest dune, feet sliding under him as miniature yellow avalanches marked his passage. He reached the top and looked down at her. She smiled, leaning lightly on her staff, the crown of living green ivy around her head. He marvelled at how unchanged she was: how she still smiled even when sad, at how she instinctively placed herself to catch the sunlight, not out of any great vanity, but because she liked to feel its warmth on her face.

But then, Freya had never pretended to be anything but herself. He'd just neglected to ask her whether that self was an agent of Time, on a mission to manipulate the future to Time's grand design. He stared, not minding that he did so.

She stared back at him, her eyes narrowing in contemplation. At length, 'I'm sorry,' she said.

He took his time to answer, not moving to join her, looking down from on high. 'Time, in his infinite wisdom, seems to think I still love you.'

'Is he right?'

'Quite possibly.'

'So.' She nodded thoughtfully. 'You gave your soul to him after all. I didn't think you would.'

'No, actually, I didn't.'

'He said to trust you. He said you and he had reached an understanding.'

'Yes, we have. But I'm still free. Still me. The question is, are you still you?'

She walked a few paces towards him, craning her neck to see him against the burning sun, climbing up the dune to get level. Closer now, she studied his face, looking for signs of age or despair, and finding none. 'I am more me than you are you,' she replied. 'For I only have one being sharing my heart. You have thousands.'

'Did you ever feel like telling me?'

'At first, no. You were just the next assignment. I am a Daughter of Love, it's my blessing and my curse to have many love me. You were no different from the rest.'

'There's a word for that, and it isn't pretty.'

'I know, but the Sebastian I love knew that anyway, when we first met, even if he didn't understand the real reasons.' She sighed. 'Anyway, as the days went by I began to like you more than I had the others. And I began to like you more and more. Until one day I woke up and realised that I had fallen subject to my own trap, and not only did you love me as I intended, but I loved you.'

'It sounds like a fairytale story of the unconvincing kind, with talking bunnies, occasional bouts of song and dance and happy ever after.'

'My favourite kind.'

He frowned at her. 'I . . . don't believe in all that any more. You've succeeded in taming the Bearer of Light to your cause. But you went too far. He just doesn't believe.'

'Then what is he fighting for?'

'I . . .' His voice trailed off. 'Time knows,' he said, shaking his head.

'I love you, Sebastian.'

'You say it so well. How many times have you said those words to a hundred other waiting ears? And was the performance always so consummate?'

'If you came here not to believe, why did you trouble to find me?' she asked, slipping her hand into his.

He turned her hand over, looking at it from every angle. At length he hung his head, and murmured, 'I have no idea.'

'Do you want to believe?'

'I'm too old. I've seen too much.'

'There may be a miracle. You may believe.'

'Miracles aren't two a penny. And even if they were, I've no coin left to spend in that particular department. I'm hoping for a miracle to strike in three days' time. I don't believe it will.'

'You are the maker of miracles, Sebastian.'

He stared down at her, and wondered what he should

say. *I do not love you, yet soon I'll be dying like a knight errant for his lady. And this is hardly the action of a practical survivor, Prince of Darkness. There must be a motive for this mad course. And love is as good a cause as any.*

'I can't make miracles when I'm dead.'

'Whoever said anything about dying?'

He stared at her for a long time, wondering. 'You haven't changed, have you? You're just like you were. Only now I realise that what you were isn't what I thought you were. Strange, that. I've seen so many minds, and at some stage in my life I know I've touched yours. But I never saw. Perhaps I wasn't looking properly.

'Perhaps not.'

There was an uncomfortable silence. He felt somehow too large for his own body, was aware of his arms hanging loose, of the way his left foot stuck out to one side in the sand while his right pointed straight forwards, of how his eyebrows tried to compete for space on his face, of how his mouth was dry and his fingers limp at the ends of his heavy hands. Finally he couldn't help himself. 'Miss me?' he asked.

She made a show of considering, sucking in her cheeks and pursing her lips. 'Not the cooking,' she admitted. 'You were always a dire cook.'

'What's the point of having the world at your feet if you can't go to restaurants?'

'That's a decadent attitude and you know it.'

'There are thousands of restaurants in New York alone. We could have gone to a new restaurant every night in any city and any country we pleased. And what did we do?'

'I offered to cook.'

'Freya, now that the end of the world is coming I can safely say that your duck in orange sauce was possibly the most repulsive meal I've eaten in all my life. We have both spent too much time learning the languages of the three worlds and studying the art of survival to learn how to cook anything more challenging than baked beans on toast or bacon and egg sandwiches.'

She laughed, but not very much, eyes never leaving his. When the silence returned again, it poured across the desert like a sandstorm.

He wasn't entirely sure whether he kissed her or she kissed him, or whether it was something mutual. It was nothing spectacular: no choruses of sobbing violins or choir of angels marked the event. Just the silent wind and the trickling of sand.

'Am I interrupting something?' asked a voice.

Freya immediately pulled away from Sam, raising illusion to cover herself. He watched the air around her distort, hiding her features from him.

Tinkerbell clambered over the dune and peered at Freya like a blind mouse trying to spot the cat. 'Uh . . . do I know you, love?'

'I'm no one special.'

'You two were kissing.'

'We're old friends,' snapped Sam, brushing himself down. 'Was there something I can do for you, Tinkerbell?' he asked, and felt Freya's amusement at the name.

'Just wondering if we should be off.'

'Yes, of course. Pressures of time, and all that.' He smiled and shrugged at the blurred features of Freya. 'Perhaps . . .'

'Some other time,' she agreed, and without another word turned and began to walk across the dunes.

Tinkerbell watched her go. 'Who the hell?'

'A bishop on the board.' Sam saw the look on Tinkerbell's face and grinned, albeit half-heartedly. 'Come on,' he said. 'There's a lot to do before the game is won.'

FOURTEEN

Position of the Enemy

They Waywalked to Earth, Sam leading the way. When he offered Tinkerbell his hand, Tinkerbell looked down at it as if Sam were mad. But when he saw the gaping Portal, white mist pouring out from it, he changed his mind. In the Portal Sam felt Tinkerbell's hand turn hot and clammy as they passed through towards Earth, and against the whispering of the Wayspirits his breath sounded loud and fast. Sam had never seen Tinkerbell afraid, but was willing to swear it was fear that drove Tinkerbell in such haste through the Way of Earth.

They emerged in darkness, and cold.

'Where are we?' asked Tinkerbell, blinking up at unfamiliar stars through his sunglasses.

'Siberia. There's no one here to see us,' Sam explained.

'You could have found somewhere more pleasant, if you tried.'

'You'd be surprised. There's always some kid somewhere playing hide and seek who spots you. Or some
fanatical mortal with a taste for the occult who hangs
around Portals and gets down on his knees to the first
person who comes through it. Or tries to disembowel
them for chicken feed. One or the other. Come on.'

He led the way back again. Not focusing on a particular destination, because he didn't have one. But
seeking . . . the night. The edge of night, though. In Hell
it was either night or day, with twilight usually somewhere over the Whirlpool Ocean. What he wanted was
night within the desert, where the sun hardly ever set.
Not proper dark night, because that would mean going
deep into Seth's power. Just the fringe of night, the very
outskirts.

They stepped from the Way in a place where the sky
was running from blue to pink to purple to black as far
as the eye could see. The Portal opened on to a cliff,
where a few half-hearted shrubs were attempting, and
failing, to grow. Below, and to the north, night was
spreading across the land like a newly breaking flood. To
the south the desert was as bright as it had always been,
the sun sitting high in the sky with no intention of
budging.

Tinkerbell looked thoughtfully in the direction of the
moving sea of darkness. 'Seth's doing that?'

'Uhuh. He's a Son of Night, to him that kinda thing is
simple. On a good day he can also manage eclipses of the
sun, but not in the proper astronomical sense.'

'And somewhere in there,' Tinkerbell nodded towards
the moving shadow, 'is an army?'

'Yup. Hidden away so we can't see.'

'Why do you want to see? We've got a rough idea. Thousands of Hellish troops under the command of Seth, Odin and Jehovah.'

'I want to see. It's important to me.'

Tinkerbell looked Sam up and down with a frown. 'The master said you were one of us now. I think he lied.'

'You don't trust anyone, do you?'

'Especially not the master.'

'And you call me the optimist.' Sam indicated the darkness. As if to himself he said, 'Even if there are thousands of people in there, they'll all be dead in three days' time. They'll reach their destination, they'll fight the Ashen'ia and most likely destroy them. Then they'll storm this city, and the city will destroy them. But not before they've managed to raze it to the ground.

'And then Seth will saunter into the city and pick up the key to Cronus's prison and all that death will have been for *nothing*. Thousands dead, for nothing.'

'Then stop it.'

'I don't have the power.'

'That's a lie, and you know it. You're the Bearer of Light. Call on the Light now! Send it out into the world, send it into the night and dispel Seth's power! If you genuinely are Ashen'ia, you're sworn to destroy him!'

'The Ashen'ia wish to use me; why should I even try to help them?'

'The Ashen'ia are your only ally against Seth.'

Sam looked at Tinkerbell, and laughed. 'You still believe that? The Ashen'ia are pawns. Sacrifices to Seth, to make him—' He stopped, staggered a few paces, put his hands to his ears. Voices roared in his head, screaming. *You're slipping, Sam . . .*

He managed to gasp, 'The Ashen'ia will die. The armies of Seth will die. The city will fall, the key will be found, Cronus will be freed. And there is nothing I can do about it!'

'Then why did you want to come here?'

The voices were fading again. *I almost told him. And then I couldn't. The Light is life, and life wants to live. Even if thousands die.*

'I . . . wanted to convince myself of something. You must believe me. If I could do something to save the lives of these men, I would.'

'What's your deal with the Ashen'ia, Sebastian? What did they offer you?'

Sam turned back, looking at the darkness. 'A life. They'll kill someone very dear to me, unless I do what they want.'

'You were negotiating with the master himself, weren't you? Who is the master?'

Sam said nothing.

'The master doesn't want you to weaken Seth at all, does he? And while they hold this one life hostage, you just won't do it. Even though there'll be a battle in which thousands die? Thousands of lives for one? Is that moral? Or are you like every other Prince of Heaven – who cares how many mortals die, so long as the immortals' petty feuds survive? Is that it?'

'Give me an alternative. Tell me how I can save these people's lives without changing anything.'

'So you're going to mope around for three days and hope something happens instead? That's your brilliant solution to all the universe's problems?' Tinkerbell folded his arms and spat on the sand in disgust. 'How pathetic.'

'Thank you for that, Tinkerbell.' Sam looked once more towards the darkness, then turned away. 'Come on. I need to think.'

They went to Earth. Tinkerbell sulked, and wasn't much of a companion. They walked down from the Soho Square Portal in the direction of Piccadilly Circus, and then further east, towards Covent Garden.

'Where are we going?' asked Tinkerbell as they passed through Leicester Square.

Sam looked around. He wasn't sure. At the Odeon workmen were toiling to dress the cinema up in preparation for yet another première. Outside the huge cinema complex, next to what was possibly the worst take-away pizza shop in the world, dozens of people were queueing to get in.

Sam wondered how they had the time. On the other hand . . .

'Let's go to the pics,' he said.

In the darkness, he sat, knees up to his chin, and thought. The film was something mass-market, with a famous star falling for a sexy and if possible even more famous star, in their 'charming whirlwind romance set against the background of Paris in the early twentieth century, essential viewing for all the family'.

He wasn't really following the story. Tinkerbell sat next to him, munching on popcorn and looking as if he'd like to hit either one of the leads. Not, Sam realised, because they were particularly bad, but because going to the cinema wasn't how Tinkerbell saw his assignment to protect the Bearer of Light in a time of crisis.

If only he knew. In the darkness of the auditorium, surrounded by rapt humans, their minds all focused on the same thing, he could concentrate without the irritating buzz of numberless wild and whirling sounds, feelings and sights around him. Just one soundtrack, just one spectacle, and he could ignore that. For once he didn't have to worry about being surrounded by others, because this crowd was responding, essentially, as One.

He remembered.

Before Seth, before Freya, before the Pandora spirits and before the lonely reaches of exile on Earth, there'd been Heaven. In Heaven, he'd fought against the Eden Initiative. And to everyone's surprise, including his father's, he'd won.

Eden Portals were hard to sense, especially after they'd been so thoroughly warded by a Greater Power. Three times he'd thought he'd sensed one, and three times they'd turned out to be Earth Portals. He'd been half prepared to give up, until he saw, hidden at the base of a rolling green hill, something unnatural sticking up through the trees. Sam walked towards it, pushing his way through overgrown bracken and thorns towards the sound of running water, following his instincts. When he stepped from the trees into bright sunlight he saw what it was that was so unnatural.

It was like a totem pole, except it was carved out of pure white marble. It stood on the bank of a shallow, bouncing little stream, and was aligned to catch the sunlight and reflect it in a thousand directions at once. At the bottom of the pole was a sculpture of a sleeping lion, above that a dog's head, then a snake, an eagle, a hawk and, capping it all, a rough, chipped carving that might have been a man, if men were square. His body and limbs were lumpy and disproportionate; but the face was perfectly carved, with melancholy eyes and a faint, sad smile, that seemed to say, 'I see you too'.

One arm of the figure was pointing towards the river. Sam turned to follow it, and in that moment, when he'd been least expecting it, felt a Portal tug at his senses. He probed again, eagerly, trying to recover the signal. Above the stream, yet sitting directly between the two banks, a silver doorway opened, grudging and slow.

Sam probed it, and felt the warm signature that all Earth Portals were lacking. Earth Portals were cold compared to this, just like Hell Portals felt downright icy. He pulled off his shoes and waded out over the stony bed of the stream, the cold water pushing at his ankles with surprising force.

He stopped in front of the Eden Portal and examined it. It looked like any other Portal, but just inside the boundary he could sense . . . what? Very tenderly, he pushed his mind into it. He felt power pull at him almost immediately. He tried to steady himself as his world filled with white mist, rushing past him at high speed – yet he hadn't moved; he was still standing outside the Portal. Ahead a light grew brighter, and brighter still, filled his sight, grew unbearable and suddenly hit him hard between the eyes.

He fell back, landing in the stream, his hands slipping on the loose stones underwater and sending up enough of a splash to soak whatever part of him had still been dry. The Portal snapped shut, with a promptness that seemed almost righteous.

Sam sat in the water, feeling cold and foolish, hoping no one had seen. Eventually he pulled himself up, dripping all over, and, full of heightened determination, called the Portal back. It opened quickly, as if nothing had happened.

He glowered at it, and once more extended his mind, but this time far more slowly, fearing danger. His mind brushed the edges of the wards as he skirted along them, noting how thick they were, and marvelling at the strength of the Greater Power that had written them.

The wards were not, as he'd previously thought, unique to any one Portal. They'd simply been thrown up through the Way of Eden at the mid-point between Heaven and Eden, so that no matter which Portal you entered, nor where you were going, you would hit them, and be repulsed.

A pity, then, that they were flawed. All it would take to puncture the wards was a punch from Darkness, and Sam didn't doubt that his brothers were eager to deal the fatal blow.

He withdrew his mind, but kept the Portal open. He wondered why he was doing what he did. Because he genuinely feared Darkness? Perhaps. Or because he wanted to prove a point to his brothers, prove that the bastard Son of Time was no less a fighter than they were and might just be something more? Perhaps that too.

Fear and pride. Never a great combination, thought a part of his mind that always said the wrong things at the wrong times.

Oh, shut up.

He took a deep breath, trying to feel strong and confident despite his soaking, dishevelled appearance.

He sent his mind into the Way one last time, and broadcast towards the wards.

<Is this what you want? Shall I seal it?>

Silence.

<I know you can hear me. I'm the Bearer of Light, I'm your son's heir. Balder's dead, your son is dead. The Light passed on to me. I know it was because of his death that you fled and sealed the Way. But even the wards of a Greater Power can be breached, if that Power's opposite attacks them. I know it's too late to make amends for his death. But if you want me to, I'll seal the wards against my brothers for ever.>

The voice was there: no explanation, no sudden revelation, no warmth, no fire, no light, just the word. It was the first time he'd spoken directly with a Greater Power, except for Magic, his mother, and his father, Time. To seek an audience with any other Greater Power was supposed to be a complicated procedure, full of ceremony and magic. But with his mind brushing the wards of the Greater Power in preparation of what might well be a breach, as Sam reasoned it the Incarnate of Light and former Queen of Heaven had no choice but to respond.

He was right. <How?> The voice wasn't anything particularly special either, which was another surprise. He'd expected something musical, soft, motherly. It was just a flat question, demanding answers for nothing.

<Shadow,> he sent, suddenly uncomfortable with the reality of his situation. *Time above, I'm really going to do it, just to prove a point. And to keep Darkness out, always to keep Darkness out, because I'm afraid of what will happen if she's summoned . . .*

<Explain.>

<Shadow has no opposite. A ward drawn of shadow cannot be breached, except by the one who drew it.>

<Then I will be dependent on your good will.>

<You trusted the first Bearer of Light.>

<He was my son. Balder, Prince of Heaven, Son of Time and Light, the Bearer of Light . . .>

<Why not trust the second Bearer of Light?>

<The Light that you carry and the Light of which I am Incarnate are two different entities. I bring the warmth, the comfort, the joy and the brightness of the new day. You bring destruction. The Light and Light are different, I have no reason to trust.>

<Then the Way of Eden will be breached.>

Silence. Then, <Why are you doing this?>

<My brothers will summon Darkness. I am . . . afraid of what will happen if they do.>

<Darkness brings discord.>

<Yes.>

<She is also very hard to get rid of, my sister Darkness.>

<Yes.>

<You fear using the Light against her.>

<Yes.>

<You fear losing your mind in the process.>

Very quiet, hardly a murmur. <Yes.>

<You think sealing the Way for ever is the answer. You need fewer minds to write wards in shadow than to destroy a Greater Power. I understand now. Fear, not kindness, motivates you.>

He bristled a bit at that. <Look, lady, do you want this done or not?>

<I have not said. This is your own idea. You are afraid of the Way being breached.>

<So,> he snapped, <are you.>

Silence. Finally the Queen whispered, <Yes.>

<Why?>

<I fear Time's children. They killed my son.>

<You are a Greater Power!>

<And you are the one who can destroy us. Doesn't that send a tingle through your spine, Prince of Heaven? You could turn on Time himself and throw him from the throne of Heaven, take the crown, write the universe in your own image . . . but wait, I forget. You are afraid, aren't you?>

<Sod this,> sent Sam defiantly. <If you want Darkness to descend on the Way of Eden then fine, you tidy up after.> He began to withdraw his mind, knowing she wouldn't be able to let him.

<Wait!> He waited. <What do you want in return for this?>

<I hadn't really thought that far.>

<If you succeed, which is unlikely, call for me, and ask. Should you fail, and your brothers do indeed summon Darkness, I will give you protection in Eden. Because you tried.>

<Thanks.>

Silence. He probed. Nothing there, except the wards. He wondered whether he should turn round and walk away.

You are afraid.

Yes.

She is very hard to get rid of, my sister Darkness. You fear using the Light against her.

Yes.

You fear losing your mind in the process.

It was a choice, he realised, and felt relieved that something so big could be boiled down to a simple option. Let his siblings summon Darkness, in which case he, the Bearer of Light, might have to tap the minds of thousands and thousands to dispel her. Or seal the Way of Eden for ever, a process that would require far less power and therefore ran less risk of turning his mind to jelly.

Put like that, there was only one way forward.

FIFTEEN

Asgard

You must have seen I'd close the Way of Eden.
   I saw it. But I did not think you had the strength.
   Sitting in the cinema, Sam opened his eyes and looked across at Tinkerbell, chomping on his popcorn with a determined grimace, as if to make as much noise as possible.
   I will give you protection in Eden. Because you tried.
   Protection.
   He remembered.

To close the Way of Eden for good, certain provisions were necessary. One major ward, to prevent anyone sneaking up on him while he was, well, engaged. One minor shield, to hinder anyone from scrying his intent. One bottle of the most alcoholic substance he could find on Earth at that time, in the event of failure or success alike. Either way, he thought he'd probably need a good drink. One sword and dagger, just in case someone decided to break his wards and stop him by more violent means. He didn't put it past many of his brothers. One set of clean clothes and a towel, in case the shock was enough once more to bowl him over into the stream. Assuming, that is, he'd be in a fit state to change.

His provisions assembled, he opened the Eden Portal for the very last time. The thing was to push fear to the back of his mind. If he focused on his fear, that fear would be drawn to the forefront of every mind the Light touched, and the wards that he'd draw would be of fear, rather than shadow. Think shadow. *Think . . . think careful. Don't rush.*

He raised his hands, but still didn't touch the Light. His fingers met, weaving themselves around a hollow between his palms. He closed his eyes. Still he didn't touch the Light. *No fear. No emotion, no nothing. To feel something is to give that feeling strength, amplified through the Light. Shadow feels nothing, Shadow has no strong opinions, Shadow does not love and hate, it is the ultimate non-extreme, yet it encompasses everything that* might *be.*

Nothing can breach wards drawn in Shadow.

And there it was. He hadn't even noticed. It had slipped into his fingers without burning, without the usual roaring in his skull, without the usual baying for blood. No feelings this time. Just shadow. The Light filled his cupped hands and hung there. He looked at it with a strange expression on his face, wondering what he should be feeling.

No feelings. The Light wouldn't permit it. It knew what he wanted to achieve, and wasn't going to let a simple thing like personality or free will mess it up.

He closed his eyes against the brightness of it, and opened his fingers. The Light spread outwards in total silence. He felt the first mind a second later, felt its surprise at seeing a wall of burning bright whiteness, too bright to look at, racing across the land at waist-height. It was a beehive. Only one mind, he noted with surprise. Bees thought with just one thought, Many in One, and only One of the Many.

Then more minds, bringing with them more complicated thoughts. Angels, turning as the Light passed, running their fingers through the bright wave, marvelling at it. Avatars joining the throng, voices beginning to lose identity as the quantity increased tenfold in just a second, when the Light touched the city of Arcadia.

Somewhere in the roaring mass of thoughts, a tiny Sam slapped his fingers together, closing them tight. The Light froze, retracted, raced back across the land towards Sam, slammed into him like an express train and then past, into the waiting maw of the Eden Portal.

The voices in Sam's head fell quiet. At least, they were quieter. They still roared, still howled, and drowned out everything that made Sam what he was, screaming their individuality so loud that no one had an identity. All those voices melding into one cacophony. But this time there were no stro. ; emotions – no fire, no light, no dark, no anger, no hate, no love, no fear. Just the quiet roar of a thousand minds thinking thoughts that were neither good nor bad. Trivial things, mostly. Where was the paperwork? Where is the pen? No 'me' or 'I' or 'we' or anything to give anything a personality. Just flat, impersonal nouns, filling Sam's mind.

The sidhe, faerie of legendary power, so Sam had once

been told, had a skill that few other races possessed. They could step sideways through reality, into the world of shadow. And the deeper they went, the more distant the real world seemed, until past and present merged into one and they could walk through walls, so insubstantial was this world they inhabited. Sam now understood how it felt. Everything seemed a thousand miles away, and though he faintly registered the fact that he was drowning, falling into a whirlpool of voices from which he couldn't escape, he didn't care. There was just no point. It seemed so irrelevant. Why bother?

Wards. Write the wards, whispered a tiny, tiny voice that might just have been his.

Write them now! A jolt across his mind, like electricity. Extreme emotion, one voice in the many, panic-filled. His voice, in the Many the only voice aware of what was going on, desperately clinging to a huge cliff, while below the seas of minds boiled. Screaming useless instructions. Sam to the Bearer of Light, come in please. Bearer of Light, can you hear me?

Somewhere, a small, dark man standing before an open Portal raised his hands and began to move them through the air. They trailed white sparks as he drew, so that soon the air around him was on fire with swirling patterns and shapes. He tied a knot here, a knot there, looped one line of fire under another, until before him a lattice of burning fire stood in all its complex glory. With a gesture, he pushed it, white eyes not seeing, towards the Portal. It drifted inside.

There was a long silence in which the white-eyed man stood there, hands limp by his side. Then the light in the Portal suddenly dimmed. Silver mist turned grey, darkened almost to black, and lightened again abruptly. Something hard and fast and dark exploded out of the Portal and rammed into the man, sending him flying backwards until he slammed up against his own major ward. He struck it in a shower of blue sparks and fell to the ground.

The dark thing picked itself up – and up and up – and went on expanding upwards until Sam had to crane his head to see it. The Incarnate of Shadow stared emotionlessly down at the man who'd created such a perfect replica of itself in the minds of men. Then it, and the Portal that it had come through, winked out, and Sam was alone.

Almost alone.

So many voices filling my ears, yet they speak as One, and they say the same . . .

He staggered to his feet, got a few paces and crumpled again. *We are the intention and the act, the strength and the weakness, the light and the dark.*

And yes, we are shadow too. All that life, when melded together – everything is contained in it. Light, dark, shadow, individuals, collectives . . .

He could hear voices screaming louder in his head, emotions creeping back up through the layer of shadow he'd written across their minds, growing indignant, growing powerful, growing loud.

The Way of Eden, said a mind that might have been Jehovah's.

It's sealed! wailed a mind that could well have been Odin's.

And somewhere behind it all, another mind, just on the edge of hearing. *My son did it. I made him too well . . .*

And no matter how hard he tried, he couldn't quite hear his own mind. *Where am I? Am I you? Am I you?*

And me?

And me?

And me?

And me?

And me?

Go away, leave me alone, go away, go away, go away!

Somewhere by a small stream in Heaven a small figure ran into the forest, where the shadows ate him up.

In the cinema, Sam opened his eyes, which glowed. 'Tinkerbell,' he said quietly.

'Uhuh?'

'I've got it.' He rose to his feet.

'Hey, the film! She's about to tell him that she—'

'Another time, Tinkerbell.'

'Ah, hell.' They elbowed their way into the light.

Out in Leicester Square, Sam looked around, blinking in the sun. A group of Japanese tourists were posing in front of a theatre that advertised 'a glittering, exciting play – I laughed myself silly', a man in a ragged army coat was walking his pet ferret while a pair of girls pointed at him and giggled, and the rest of the mass of humanity likewise moved back and forth with no understanding of what was at stake.

'Where's the nearest Heaven Portal?' he asked Tinkerbell.

'You don't know?'

'I haven't been to Heaven for over two thousand years.'

Tinkerbell frowned, turning this way and that. Finally

he pointed. 'That way. Up Long Acre. Why are we going to Heaven?'

'Because there's someone really influential who owes me a favour.'

'Anyone I know?'

'I doubt it.'

'And you ain't going to tell me?'

'And spoil the surprise? Why on Earth, or any other world for that matter, should I do that? Besides, what I have in mind might piss people off.'

Tinkerbell sighed. 'It's been a bad century, right?'

'You're getting the hang of it.'

The Portal was where Sam had least expected it. 'In there?' he asked, looking up at the huge building.

'Uhuh. The Masons built their castle bang smack on top of a Heaven Portal.'

'Exactly why?'

'I don't think they realised they were doing it. They were probably looking for somewhere central, but with a feeling of mystery about it.'

Sam looked up again at the huge white building with its central tower that dominated the skyline. 'And they built it on a Heaven Portal.'

'Sure did.'

'But I'm not a Mason.'

'Me neither.'

'So . . .?'

'Generally, I find that what gets the best response is barging in there, walking straight up to the Portal and going through as though there was nothing wrong.'

Sam stared at him with wide eyes. 'You're kidding.'

'Who are the Masons going to tell? The police? Who's gonna believe them, anyway? They'd think it was some hoax by the Masons to get free publicity.'

'A secret society wants free publicity?'

'Look up at the building, pal.'

Sam looked again. Situated at the end of Long Acre, in the heart of London, it did make a dramatic impression. 'Okay, I get your point, but I want you to know that in principle I'm utterly opposed to it.'

'The universe is going to end in three days' time. Take a risk, okay?'

So Sam did. He walked straight up to the doors of the Masons' building, pushed them open, strode confidently across the foyer as if he knew exactly what he was doing, felt the Portal directly ahead, reached out to touch Tinkerbell's arm and opened the Portal. By the time the man in the dark suit by the stairs had turned and said 'Excuse me', they were already stepping through the silver doorway and into the Way of Heaven.

It was for the best, thought Sam, to make a speedy entrance to the Way of Heaven. All those memories of Heaven, and over two thousand years hadn't eroded them. Perhaps if he'd waited, thought about returning to Heaven, he wouldn't have done it. Maybe he was afraid of what might happen, of what he might remember that he'd tried so hard to forget. By charging straight through the Portal, however, he'd left himself no time to consider.

It was like any old Waywalk. The image was clear in his mind, not dulled by the years spent away. Yet, though it was clear, the journey was hard, the Portal at the other end reluctant to open, the distance seemingly too long. What had changed the Halls of Asgard, that the Way of Heaven now had difficulty recognising the images he was feeding it?

He could feel Tinkerbell's fear rising as the Waywalk grew long, hear him struggling to breathe as the air began to run out. Still Sam kept walking, focusing, keeping the image in the front of his mind. A Portal opened ahead, and he almost ran for it, breaking from the Way of Heaven and gasping down lungfuls of air.

He'd chosen this place because here, in the caves of Asgard, deep beneath Valhalla, there were numerous Portals and few people to watch them. Asgard was a place of shadows, spirits and sharp knives.

Or had been.

'Shit.' Sam looked round the dark passages at fallen timber, piles of stones smashed from the walls, torches burnt out, swords stained with blood left lying on the ground, smelled the death, heard the cold wind, felt the emptiness.

'Holy Hells,' muttered Tinkerbell, looking round. 'What happened here?'

'I expect someone tried to put up a fight against Seth, Odin and Jehovah. And got screwed for their pains.'

'Are they . . . all dead?'

'Probably.'

'Who lived here?'

'Valkyries, mostly. Asgard was like a prison, but it was riddled with Portals. They were the only way in and out, you see. You had to be a Waywalker to get in. It was a way of ensuring that Feywalker prisoners or faerie or even mortals who'd used just a bit too much magic in the wrong way didn't escape.'

'This?' asked Tinkerbell, nodding at the ruined passages. 'Asgard?'

'Uhuh. Valhalla is directly above.'

'Why've we come here?'

'Because it *is* so riddled with Portals. Of every kind.'

Tinkerbell gave Sam a shrewd look out of the corner of his eye, while picking his way over a pile of rubble. 'But there are two kinds of Portal in Heaven – Eden, as well as Earth.'

'Tell me about it.' Sam sniffed the air, trying to sense the nearest Eden Portal.

'Why do you need both? You *sealed* the Way of Eden.'

'I know that too.' Sam pointed down a dark corridor. 'This way.'

'Am I just being thick, or don't I get it?'

'That's a silly question and you know it. You might be thick and not get it, or you might not get it yet not be thick, or you might be thick yet get it. There is no one answer.'

'What do you want with the Way of Eden?'

'I'm owed a favour, didn't I mention?'

'I don't like here. Couldn't you have chosen somewhere else?'

'Asgard has a higher proportion of Portals per square kilometre than any other area in Heaven,' recited Sam from a long, long time ago. 'There's at least one Eden Portal every seven hundred yards. The difficulty is in pinpointing *which* seven hundred yards.'

He turned a corner, saw a rockfall that blocked the passage and sighed. 'Do you ever get the desire for a golden ball of thread?'

'What?'

'Ever meet Theseus?'

'Before my time. I'm only a few hundred years old, you know.'

'Ah, the innocence of the young,' sighed Sam, stepping carefully round a door that had been smashed off its hinges by some unknown force. 'Anyway, you know how Theseus really beat the monster in its labyrinth?'

'Do tell.'

'He was a Feywalker. He hung around the Way of Fey, lured the monster in and left it there to get lost and die. He then snuck out through the Fey Portal and presented himself before the king with a dirty great big sword and a smug attitude.'

'Let me guess. You didn't like him?'

'We did meet once. He was arrogant. He told me I was a demon of the nether pit and would roast in damnation for ever, and that he, the divine, couldn't be touched by me.'

'What did you do?'

'Set his pants on fire.'

Tinkerbell thought about this. 'You have a nasty streak, don't you?'

'Pal, I'm the Devil Incarnate!'

'I thought you didn't believe in conforming to expectations.'

'Sometimes I make an exception. Ah.'

He stopped and beamed at what he saw. Another corridor. Tinkerbell peered down it. 'It's a dead end.'

'It's the answer to a lot of problems.'

'Do you mind me asking, but who are you trying to double-cross this time?'

'I asked you the same question, and you wouldn't answer. So why should I?'

Tinkerbell looked worried. 'Pal, I'm here to *protect* you. That means from yourself, if necessary. But I can't help you if you piss off some Greater Power and get struck by lightning.'

'Don't worry, nothing bad will come of this, I promise.'

'I'd love to have faith, really. But you push belief.'

'Calm down. Why are you so edgy?' As soon as Sam heard his own words he realised, *Hell, he is edgy. Why? What is it about this place?*

'Just making sure everything's going to be okay,' said Tinkerbell, raising his hands defensively. Too relaxed now, a sudden shift of gear, a loosening up that couldn't be natural.

Now it was Sam's turn to be edgy. He turned to stare at Tinkerbell. 'What is it? Why are you so nervous?'

He thought he saw a shadow move, thought he heard a whisper on the air. *Danger . . .*

'Look, can't we find another Eden Portal? This place is dangerous. It might collapse at any moment.'

'This place is dead, Tinkerbell. There's nothing here to harm either you or me.'

A faint, chill breeze, and again, the whisper. *Who's there?* Sam's head turned, and he strained to catch the voice again.

<Help me.> A distinct signal now, but still just a whisper. Someone was directly broadcasting into Sam's mind.

<Who's there?>

<Whoever you are, help me.>

<Who is that?>

'Why would Jehovah destroy Asgard?' asked Sam

softly, eyes flickering back to Tinkerbell. 'What's his purpose?'

'Look, let's go.'

<Please. I'm dying.>

<Who are you?>

Tinkerbell frowned. 'You're broadcasting. Who's there? I can almost hear, but —'

<Help me.>

<Which way?>

<Down. Always down.>

Sam started forwards, but as he passed Tinkerbell, the other's hand shot out and caught him by the shoulder. In the gloom, Tinkerbell's eyes burned brightly. 'Is he calling you, is that it?'

'You know who it is?' asked Sam.

'We leave here *now*. We shouldn't have come!'

'Tell me who's calling.'

<Down, always down . . .>

Tinkerbell's grip tightened to the point where it became painful. 'We get out of here!'

'You know something, Brian Hunter, and I'm not budging a step until I know it too!'

<Is it you?>

<Who? Who do you think I am?> 'Who's trapped in Asgard?' demanded Sam, pulling free of Tinkerbell. 'And why do you know about it?'

<Brian? Are you there? Have you brought him yet?>

Sam froze.

So too did Tinkerbell, who must also have heard the thought that filled Asgard with its pleading. Or perhaps he saw it in Sam's eye. Whatever the cause, he swung his fist. Sam ducked, felt the fist pass him by a hair's breadth and fled, leaping over fallen debris and running for all he was worth. He was a first-generation Son of Time while Tinkerbell was just third generation, his heritage distilled by mortal blood, however potent. Sam could still win.

He heard a cry behind him. 'Lucifer!' He didn't answer, but pelted through the darkness, fighting fear and running, always running. He saw a flight of stairs to his right and took it. *Down, always down.*

In the stairwell he turned, saw Tinkerbell racing towards him, scowled and threw up his hands. Scattered across the floor, the undigested bites some monster had taken out of the walls themselves, the bricks began to move, flying down the corridor towards Tinkerbell. Tinkerbell threw up a shield, but it was weak, third-generation magic. Sam tore it down with a gesture and saw a brick catch Tinkerbell on the shoulder. Another scraped along his cheek, leaving a line of blood, another struck his up-flung arms, another caught his knee and sent him staggering to the ground. Sam let the rest fall harmlessly to the floor and yelled at the panting, battered Tinkerbell, 'You said yourself – I'm the Son of Magic!'

Tinkerbell made no answer, clutching his bleeding leg. Sam ran down the stairs. Gloom deepened to darkness. He summoned light, a glowing white ball that hovered around his head, but it was barely enough to illuminate the stones beneath his feet. With a gesture he sent it skimming out ahead of him to light the path. Here there was no light, except what he summoned. He heard the voice again.

<Hurry. I'm dying . . .>

<Calm down, calm down. Chances are slim you'll die exactly this *second*.>

<Who is that? Where's Brian?>

Sam saw another flight of stairs, a well of darkness
that his glowing sphere of light could hardly penetrate.
He summoned more light still, three balls circling around
him in ever-increasing orbits, and sent a fourth skirting
the passage ahead of him as he descended the stairs cautiously. The stairs were a spiral, the ancient stones loose.
There was no rail, and the stone when he pressed his
hands against it was warm to the touch. He could smell
magic. The place reeked of it, and the smell was getting
stronger as he descended. He kept climbing, fingers tap-
dancing along the side of the stairwell.

At the bottom he stumbled, hardly aware that he'd
reached it, and peered through the darkness. A heavy
wooden door looked like it had been smashed open, the
wards above it shattered by the impact of heavy magic.
Beyond was a room full of brutally sharp metal things
that looked too large to be a surgeon's kit and too sinister to be a juggler's. He passed through it, pushed open
a door torn by the impact of many weapons and saw the
cage. It burned his eyes with magic. Wards of every kind
were inscribed across it, thick, thick wards, the kind of
thing that a Greater Power might weave. The cage
looked large – at least he couldn't see the back of it – but
then the darkness was everywhere. He edged forwards
and touched a bar. The shock made his arm go numb. He
leapt back with a yell.

'It does that,' said a weak, hoarse voice to his right.

He followed his ears. The man inside the cage was old,
thin white hair falling over a body so worn by age and
hunger and disease that it was little more than a pile of
bones that looked far, far too frail to support the sagging
white skin that bound it all together. The eyes were

sunken, which made the nose look far too large, and the thin hair was so worn away that the ears stuck out ludicrously, with nothing to disguise their strange disproportion. He was covered with scars, and wore just a few rags which were themselves filthy – what with, Sam couldn't tell.

'Who are you?' asked Sam. 'Were you the one who called for help?'

'Yes. Where's Brian?'

'He had to wait. I've come instead.'

'Have you got food?'

Not taking his eyes from the man Sam opened his bag and produced the much-despised chocolate bar. The man stirred, staggered to his feet and worked his way along the cage, holding his hands out hungrily. 'Food can pass through. They didn't want me to starve, no, no, they didn't want that.' He laughed, a hacking sound that Sam half expected to kill him, as his entire frame vibrated with the effort of it.

Sam passed the chocolate bar through the bars, cautiously. The man took it, then one thin hand lashed out and caught Sam's wrist, held with a surprising strength. Two terribly sane eyes in a mad face looked out as he dragged Sam's wrist into the cage, and hissed, 'Everyone's dead except you and me.'

'Who are you?'

The man abruptly let Sam go and stepped back, waddling away from the bars as if he'd forgotten Sam existed. He tore the wrapper off the chocolate bar and began eating loudly while Sam looked on, wondering what could drive a man to this state. Suddenly the man spun and exclaimed, 'They left me to die!'

'You wouldn't die,' said Sam, taking a guess. 'You're a Waywalker.'

The man fell silent, stopped munching. Then he grinned a huge, toothless grin and began eating again. 'You're quite right, young man, well done, quite right, you'll go far. And you, I think, are also a Son of Time.'

'Yes. How did you end up this way? Waywalkers don't age.'

'*They* did it to me, all because . . . because . . . where's Brian?'

'How do you know Brian?'

'He . . . he killed them. Because of me, to help me – isn't that nice? – because of me. He came here with his friends and killed them.'

'Brian killed the guards? With the Ashen'ia?'

'Is that who they are? Ashen'ia, eh? Ashen'ia, a tree of the tropical region in the tropic of Cancer, with large pink fruit and birds. That's right, isn't it, that's right?'

'Why did Brian kill them?'

'They were going to let me die, but you . . . you saved me, didn't you?' He raised the chocolate bar in delight. 'You brought this, you . . . you're a good boy, aren't you?'

'If Brian wants to help you, why doesn't he let you go?'

'Can't breach the wards, doesn't have the power – he's just a grandchild, he doesn't know real power, he can hardly Waywalk!'

Sam looked up at the wards, then stepped back to look again, adjusting his position until he had the best view. The man watched from the cage with worryingly shrewd eyes.

A Waywalker wouldn't be able to breach something this thick.

*But if you could identify the principle component of the wards —
say, if they were based mostly on Night — then the Bearer of Light
might be able to breach them by targeting with the opposite power.*

*Which raises the interesting question — who is this guy, that he
should be locked away by wards so thick you need the Bearer of
Light to bring them down?*

Sam looked at the little man, now pacing up and
down, beating his hands against his sides as though
trying to fly. He said, 'Brian wants you free?'

'Yes, he's a good boy, is Brian, a good boy.'

'He needs the Bearer of Light to do it?'

'Yes, that's right. He'll bring the Bearer of Light, the
Bearer of Light will destroy the wards, always the
Bearer of Light, even though I killed him last time we
talked, but then Brian knows what he's doing, does
Brian, he knows—'

I killed him the last time we talked. 'You're Loki.'

The man stopped dead, looking up at Sam with fear in
his eyes. 'I didn't do it,' he whispered. 'I didn't do it, I
didn't mean to, please don't.'

'You killed Balder.'

The man was backing away, raising his hands to
shield his face. 'No, I . . . I didn't do it, I never meant to,
it was him! Cronus did it, I couldn't stop him. I tried, but
I couldn't stop him, I swear!'

'Why does Brian want to free you?'

'Please, I'll be good, I promise. I won't hurt anyone
ever again.'

'That's why Brian needs me, isn't it? To breach the
wards?'

'Left me here to die, I swear I'll be good . . .'

'Loki!'

The old man stopped, stood still, then tried to pull himself to attention. 'Reporting, sir!' he stuttered in what was supposed to be a brisk, business-like manner but fell nearer a sob.

'I am the Bearer of Light.'

Loki looked Sam up and down. 'No,' he said. 'He's got blond hair, I know, I killed him myself.'

'I'm his heir. I'm Lucifer. I am the Bearer of Light.'

'Pleased to meet you, sir, may I offer you our cut-price range of bath salts?'

'Loki! Listen to me!'

Loki turned, smiled, began to rub his hands, massaging warmth into them. 'The grand old duke of York had ten thousand men, sir. Did you know that?'

'I'll free you, Loki. I'll let you go.'

'Why'd you do that, Mr Lucifer, why'd you do that? Just a doddery old man, Mr Lucifer, nowhere to go, no family, not even a hill to march up with my ten thousand men, why . . . why'd you do that?'

'I'll free you, if you tell me who Brian wants revenge against.'

'Oh, that, that's obvious, what a silly question, and such a nice young man too.'

'Tell me, Loki. I'll set you free.'

'He wants Jehovah, of course. Big brother Jehovah, little Jehovah, big Jehovah, Jehovah the medium, Jehovah, size sixteen, shoes size eleven, height six foot—'

'Why? Why does he want revenge against Jehovah?'

'Never get into religion, boy, it's never healthy, medium height, average size, normal colouring—'

'Loki! Listen to me!'

Loki's eyes flickered past Sam, and his face broke into a grin. 'Brian, is this man nice?'

Sam turned, reaching for his dagger. The fist caught him across the jaw and he fell back, hitting the ground. Tinkerbell loomed, possibly the most looming figure Sam had ever seen, dark in every sense, an axe drawn in one hand. Sam tried to crawl away but Tinkerbell slammed a foot down on Sam's chest, knocking him backwards. Sam raised his hands to call magic and froze as the axe sliced through the air. He closed his eyes.

Death failed to come. He opened his eyes, and wondered whether that had been such a great idea. The axe was hovering a short distance from his neck. His heart raced, his stomach churned. He heard Loki say, 'Oh. So he's not nice?'

Tinkerbell's eyes didn't leave Sam's face. 'He's nice, pups. He's just slightly over-enthusiastic.' To Sam he said, 'We shouldn't have come to Asgard. You could have told me, I would have talked you out of it.'

'At least I keep you on your toes,' Sam answered, eyes not leaving the axe.

'We're leaving.'

'Already?' asked Loki. 'You've only just arrived! Keep grandpa company a bit longer.'

Sam's eyes narrowed. 'A Son of Night, not a Son of Chaos,' he breathed. The axe wavered a little bit closer to his throat, but Sam ignored it. 'No wonder you lie about your grandfather. Your grandfather murdered Balder.'

'And he's suffered for it.'

'You have followers within the Ashen'ia, I was told as much by the master. You led them here. You destroyed the guards, killed everyone, but left your grandfather alive. Because you want to free him?'

'He's suffered enough,' said Tinkerbell through gritted teeth.

'You need me to breach the wards.'

'Yes.'

'Then killing me might not be such a great idea.'

Tinkerbell smiled. 'This axe won't kill you, Lucifer. It'll put you in a regenerative trance for a week after I slit your throat; and when you wake up, all cold and scared and drained, I'll slit your throat again. And when you wake up again, I'll kill you again, and again, and again, because that's the advantage of being a Waywalker. You can suffer, you just never die.'

'I'd free him anyway,' said Sam flatly. 'I'd do it now.'

'No. Not now. Not yet.'

'Why?'

'He gave his blood to Cronus. That's the kind of bond that can't be broken by Time. If you freed him now, it would be Cronus, not Loki, who came out of that cell.'

Sam felt ice start to creep through his blood. Tinkerbell smiled a sad smile and nodded very faintly. 'For the bond to be broken, Cronus must die. For Cronus to die, he must be freed by one he trusts. By Seth, to be exact. For Seth to believe that he is doing the right thing, he must have opposition when he tries to free Cronus, otherwise he won't believe that what he does is his own action, rather than that dictated by Time. Opposition is provided in the form of the Ashen'ia. The Ashen'ia will die. Cronus will be freed. You will destroy him. The bond between him and my grandfather will be broken. Loki goes free. Who's the master, Sebastian?'

Sam let his head fall back against the floor. He put his hands up to cover his eyes and said, 'This is such a bad millennium.'

'Jehovah's the master, isn't he?'

Sam nodded, feeling weak and wretched. *Everyone seems to be trying to free Cronus for some reason or the other. Except me.*

'I thought it would be so. I wanted proof, you see. If the Ashen'ia really are just a part in Time's conspiracy then Time will want someone to guarantee that they get destroyed and Seth achieves his aims. Jehovah seemed the obvious candidate to play that double game. Send Seth his to fate and the Ashen'ia to theirs. Jehovah is the master. Jehovah will ensure that Cronus is freed.'

'You did better than me,' said Sam sourly. 'You saw the truth, and I didn't.'

'You're trying to survive. I understand that.'

'If I do destroy Cronus, I'll probably be killed in the process.'

'No. You'll simply go mad, lose your mind, lose your identity, lose everything that makes you who you are. You won't die.'

'Forgive me if I don't find that a reassurance.'

Tinkerbell shrugged, pulled the axe away, offered his hand. Sam glared it at, but reluctantly let Tinkerbell help him up. Loki was staring at the pair of them. 'Cronus is coming? Cronus is going to be free?'

'It's all right, pups. Lucifer will stop him.'

'But . . . but he's coming! He's everywhere, he's coming!'

Sam frowned. He could hear something in Loki's voice, something like . . . 'Erm . . . Tinkerbell?'

And there it was, the translucent film spreading across Loki's eyes, the grating quality entering his voice as he turned to Sam and said, 'Hello again, little light and little fire.'

'Hello, cowardy Cronus.'

Loki's hands lashed out, striking the bars. Sparks flew from them but still he gripped, grinning as the wards fluctuated up and down. 'Little light and little fire is going to die,' he said.

'Cowardy Cronus is thick.'

Tinkerbell said nothing, edging away from Sam, as though afraid he might catch something from the man who dared talk to one of Cronus's possessed.

'Have you ever considered what it would be like to serve me?' LokiCronus said.

'Excuse me? Little light and little fire, the guy who you tried to kill while possessing Thor, *serve* you?'

'You can't be happy serving Time.'

'Who said anything about serving anyone? I'm *me*. I believe very firmly in the independent spirit.'

'Little light and little fire is just a pawn.'

'Little light and little fire will find his own path, thanks anyway. Now bugger off, because you know as well as I that it's nigh on impossible for a Greater Power to sustain possession for more than a few minutes. Let alone a Greater Power who's been behind bars for a few million years.'

'I destroyed Balder. I can bring you down too.'

'Delighted, I'm sure. But you haven't brought me down, have you? I'm still up and running and waiting for something interesting to happen. And pal, I don't think you *are* going to bring me down. I'm going to kick Seth hard in the arse and leave you to rot, because I don't like you any more than you like me.'

'I will destroy you.'

'And I'll become a great cook.'

Almost grudgingly, the film faded from Loki's eyes and he staggered back, clutching at his face and wailing, 'Doddery old man, leave a doddery old man alone!" Sam watched him with pity on his face, but didn't move.

'You just faced down the former master of the universe,' said Tinkerbell.

'Look, either he remains locked up, in which case he's no threat to me, or he gets freed. In which case I either get driven stark raving mad destroying him, or die in the attempt. Whatever happens, he can't touch me.'

'Have you realised what happens if you use the Light against him? To destroy a Greater Power you must touch the mind of everything that lives – and even Cronus, to a small degree, shows signs of life. You'll touch his mind too.'

'And yours, and the mind of Time and the minds of everyone else in the universe – but, you know, I don't think I'll be in a fit state to take notes, do you?'

'I'm sorry it has to be like this, Lucifer.'

Sam sighed, brushing off dust that wasn't on his clothes. 'Tinkerbell, I need a favour.'

'What?'

'Five minutes alone with an Eden Portal.'

Tinkerbell's eyes narrowed faintly. 'Who are you double-crossing now, little light and little fire?'

'The whole goddamn universe, pal.'

But Tinkerbell gave him his five minutes, which was more than enough.

SIXTEEN

Unpaid Debt

In the tunnels of Asgard, the Eden Portal looked like any other. But then it always had, since the wards were written on the inside.

Sam slipped his mind into it, recognised the wards. After all, he was the one who'd written them. Seeing his own handiwork, he marvelled at its strength. So much power, tapped from so few minds, to create wards that if anything were even thicker than those made by Light herself. They lay across the Way of Eden like a giant blanket across the horizon so that, whatever way you turned, still they were there. Grey and unobtrusive, but as hard as rock. You couldn't puncture wards like that. They'd just absorb the attack. There was nothing extreme here, and nothing extreme would tear the wards, yet at the same time anything less would be a drawing pin against a blue whale.

He called, nonetheless. <Lady.>

She answered instantly. She must have been waiting for him to speak. <Son of Magic.>

<There was talk of protection.>

<That was thousands of years ago.>

<Has the offer died?>

<No. I merely marvel at your memory.>

<I need protection.>

<Then step through. I will not bar your passage to Eden, you are welcome here, Bearer of Light.>

<It is not for me. There are, I suspect, simply too many other forces at work against my purposes. I need you to protect one who is dear to me.>

<I can do that.>

<I need you to protect her against Time.>

Silence. Then, <You ask a lot. He is King of Heaven.>

<You are Queen of Eden.>

<I have shut myself away from the doings of him and his Children.>

<She is a Daughter of Love. She will do you no harm. Nevertheless, Time would harm her.>

<You defy Time to request this?>

<Yes.>

<Then I fear you shall not be long in this world. I can protect only one from Time's anger.>

<One is all I ask. I need you to keep her safe.>

<Love is a dear sister of mine. I was always close to her.>

<Guard her Daughter for me.>

<Tell me the child's name.>

<Freya. She has given her blood to Time. He has threatened to possess her and destroy her.>

<I can protect her. Where is she?>

<Hell. Can you find her there?>

<She will be safe, I promise. But this pays all debts I owe you, Bearer of Light.>

<Soon, lady, soon it will be all over anyway.>

<Good luck, light and fire.>

<Little in both, so I'm constantly told.>

<The ones who fear you tell you that. You make miracles. Balder would be proud of you.>

She was gone.

Sam sat in front of the Portal and marvelled. He got to his feet and began to smile all over. He walked down the corridor.

Tinkerbell stood at the far end. 'Lucifer,' he said in a low voice, 'who've you double-crossed?'

'Like I said, the entire goddamn universe.'

'You seem very happy about it.'

'Tinkerbell, you would not believe. Come on. I need to scry.'

A simple target. They went to Trafalgar Square, and Sam sat on the edge of a fountain, looking down into the clear, toxic water. True to tradition, a hundred pigeons scurried towards him for food, then sensed, with better instinct than humans, who he was and hastened off in the other direction.

He stared into the water. Simple scry, no need for precautions. Just one mind to another.

<Freya.> Silence. <Freya, can you hear me?> Silence. <Freya, it's Sebastian. Are you there?> Silence.

<Sebastian? It's all right, Sebastian, I understand, I'm safe, she's given me—>

And the water that Sam stared at rippled, shifted, and

exploded in his face. He staggered back, wiping the water from his eyes. Tinkerbell had leapt to his feet with a cry of 'Shit!' and now followed his look of surprise with a wry smile. 'That, I take it, wasn't what you meant to do.'

'I think I've pissed someone off,' said Sam.

'Anyone I know?'

'Oh, just the ruler of the universe. Come on, let's leave.'

'You've screwed Time?'

'Only in a polite little way.'

They walked briskly towards the river, past busy Charing Cross and along the Embankment.

'Why exactly have you done this? I thought you and he were getting along fine.'

'He said he'd kill someone very dear to me unless I did what he wanted. I've now removed that option from him. One of his Queens is offering her protection.'

Tinkerbell stopped, and seized Sam by the arm. 'Oh no,' he said. 'I know about this. You get Day involved and Night tries to kill her. You get Fire involved and Water tries to kill him. You get any Greater Power other than Time involved and—'

'The Queen of Eden, Light Incarnate, is protecting her. When I sealed the Way of Eden I removed the reason for my brothers to summon Darkness. Darkness is Light's opposite, but she is weak, not acknowledged as a Queen of Heaven, and Light hides herself away in Eden, where no other is allowed to set foot. For preventing Darkness being summoned, Light owed me a favour. I've just called on it. Time will not move against one of his Queens, nor will the other Greater Powers,

because Light is Queen of Eden in her own right and
greater by far than any of her sisters. *That's* why Time
had Balder by her – the greatest, golden child by the
greatest, golden Power. No one will act against someone
who is under Light's protection.'

No one except things like Cronus.

'Let me guess. They'll act against you, who arranged
the entire business?'

'Yeah. That's the only real drawback.'

Tinkerbell's smile was beginning to look painfully
taut. 'So. You've won?'

'Not yet.'

'But . . . you might not have to destroy Cronus? Time
has lost his hold on you?'

Sam saw. Slow and deliberate, he interlaced his
fingers and began twiddling them. A tiny, tiny gesture
that might just be attributed to nervousness, but could be
something more. People on the busy street gave them no
attention as he stopped and looked at Tinkerbell. A
tourist boat on the Thames passed, the loudspeaker
commentary declaring, 'And here we see the fascinat-
ing . . .' and passed out of earshot. Sound carried well
across water.

'You're a strange man, Brian Hunter. Tinkerbell. You
told me I should try to save the lives of thousands.
Potentially, that's what I've now done. I'm free to stop
Time in his plans, where these same thousands die.

'Yet though you seemed to put the lives of the many
before the one, still you'd see many destroyed – for one.
For a doddery old man who murdered the Son of Light,
sold his soul to the enemy of his father, lied and tricked
his way through his youth and finally lost his mind. For

him, you would not care that I died. Why? Because he's your grandfather?'

'If Time's lost his hold on you, Sebastian, you no longer have any need to destroy Cronus.'

Sam seemed to not hear him. 'You spoke of revenge. Revenge against a Waywalker? Who? Who do you want to see destroyed?'

'If Cronus isn't going to be killed, then Loki will not be freed.'

'It must be connected to Loki. A Waywalker connected to Loki.'

'Lucifer.' Something in Tinkerbell's voice caught Sam's attention. He looked up, frown still on his face, fingers still twiddling. 'I can't let you ruin this,' said Tinkerbell.

'I thought you'd say that.'

Tinkerbell hesitated. And as Sam threw the coiled magic, unwinding from his fingers like a spring snapping open, Tinkerbell smiled. He knew, Sam realised. He *knew* about the magic in Sam's fingers, and hadn't done anything to prevent it from building up. Even as it struck him across the side, and spun him round in a circle just in time to hit Sam's counter-spell and get shoved to one side, he knew. Even as he hit the edge of the wall that lined the side of the Embankment, pivoted off it and fell into the river below, he knew. He knew that Sam was going to hit him with the spell, and hadn't done anything.

As Sam leant over the edge of the wall and looked down to see Tinkerbell surface from the river and pull desperately at the harsh yanking of the tide, he wondered why.

SEVENTEEN

Conquering Time

More memories, of old times.

He'd naively thought that he could just close the Way of Eden and return home to his roomy bed-chamber in Elysium. He'd been wrong.

Three hours after Sam had set the wards in the Way of Eden, his mind had cleared enough for him to dare head home. The guards at the gate of the city had let him pass, recognising him for a Waywalker. But he'd seen it in their look. They knew that his eyes, usually black, were now turned grey as the noise of the Light faded from his ears, darkening the whiteness of his irises with them, so that his eyes returned to normal only by degrees. They were afraid of him.

His room hadn't actually been in the palace, but in a street near it. He was, after all, just a bastard Son of Time, rather than the genuine article.

The house was a burning wreck.

He heard the minds of the people around him, heard them knowing what he should have known – that his own brothers had burnt his house down as retribution for sealing the Way of Eden. It was unlikely they would stop there.

And in that sea of minds, that he was still half aware of as the effects of the Light faded, he felt two others that were neither focused on the crowd nor on the gutted house, but were entirely dedicated to watching *him*. And these minds were . . . *cold*. It made his fingers tingle just to touch them. They reminded him of snakes, but at least snakes had a genuine motivation for killing. These creatures existed to kill for no other satisfaction than the murder itself. And they were about to kill him.

It was that revelation that prompted him to shield himself behind a distortion spell. Which was why the first crossbow bolt only bounced off the cobbles nearby, and why the second embedded itself in a door inches from his right ear. He ran, but knew he wasn't about to lose these assassins. Firedancers were persistent. He fled to the palace, where he thought that perhaps he might receive protection. The guards were, after all, sworn to protect all Children of Time.

Indeed, the ordinary guards did not attempt to stop him. But he felt fear grip him again when he entered the populous great hall and saw Jehovah whispering to his archangels. Catching sight of him, Jehovah rose to his feet, touched the archangel Michael on the shoulder. Michael turned, saw Lucifer too, and advanced towards him. The other archangels followed, spreading out around Michael to form an arrowhead of tight faces and drawn blades. A space cleared between them and Sam and, imperceptibly, the crowds in the hall shuffled to seal the doors with bodies.

Sam looked round for help, and every eye he caught avoided his gaze and fell elsewhere. At the end of the hall Jehovah rose to his feet and stared mercilessly down as the archangels formed a ring of metal around Sam. Within it Sam turned like a trapped animal, before facing Jehovah once again across the silent hall.

Then, without warning, he smiled.

'You know I was right,' he called out, loud enough for Jehovah to hear.

'Time will tell,' replied Jehovah.

Continuing to smile, Sam shook his head. 'You never knew the extent of my power.' He didn't move a finger, didn't say a word, but vanished where he stood. The archangels stirred in consternation, but still the silence filled the hall, pouring in from every direction.

'Don't move,' snapped Jehovah. 'He's within the ring of steel. It's illusion. Stab him, and you'll see.'

So, tentative at first. then gaining confidence, the archangels lunged and stabbed at the empty air beyond their swords – which nonetheless appeared to come away clean.

'You can't do it,' called out Jehovah. 'You can't sustain illusion like that, and escape.'

There was no answer, except, high above, a window cracked with a dull ripping sound. All eyes went up. No one there. Each gaze danced round the room as one after one every window cracked, but none shattered.

'Where are you?' called Jehovah.

They all saw it. Lights darkened throughout the hall, the sunlight through the shattered windows seemed to grow faint, the darkness crept out of every shadow and thickened.

<I am everywhere. There's a part of me in every one of your minds. Just as there's a part of you in me. I know your weaknesses. I know you're afraid of the shadow, if not of the dark.>

Shadows crept across the hall, shadows with claws ready to rip, shadows that danced nimbly through the people and, as one, converged on Jehovah.

'Where are you?' repeated Jehovah.

<Inside you. And you, and you, and you, and you . . .>

And me, and me, and me, and me, and me.

<And inevitably, everywhere else too.>

A window smashed at the far end of the hall, but no one noticed it. They were too busy watching the shadows that danced round them and which, for each individual, summoned up the worst nightmare that leered in the dark corner of their minds.

So no one saw the small, dark figure, trembling from strain, pale as the moon, pull himself through the shattered glass, bleeding from cuts by a dozen swords. You couldn't maintain a complete enough illusion to hide for long from a Waywalker. Nor could you just magic others' weapons aside as you flew to safety. You had to compromise.

'You will die for this, Lucifer!' screamed Jehovah, realising that his target was lost.

Unoriginal, thought Sam, but said nothing. There was already too much being said, *and me, and me, and me, and me, filling my head, no escape . . .*

The silence flooded in, and suffocated everything it touched.

❖

The priority was to get a message to Seth, preferably without getting killed in the process. If he asked to meet Seth as himself, he knew Seth wouldn't come. The only alternative was to force the message on to him.

Sam Waywalked back to the edge of the night.

It was a strange sensation, standing between day and night in a pink desert, with nothing around for hundreds of miles and yet knowing, *knowing* that somewhere in the night an entire army moved, trudging slowly towards Tartarus. Sam didn't stir from the Portal, fearing being caught unawares by attackers, and wanting a quick line of retreat. He laid out his remaining Molotov cocktails and loosened his sword in its scabbard, looking round at the bare landscape and questing gently for any sign of danger.

He felt nothing. The Portal stood smack in the middle of the desert, there being nothing alive for miles around to warrant it being protected or sheltered by nature. Any features that might once have stood around the Portal had been eaten away by the sand, and now only it remained, an empty patch of air behind Sam that just happened to be slightly more interesting than every other patch of empty air.

He cast his mind into the night. <Seth,> he sent quietly. No answer. Louder, then. Why not? <Seth. Seth, I know you're in there.>

Silence, but just on the edge of sensing . . . another mind brushing his own? <Seth, I need to talk to you.>

A stirring of thoughts. Then, <Hello, little light and little fire.>

Sam smiled, and wondered that he should be so relieved to hear his enemy's voice. Then his smile faded again and he tried to speak seriously. <You're in danger. You've been deceived, deceived about everything, you're being led to your death, Time has planned it . . .>

And another mind slid into the gap between Sam and Seth's. <Little light, little fire,> it whispered.

<Jehovah? Jehovah, get out of it now! Let me speak to Seth!>

<I'm sorry, little light, little fire. You cannot win.>

<You never knew the extent of my power,> snapped Sam. <Even now you don't know it. Get out! You cannot stop me!>

Seth's mind, breaking in. <Jehovah? Does little light and little fire fear? Does he run? Does he hide? You said he would.>

<Lucifer is mine,> hissed Jehovah.

<Seth! Jehovah has—> began Sam, and felt the wall descend again.

<Give up this folly, brother. You cannot win.>

<I will save thousands of lives! Cronus doesn't have to be freed, there need be no war. I will not let you destroy so much for so little!>

<You did well to get Freya such . . . substantial protection; to get her to Eden. But you must realise that this conflict is inevitable. With Freya as Time's pawn, matters were simpler for us all. Simpler for Time because he had your cooperation, simpler for me because I did not have to find a way to force you, simpler for you because you did not have to be forced. You need to understand – you cannot win. Now we will simply force you rather than persuade you.>

<Freya is safe, Freya is free, you cannot touch her!>

<No. But I can touch you, can't I?>

Sam hit him. He hit him with everything he had and
felt Jehovah stagger back in shock, felt his head fill with
buzzing. And then, sensing Jehovah's pain as every
blood vessel in his nose burst, he hit him again with just
a little bit more, that bit of magic inside that he'd never
let anyone know about.

Always play your cards close, that was the rule. No
one knew what a Son of Magic's potential was, no one
understood how much he'd hidden.

Sam hit Jehovah again, and again, and again, feeling
Jehovah's mind buckle under the pressure of his own,
and even when Jehovah's shields failed he struck yet
again into the soft, malleable parts of Jehovah's mind,
driving home centuries of hate and anger, turning his
emotions into magic, his magic into arrows, and firing
those arrows with unwavering aim.

Another mind slammed in front of the stricken
Jehovah, another voice.

<Lucifer!> screamed Seth. <You cannot win!>

And just behind Sam, calling his name softly, 'Lucifer.'

Sam staggered and turned. Thor smiled, leaning on his
axe. 'Little light, little fire,' he said. 'You think you can
fight your way to freedom?'

Sam drew his sword but didn't attempt to rush Thor,
leaning on the blade instead and drawing heavy breaths.
He felt emptied of everything; the last attack had taken it
out of him. 'It's a trap,' he said. 'Cronus sees through your
eyes, let him see my words! You're being led into a trap.'

'You're lying to save yourself.'

'Please, listen to me,' begged Sam, edging away as
Thor advanced. '*Listen!*'

'It's too late, little light and little fire. You've lost.

You've been losing for centuries. In fact, I don't think there's a single battle you've ever won.'

'You people always underestimate the plucky little guy. Last time we fought, you limped away with a dagger in your leg.'

Thor patted his thigh. 'I'm feeling much better, thank you. And I don't plan to make the same mistake.'

'That's what they always say. "Sell me your soul, Lucifer, go on. I won't underestimate you, Lucifer. Run and hide, come and fight, it's all for a good cause, Lucifer, One sacrifice for the Many, Many for the One, it's all the same, Lucifer." It's bullshit, but it's all the same to certain people, isn't it?'

Thor took a step towards Sam, who dropped his sword and held up his other hand. A bottle full of petrol was clasped there. 'Do you know what this is?'

Thor shrugged, but magic rose around him, thick magic to ward against fire. Sam smiled and shook his head. 'No, no, no. You've got entirely the wrong idea. I'm not going to use this on you. I'm going to use it on them.' He pointed behind Thor.

Thor grinned back. 'No. I know that trick far too well, Lucifer. You don't catch me out with it.'

'Suit yourself,' said Sam. 'Tinkerbell will be pleased.' Thor frowned, recognising something in Sam's face that shouldn't have been there.

Sam heard the thunk of the crossbow. Thor must have heard it too, because he moved in the way that only Cronus might manage, becoming a blur and snatching the crossbow's quarrel out of the air. A sopping wet Tinkerbell, flanked by at least a dozen Ashen'ia, was already reloading.

Thor spun on Sam, who shrugged. 'Don't look at me. You're being led into a trap; you don't stand a chance.'

Cronus hissed in Thor's voice and sprang back as another bolt sailed through the air. Without a word he stepped back, a Portal opening behind him. Sam made no move to stop him as he stepped into the Portal, which closed upon him.

That left Sam and two dozen Ashen'ia, who didn't look at all sympathetic. There was an uncomfortable silence. Carefully Sam picked up his sword.

'Help me,' he said. 'You're sacrifices. You're going to die. Many for the One. You're going to be butchered by Seth's army and left to die. Help me stop him.'

'Don't listen,' said Tinkerbell, his eyes not leaving Sam's face.

Sam gave Tinkerbell an almost sympathetic look. 'You're going to die too, you know. You'll be in Tartarus with the rest of them, and Night will take you over, lead you to the battlefield, and there you'll die in a sea of blood with a thousand other innocent souls for a needless fight. This is your fate too. Help me.'

'Night will protect me. I'm of her blood, I strive to free her son. Night will keep me safe.'

'Time would kill his own daughter, his own son. What gives you the impression that Night is better? Night had Loki, Loki killed Balder. Night had Seth, Seth seeks to free Cronus. Is this a promising family record?'

Tinkerbell raised the crossbow, aimed straight for Sam. 'This is a steel tip, Lucifer. It'll put you to sleep, it won't kill you.'

'It'll put me out of action for days. I'll be regenerating too long to save the universe.'

'You cannot win, Lucifer.'

'I can sure as hell try.' <Seth!> He screamed the message across the land. <Seth, you are being led into a trap, Time has planned —>

The Ashen'ia heard his words, and charged. Sam lobbed a Molotov cocktail at them and brought his sword up and across as the first blade headed towards his face. All the while he never ceased his frantic transmission. <Seth, Time has planned it all from the beginning, you're luring Cronus into the open, you're . . .> Cut up, across, slash, parry, parry, parry, too many swords coming from too many directions. <You're supposed to believe in what you do so that when you free him you . . .> Parry, parry, turn, hot pain across his back, hot pain down one arm, parry, parry, turn, put magic into every twist and every spin, still too many coming from too many directions. <You believe that you're doing it of your own free will! He can sense, you see, he won't come out unless —> A face looming up large over his own, eyes covered over with a translucent film, grinning. <Unless he believes —>

A fist. An ending in the transmission. A big, dark place somewhere down below. A long way to fall. A still, silent sea lapping against black cliffs. Teetering on the edge of the fall. Pushed over. Waters closing over his head, pulling him down despite his struggles. <Seth . . .>

Eventually, darkness.

EIGHTEEN

Darkness

He woke intermittently, feeling much too large for his skin. Everything seemed out of proportion, his hands larger than his stomach, his head larger than his chest, his toes larger than his feet, his feet larger than his legs. He tried to speak, but there was no moisture in his mouth, and when he tried to move, he couldn't. He wasn't entirely sure why.

Sam could feel a regenerative trance humming away deep inside him, but it was uneasy, uncomfortable. Every second it wanted to snap, for fear of the dangers around him. But as danger became a background constant it began to work nonetheless, healing wounds, pulling at energy he didn't have, keeping him in warm, empty darkness.

He thought he saw faces, heard voices, saw needles. They were poisoning him. Giving him a small dose at a time, enough to kill an ordinary man and keep Sam himself asleep. Whenever he woke before they wanted him to, they poisoned him a bit more, so that no sooner had one toxin in his bloodstream been washed away by the regenerative system than another had replaced it.

Soon, he thought, they'd run out of poisons, his system would build up immunity and he wouldn't have to regenerate. Soon, but not soon enough. Not within three days. There were enough poisons in the world for it to take some weeks.

Run out they would, but not in time. Never in time . . .

Drifting, dreaming.

'Why did you defy me?' Soft voice, filling his mind.

Lying handcuffed to a bed, surrounded on every side by wards, poisons, poisons in the blood. Trying to speak, knowing it wasn't real, knowing there wasn't an escape. *Father . . .*

'Freya has been taken from me. Why did you take her from me?'

You would have killed her, Father. Killed her so I would destroy Cronus. Many lives for One, One for Many, no escape . . .

'You cannot win. I will now take what before you offered.'

Let me go, please let me go.

'Give me your soul, Lucifer.'

You're slipping, Sebastian.

'Let me in. I'll take the pain away. I'll purge the poisons from your blood. I'll keep you safe. Nothing shall harm you. You shall be my new golden child, and your name shall be praised as protector of the universe. You shall be welcomed in Heaven, called a hero. You shall belong once more, my child, my heir. Give me your soul.'

I always found it ironic that people were supposed to sell their souls to Satan. What use did he have for them? Go away, leave me alone.

'Let me in. It'll be all right if you just let me in. We can do this easily. No pain, none . . .'

There is a part of Us that can destroy Time. For Time is but a One, and we are Many.

'The Light won't protect you from me, Lucifer. I created the Light, and you are already slipping into a dark place inside.'

We are the intention and the act, the strength and the weakness, the light and the dark, the individual and the whole, the magic and . . . and . . .

I can't make miracles when I'm dead.

You're slipping, Sebastian . . .

Poisons in the blood . . .

'If you don't give up, I will take by force what could have been gently won. Cronus will be freed, Cronus will fall, and you will take him down. But if you let me in, I'll keep you safe when the time comes. I'll hold your mind up, above the others.'

I am many things, you are but one, a part of me. I have seen the minds of the world, and in a small way they are all part of me.

'I'll give you peace.'

Many dying for One, One dying for Many, but that doesn't matter to you. Just a part of me . . .

'Lucifer? Lucifer, why are you hiding in other minds? Why are you burying your soul? I will keep you safe. I will keep you whole. Give in to me, and it will all be over.'

Give in to me . . .

'Father?' Standing in the centre of the summoning

circle, holding the knife. A smile. Sam looked down at the floor, gazing through the swirling images until, just for a second, he saw the clock. He seized on it, dragged it up to the fore of his mind, focused on it. Raised the knife.

Give in to me . . .

He drew a line of blood across his hand and moved it, uncertainly, towards the image. The image danced and shimmered in expectation. 'Father?'

And Time sensed it. He must have sensed it because the image swirled and spun, tried to leap backwards. *There is a part of Us that can destroy Time.* He drew the knife across the image of the clock, but the knife was no longer a knife, and in his hands it left a trail of pure white fire. As bright and as white as the Light. Sam shoved his bloody hand into this tear, pressing his mind into it. A miracle would save him, that was for sure. *I can't make miracles when I'm dead . . .*

He sank into the mind of Time, feeling Time tear, ineffectively, at his own mind. There were too many minds between Time and his own. And the more Time dug, the more minds Sam tossed his way, barring his passage until Sam was sinking behind a world of other minds. Still Time came on, reaching through these other minds for Sam, rushing after him with tendrils of power to turn him into just another puppet, a servant who would live, fight and die for Time. He was crawling through Sam's blood, reaching for his elusive mind, itself a tiny, tiny dot in a sea of others, so small and insignificant it could hardly be seen.

Poisons in the blood. I have seen the minds of the world, and in a small way they are all part of me.

There is a part of Us that can destroy Time. For Time is but a One, and we are Many . . .

At the last, just one mind in all the universe stood between Time and Sam. Sam smiled, wrapped himself in the memory of this one mind, so briefly touched by the Light, and used it like a shield. And though Time tried, he could not tear through this mind that Sam had found within his own, because it tore back with equal strength.

'Your mind, Father,' Sam called. 'A part of your mind is written into my soul, just like a part of my soul is now written on to your mind. You cannot touch me.'

'You cannot win.' *It will be easier, I will keep you safe, I will keep you whole.*

There is a part of Us that can destroy Time. For Time is but a One, and we are Many . . .

'You cannot touch me,' repeated Sam, as though convincing himself of it, rolling the words around his mouth. 'But I,' he said, a gleam in his eyes, 'I can touch you.'

'Lucifer —'

Sam raised the knife made of white fire, turned and without a word plunged it into the heart of Time. His father clasped at his arms, face an oval of surprise as it changed – from Jehovah to Seth to Odin to Thor. And lastly to Sam's own. 'You . . . you would kill me?' he gasped, dragging Sam down with him to the floor.

'Kill you?' Sam laughed. 'Whatever gave you that impression? I'm merely taking out insurance.' His face darkened. He leant forwards, clutching the useless, helpless copy of himself to his chest, and whispered in his father's ear, 'Tell Jehovah where to find me.'

He pulled the other Sam into himself, two Sams becoming one, darkness blending with darkness, a big, black place somewhere down below, a long way to fall, a rushing, roaring sea thundering against dark cliffs, teetering on the edge of the fall, diving over with arms wide, waters closing over his head, pulling him to where he wanted to go.

Eventually, silence.

He thought he saw Jehovah sitting on the edge of the bed. Pale Jehovah, looking almost as ill as Sam felt. Weak Jehovah, who'd borne the ruthless brunt of Sam's mind. Sam tried to speak, and it must have been real because Jehovah reached forwards and gently poured a few drops of water into Sam's mouth, wiping away the water that spilled with his sleeve.

'Where is?' Sam managed to mumble.

'Back with the Ashen'ia.'

'What?'

'Seth has laid camp around Tartarus. It's time to go.'

What did that mean? Time to go, Time to . . . oh. Right. *That*. 'Please . . .'

'I'm sorry, Lucifer.'

'Thousands will die.' He was surprised at how flat it sounded in his mouth, a last attempt from an empty tongue falling on empty ears.

'You won't see a thing.'

Another needle. Another poison.

'Jehovah, please.'

Jehovah rolled Sam's sleeve up, carefully placed the point of the needle against the hollow inside his elbow.

'Brother, please!' begged Sam, struggling feebly, a kitten in a golem's hands.

Jehovah glanced at him. 'I'm sorry,' he said, almost inaudibly.

Sam felt the needle. He felt the burning of the poison. He whispered, 'Time asked me to sell my soul.'

'You didn't.'

'No. I asked him to sell his. I need to know. What happened to Loki?'

'Loki? Why, after he killed Balder he went on the run. To his own, to Valhalla. But even his closest brother turned him over – sent him to be imprisoned by Time.'

'Which brother was that?'

'Odin. Is it important?'

Sam smiled faintly up at the ceiling. 'It begins to . . .'

Jehovah frowned, but his face was already beginning to swim. Black static flashed across Sam's eyes. 'When it comes . . . find me.'

'Where could you be that I cannot find?'

Sam smiled faintly. 'Everywhere. But specifically, I'll be inside.'

'Inside my mind?'

'Inside your soul, brother. In the bit you sold.'

Jehovah's confused face, fading into the all-too familiar darkness.

He woke. He was very, very careful about waking, because before he'd woken all too often only to be put back to sleep with a needle. His first sensation was of how uncomfortable he was. He seemed to have been dumped on the ground with no consideration of temperature or position. The ground itself was hard and cool and smelled of nothing, which in Hell was unusual.

He let these sensations sink in, and opened his eyes.

The ground was black marble that ran into a black marble wall on which some mad child with too much time on its hands had drawn the crude outlines of dozens of men. Between Sam and the wall there was nothing more than a hand. After a little testing, he concluded that it was his own, and was reassured.

Next. Mind. Seemed intact and, when he risked probing around, he found nothing else. He didn't feel drained, he didn't feel . . . anything really. There was just the warm glow of a regenerative trance that had finally, *finally* been allowed to run its course without his system being pumped en route with several more ccs of poison.

He sat up. There was, he discovered, a slight hitch in this scheme, but then he hadn't expected his good fortune to last for long. Someone seemed to have chained him to the wall, and warded the chains in the process. Thick, thick wards using every kind of magic the writer could find. Clearly someone knew his stuff. That someone, he suspected, was Jehovah.

With his hands locked together in front of him, he fumbled with the chains around his ankles. They failed to budge. There was nothing nearby that might serve to help against the locks, and unpicking the wards would take a lot of time.

He looked round the room again. It was a dome, he realised. A giant dome made out of the same black material throughout, and illuminated by torches that burned with a bright blue flame that didn't eat at the torch itself. Coldfire, probably. At one end of the room was a giant pair of black iron doors and, at the other, a smaller, narrower entrance.

On the ceiling of the dome the same mad child had drawn a giant woman's face, complete with red hair, closed eyes and a slightly sad expression. She appeared to be asleep, and dominated most of the room, her shut eyes seeming to stare down nonetheless at the black marble below. On every other wall were more of the same figures. Sam crawled along the length of his chains and, straining, rubbed against the nearest. The white line that defined it didn't come off, but he felt a slight jolt, as of magic. Yet when he probed, he felt nothing.

He slumped down against the wall, feeling wretched. He was tempted to yell for help, but had the feeling that doing so would only invite more needles.

Sam heard a clank and looked towards the giant doors. A thin beam of white light had appeared. Instinctively he curled up again, head in his hands and eyes closed, trying to appear drugged. He heard footsteps, and the door clicked shut again. The footsteps drew close to him, and he felt a hand touch his shoulder. He didn't move. The hand took his pulse and felt his forehead, testing temperature. Sam kept still, focusing entirely on regular breathing.

Eventually, the hand went away and the stranger, satisfied of whatever they'd wanted to know, began to walk away. Sam opened his eyes a crack, and saw an Ashen'ia carefully returning a needle to a small box. No need of it, clearly. Patient asleep. Alone again, Sam sat up and looked around once more.

The ground shook, knocking him to one side. Within a few seconds the tremors passed, but he had recognised the opening shots of a Waywalkers' battle. Start off with big, impressive stuff that doesn't really have much effect, see if you can shock the enemy. He pulled himself back up – and bit his own tongue in shock.

The eyes of the woman in the ceiling were now wide open, bright blue, and staring straight at him. Sam waved. The face didn't move.

He heard a click at the door again and curled up hastily, lying still. Footsteps approached, pausing near him. Then a hand reached down and placed something by his side. He felt the same hands touch his wrists and heard the click of the locks coming undone, even though the weight of the chains still remained. The footsteps began to retreat.

He rolled over to look at his rescuer, and the chains clinked. The man froze, his back to Sam, but still Sam recognised him. He looked from Tinkerbell to his free hands and feet, to the silver sword and dagger at his side.

Finally he said, 'I can't believe I'm going to ask this.'

'Best not to ask, then.'

'Perhaps if you could save me the bother? Begin with "because" and let your imagination do the rest.'

'Don't get me wrong, I still don't think you can win. It's far too late for that,' said Tinkerbell, not moving.

'But?' prompted Sam.

'I think . . . you deserve a chance, even though I know it's a false one.'

'Hum.' Sam considered. 'I take it you don't want Jehovah to know about this.'

'No. It doesn't matter, though. You're still gonna lose your mind. Inevitably.'

'If I know where to find my mind, how can it be lost?'

'Where will you find it, when so many other minds are drowning you?'

'Everywhere.'

'That's a lot to look through.'

'I won't be alone.'

'Yes, you will. You'll be together with other minds, but you'll be more alone than you've been in your entire life. I thought you deserved a chance to avoid that.'

'Even though you think I stand no chance anyway.' Sam smiled and pulled himself up a bit further. 'Thanks, Tinkerbell.'

'Don't mention it,' the other man said, and hurried from the hall before Sam could say anything more. Tinkerbell, Sam concluded, was not comfortable with being at heart a good guy.

He waited a good few minutes before carefully pulling himself to his feet. Tinkerbell, he found, had even supplied his old sheaths and straps.

Feeling happier, he looked up at the face on the ceiling. It was still staring at him, but now something else had changed. It had acquired, he realised, a hand, where before there hadn't been one. It seemed to be open, as if in a greeting.

The world shook again. Strike and counter-strike. Sam kept staring at the hand. He could taste on the air the bitter tang of magic. But it wasn't magic with aim or intent, just a general background roar that rose from the floor like mist and filled the room. He waved a hand up and down, and sparks flashed from his fingertips. Something was building up a charge like nothing he'd ever seen before. He backed away from the centre of the room and bumped against the wall.

It was burning hot.

Holy Hells. Sam back-pedalled hastily as the figures

across the wall began to move. Tiny degrees of motion at first, hardly noticeable as one outline twitched along the side of the wall. It was flowing like oil in water, as seen through very clean glass that kept everything two-dimensional. Sam kept on backing away, suddenly aware that he was surrounded on every side by moving figures. He felt more magic, of a different taste, and glanced towards the entrance. Through the crack between the two doors, what little light had shone was now dimming, passing into shadow and then through to darkness. With it came an unnatural cold that rolled across the floor in a tide and made his breath condense.

This wasn't part of the general background charge, though. This was Seth and his power. Sam tried to call out. <Seth! Seth, it's a trap!> Whatever spell Seth was involved in, it was too deep for Sam's voice to penetrate.

He looked round the room again and felt his stomach do a little backflip as a figure *reached out of the wall*. A single, pure white hand clutching a pure white sword extended itself from the wall and flailed in the air for a few seconds before returning to the wall.

Please tell me this isn't as bad as it looks . . .

More hands now were flailing, turning the walls into some strange animal with black skin and white spines that protruded and flapped about like fish out of water. After the hands came white arms, sickly white, followed by white shoulders and white chins and white faces capped with white hair. From every side they came, men and women of every age, all as white as ghosts, stepping from the walls.

Behind them they left nothing, not a dot to suggest they'd been there. Some carried white swords, some white axes. The majority, however, carried scythes. Endless tiny scythes, as white as the hands that held them. And when the last figure had stepped from the wall they all turned towards the centre of the room and stared with pupil-less eyes at nothing.

Sam waved a hand up and down. Still they stared at nothing. He stood on one leg and stuck his tongue out. Still they stared. He felt a mad surge of laughter well up inside him and he bit his lip to keep it in.

The white figures stood, and did nothing. Sam remembered Jehovah's words. *Time, for their crimes, bound the souls of the slaughtered citizens to their city for ever.*

Tartarus. I'm in Tartarus. And these are the local residents.

He remembered something else. *Anyone entering the city who doesn't bear the mark of a Greater Power will be destroyed by the spirits that guard it.*

As if reading his mind, every eye in the room suddenly seemed fixed on him. Heads turned in unison, a hundred empty eyes stared at him. There was a thud as a hundred feet took a step towards him, again in perfect unison. He looked up at the figure above, who had lost her pupils and irises yet still managed to stare at him as though reading him like a book.

He looked to the people advancing, chose one at random and spoke in a low, urgent voice in Elysian. 'I am a Son of Time and the Bearer of Light. You cannot harm me.' Another step, another. 'I bear the marks of every Greater Power in the whole sodding universe! Their minds are inside mine, mine is inside theirs, we are One!'

Another step. A ring closing around him. He shut his eyes and cried in a tight, scared voice, 'I am the intention and the act, the strength and the weakness, the individual and the whole! I am . . . *becoming* . . . all that lives! It is becoming me!'

Silence. No death, though, which was a pleasant reassurance. He opened his eyes just a bit. A hundred empty eyes stared back at him. A hundred blades hung poised for the kill, and remained exactly that – poised. Then, with an audible snap, the scythes went down and the eyes flashed past Sam as if he wasn't there. The white people wheeled about and began to march to the doors, streaming by, parting and closing around Sam like a river round a boulder.

Sam waited until they were gone, and looked at the figure above. Still the empty eyes were open, but they seemed less intent on him now. The ground shook again and he turned, heading for the doors.

Outside, darkness had fallen. Thick, cloying darkness, cold in more sense than one. Night was the Incarnate of more than just an absence of the sun. She embodied everything that was fearful in the dark, all the childish nightmares, all the creatures that stalked under the moon, all the magic and the mystery. Seth was a Son of Night, and could call on this.

Even though the darkness was complete, deeper patches moved within it, and sounds rose and fell, half-heard and gone as soon as Sam turned to find what made them. Although no light was present, still it managed to play tricks. Sam thought he saw teeth flash. He thought he saw a hand with a knife dart out of a shadow and disappear again. He thought he saw a pair of glowing eyes. He thought he saw . . . and knew it was silly, prayed it was silly. He wasn't seeing a corpse. To prove it he summoned a small sphere of light and marched boldly towards it. The corpse turned out to be nothing more than a white shutter in a black marble house, on which a pair of stone pillars had thrown peculiar shadows.

By the warmth of his little sphere of light, he managed to penetrate more of the darkness. He was in a street of houses. On some, white figures were pulling themselves free, stepping off the walls, at least one figure per house. Bound for ever to Tartarus, they had been called in its defence against Seth.

Which reminded him. He looked up and saw fires burning along a high black wall, eclipsed occasionally by figures passing across them. Ashen'ia, no doubt. They, having sold their souls to a Greater Power, would be safe within the city from the city's guardian defenders. To some small degree they could use its walls to defend themselves.

Poor fools. If by a chance you look like winning, the Powers you sold your souls to will simply take control, and ensure that you die anyway.

Another thought crossed his mind. *Cronus is a Greater Power. Thor . . .*

Sam began to walk, quickly. He found the nearest fires and headed towards them, breaking into a run as the street shook again. It wouldn't be long before they began the serious magics, the real world-breakers. He saw a phalanx of white people ahead and pushed through them. They offered no resistance.

The wall still seemed a very long way off when the catapults let fire. They were clearly aimed to smash a way through the walls. But the first shots were misjudged, and the flaming missiles from the catapults flew straight over the walls and exploded on the houses inside, raining down fire on every side. Or perhaps that was the point – destroy the houses that the spirits are tied to in order to destroy the spirits themselves.

The Ashen'ia on the walls, seeing that the attack had really started, began to yell. It was, Sam suspected, supposed to be a war chant, but sounded more like a very bad close harmony chorus trying to do rap.

He heard drums beating in the distance, and recognised them as belonging to one of the Princes of Hell. Troops were attacking . . .

More balls of flaming death began to descend. There was a direct hit somewhere on the walls and the Ashen'ias' war chant faltered. Missiles rained down on the city behind the wall, turning the artificial night orange as they passed. Yet when they hit there were no screams. There were no living creatures to suffer.

Sam felt new magic join the already suffocating stench that filled the air along with the smell of smoke and sulphur. From all around, complementing the night, fog began to rise; Sam's narrow range of vision shrunk yet further.

The fog, against expectations, didn't dull the noise of the drums. It seemed to amplify it, and their low boom carried through every street, bounced off Sam's ears and hummed up through his feet. He smelled death and fear. *Odin. This is Odin's work. He's a Son of War; he's trying to get to you.*

The walls shook again. The rain of burning stones and sulphur had turned into a storm. They didn't stop coming, filling the sky with fire as they poured down. Sam heard the hiss of the catapults being released, the crackle of the stones racing through the sky, the thud and roar as they struck, the drums, the battle cries of the Ashen'ia, and he marvelled at how deathly silent the city would otherwise be. Without war, it would be utterly still, the endless sunlight of the desert catching the black marble and the sleeping figures within to make the city rather beautiful. If anything, that made him more desperate. He ran faster.

Sam saw a dark stairwell leading into a tower in the wall, and sprinted up it. He reached the top as Seth's army began their own war cry, hammering against their shields and sounding no more convincing than the Ashen'ia.

There were more of them than he'd imagined. Seth must have been pressing thousands into his service as he swept through Hell, threatening to destroy them with the power of the Pandora spirits unless they did what he wanted. They stretched across the desert, looking almost pretty, a hundred thousand specks of fire in the darkness, like a galaxy seen from Earth. Hundreds of catapults, loading and firing. Sam could sense demons, angels, avatars, even some humans in the throng. All going to charge the Ashen'ia, all going to die. For One. Many dying for the One, the ultimate inversion of the noble ideal. Many dying for his father's cause.

He could hear the Pandora spirits singing through the air. They circled over Seth's camp, waiting to attack. Suspicion, Jehovah's spirit, was there too. No doubt Jehovah was with it, pretending to be one with Seth's ambition, steering events to his own end. And yes, here came Jehovah's power, filling Seth's army with the fervent belief that they were dying for the greatest cause ever. Filled with that kind of magic, they could eat their way through the walls.

It was weaker than it had been, however. Jehovah had clearly been shocked by Sam's attack.

<Seth!> screamed Sam wordlessly. <Seth, stop!>

No one heard him. He felt the song of the Pandora spirits reach a pitch, and as one they hurtled towards the city. Still the catapults kept on flying, turning the city ablaze and shattering the night and silence. Fractured stone fell from the black walls of Tartarus, cracks spreading through the marble. Sam looked along the wall and saw a couple of lights go out. Saw the gates open. Knew how.

<Thor!> he screamed. <Little light and little fire calls you, Thor! Come to fight, Freya's lover! Come fight the one who loved her more than you ever could!>

Silence, but he knew Thor had heard him. <For Freya, little light and little fire?> whispered an answer in his mind.

Sam's mind stayed focused on the gate. Perhaps the Ashen'ia would find it. Perhaps they'd close it in time. Perhaps Thor hadn't managed to do his work properly, perhaps . . . perhaps Sam had distracted him enough.

<Come to me,> he sent, privately willing Thor away from the gates.

<I come, I come.>

He turned his mind to the Ashen'ia, even as Seth's army gave one final, defiant yell, and charged. <The gate is open! Thor has opened the gate!> he screamed at the top of his mental lungs, but even to his mind the cry sounded weak compared to the roaring of the army descending across the sand like so many ants. <The gate

is open!> He didn't know if anyone heard him or not.

Swearing, he began to run down the stairs from the tower. He'd distracted Thor, and now had to get away before Thor actually found him. Sam ran through the streets, heading away from the fires that blazed in the city. The catapults started anew, but they weren't targeting the walls any more. They were trying to level the city, house by house, destroying the spirits bound to each one. *Which means Seth knows the gate is open.* <Seth's coming through the gate!>

He kept on running, ignoring the sky of fire above. The earth shook again and he heard thunder rumble as dark clouds began to move in, faster than natural. Lightning struck, somewhere near. More tremors, this time more violent. Tremors increasing as the three Waywalkers outside the city combined their power to tear the ground itself.

Sam staggered and fell. He landed with his palms pressed to the earth and through that connection tried to sooth it. But they were three and he was one, and not even he had that much power. The tremors increased again, picking up the whole world and tossing it around as if in a washing machine, only with fire and lightning serving as soap and water. Sam heard stonework crack, heard the terrible creaking of ancient masonry giving way. He closed his eyes and waited for the tremors to subside, trying to remember what he'd been told in Japan about earthquake survival. Find somewhere protected to hide or get out into the big, wide open. Neither seemed greatly available so he curled up and waited. The noise shook him most of all, the terrible cracking of a world being torn apart. And even when the tremors subsided, still the noise persisted with the clatter of falling stone, the creak of upset buildings tossed to one side, the roar of the armies, the crackle of the flames, the snapping of the catapults freeing their burdens.

As he cautiously picked himself up he heard a gentle 'whumph' somewhere to the west and saw the sky beyond the wall light up orange. He heard screams. Someone had poured a vat of boiling oil on the hapless attackers. Sam wondered how many demons Jehovah was deliberately sending against the best-fortified section of wall. Soon the Ashen'ia would begin to die. Soon there would be no one left alive apart from Seth, Odin and Jehovah. And somewhere, perhaps, Sam.

Not to forget Thor, that is.

'Little light, little fire, where are you hiding?' The voice echoed through the streets, amplified by the unnatural fog and somehow managing to carry across the sounds of war. Thor appeared at the end of the street, saw Sam, grinned.

Sam hesitated, slowed. <Seth,> he sent frantically. <Please Seth, it's a trap, call it off, make it stop.> No answer.

Thor smiled, walking slowly towards Sam, no hurry, no problem. Just a little battle against the little bastard son, nothing he couldn't manage . . .

<Seth!>

Thor, smiling. 'I can hear you screaming, little light and little fire. Screaming like a baby. Lies to soothe the night.'

<Why doesn't anyone listen to me? Why does no one believe me?>

They've all got too much invested in this conflict to be proven wrong, that's why. And besides, who ever trusts the exiled, bastard Son of Time who closed the Way of Eden?

Thor stopped a few metres from Sam. His axe hung down at his side, but Sam saw how tightly he gripped it in one hand. For a moment the two stared at each other, summing the other up. Sam had won their last two battles, but then he'd been assisted. He wasn't sure that any help was coming this time round.

Thor beamed, a madness in his eye drawn out by the orange fires raging around. 'Hear that?' he asked. 'It's the sound of war. All those people fighting and dying. It's interesting. It's part of me. I'm a Son of War.'

'You sold your soul to Cronus; you're less than you ever were. And even before, that wasn't an edifying sight.'

'Do you want to know why I did what I did, why I gave blood to Cronus?'

Sam hesitated. The temptation was to say something very rude. On the other hand, Thor was an ambulatory killing machine, and any way of surviving, even if it meant playing father confessor, counted as good.

'Do tell.'

'I did it for Freya.'

There was a long silence. 'Nope,' said Sam. 'Still pretty unedifying.'

Thor took a step towards Sam – who glimpsed a flicker of something . . . desperate? Sam had never seen Thor look like anything except a lout with an axe. He sometimes forgot that perhaps, somewhere in there, a tiny brain was screaming for attention from the huge hunk it was stuck in.

'I couldn't live without her, don't you see? I couldn't
do it! Cronus was peace, he was freedom! I couldn't go
on without Freya!'

Sam looked at Thor with something close to pity, and
wondered whether he should tell him. *He'd call me a liar,
scream blue murder and take that saying literally.*

'I somehow doubt that Freya would want you to do
what you're doing now.'

Thor's expression hardened. He stood up straighter,
being already taller than Sam, and stared at him with a
faint sneer. 'You never knew her.'

You have a point. 'You'd be amazed,' Sam sighed
wearily.

Thor's sneer expanded into a grin that distorted his
face away from humanity. 'One last, heroic stand,
Lucifer?'

'Don't be bloody daft,' Sam muttered, and turned and
ran.

Thor ran too, but Sam had the advantage of surprise
and gained a few vital metres and besides, he was
running like only a Prince of Heaven could, running so
fast that to stop was to topple like a tree. No one had
ever clocked how fast a Waywalker could run, as most
were usually in the position of having nothing to run
from. But Sam, with a lifetime's experience of being the
bastard son, the necessary child, the exile, the Devil, had
learned to run like almost none other.

Eventually, he stopped, when he felt as if he could run
no more. Here the streets were empty, calm, the noises of
battle a long way off. He put his hands on his knees and
stood in the fog, senses extended, mind racing as fast as
his heart.

Silence. The smell of smoke and death, then the screams of the dying, explosions, crashing, the crackle of flame, the occasional sound of a trumpet as it commanded troops here and there and back again.

A song drifted through the smoke, sung in a quiet pleasant tenor. 'He who would valiant be –'

Sam looked up.

'– 'gainst all disaster –'

He edged towards a building, reassured by the feeling of something solid against his back, and took a firmer grip on his sword.

'– let him in constancy –'

Shaking uncontrollably now, he leaned his sword against his knees and wiped the sweat off his hands on to his sleeves, repeating the procedure for the hilt. He tried to take slow, deep breaths; but each time he breathed in, the air shuddered down his lungs. He felt cold, and blind, and exposed.

'– follow the Master.' Sudden silence. 'Come out, come out, wherever you are.'

'There's no discouragement,' sang Sam very, very softly, 'shall make him once relent—'

But Thor was already on to a different song. 'And did those feet, in ancient times –'

'– his first avowed intent –'

'– walk upon England's mountains green –?'

'– to be a pilgrim.'

'– and was the holy lamb of God—' Silence, sudden and abrupt. 'Did they?' The voice was just a few metres away. Light bloomed around Thor, who was leaning on his axe staring straight at pale-faced Sam.

'Without Waywalking?' asked Sam hoarsely. 'You

must be joking. Geographically the idea is ludicrous anyway.'

'The Romans made it from Galilee to Albion.'

'Was one legionnaire in both simultaneously?'

'No.' Thor smiled disarmingly. 'What a pity you can't be in two places at once either. Although, once I'm finished with you, I'm sure we can arrange matters that way.'

Sam grinned a sickly grin of terror. 'Thor, or possibly Cronus – whichever you answer to – some hard-working scriptwriter sat up all night trying to think of lines like that, and even then they had to be delivered by a bad guy with a strange accent and a white cat, not to mention a hollow volcano and a portable piranha tank. Your delivery just isn't up to it.'

'Such a pity we couldn't be friends,' sighed Thor, and attacked.

Sam had learned. Forget trying to fight off Cronus and Thor simultaneously, forget trying to do something heroic, because it wouldn't work. Try and find the cavalry to save the day. He didn't parry, he didn't thrust, he didn't duck; he simply winked out of existence.

Thor's axe struck the doorframe behind Sam, and buried itself deep. Slowly, his eyebrows raised in mild surprise, he withdrew his axe and looked around. 'You can't sustain an illusion that complete for long,' he said clearly. 'I know the stories about these illusions. You still get hurt.'

No answer. Something moved in the fog. Thor turned in a blur and threw his axe. It struck another surface, but not before something dark had dived to the ground in front of it, sending up a puff of sand. Raising his hand,

Thor recalled the axe and dived after Sam, who was scrambling to his feet, a blacker figure against the darkness.

Sam ran, Thor behind him. And for every step Sam took, Thor seemed to have taken one more. Sam turned a corner, and saw a dead end.

No worries. Fuelled by a calm terror he didn't know was possible he ran towards the wall at the end of the street, and straight up it. It was magic more than physical prowess. People who ran up walls for a living were usually incapable of adding two and two thanks to their ruthless up-wall training, and Sam had never really studied the art. But he grabbed the top of the wall with magic and, hauling on it like a rope, pulled himself up on a support system as fragile as shadow.

He was on a rooftop, dull, black and about as interesting as the darkness around it. He didn't slow, reasoning that if he was capable of getting on to the roof then so was Thor, but ran again, hopping the short distances between roof and roof and running blindly in whatever direction seemed most convenient. A street ahead. *No worries.* He ran straight out over empty air, and kept on running on magic, sweat making his shirt stick to his back with the effort. *Life is one long run into the darkness, and when you do feel profound about the whole affair, it's at the most inconvenient moments . . .*

Another street. Another flare of magic. Another rooftop. The regular thumping of his footsteps as he got into his stride. Thud, thud, thud, thud . . . and just behind it another sound, accenting his own footfalls like the quavers between every long crotchet, making music out of the run: Thudthudthudthudthudthudthud.

<Seth!> he sent frantically. <It's a trap!>

He reached a street, and felt too weary to run over it. So he fell into it instead, rolling as he hit the ground and coming up with his sword raised in the guard position.

Thor landed lightly on his feet a few metres away, looking as if he'd just had an invigorating jog before breakfast and was in the mood for a cold shower and a bit of yoga. Sam backed away, heaving in lungfuls of air, pale face glistening with sweat.

'Strange thing,' said Thor, his eyes changing to the film-covered, pale eyes of a fish, voice darkening to the multi-stranded rasp of Cronus, 'but I rather imagined the Bearer of Light would be harder to kill.'

'Strange thing, so did I.'

This time he didn't run. Thor charged, and Sam was ready. He was not, whatever happened, prepared to fight Thor on his own terms. He threw up his free left hand, and pushed Thor back, hard. Thor hit the house behind, staggered, shook his head, and advanced towards him again. Sam repeated the procedure again, and again, and again, but Thor was unrelenting, and every time he came a bit closer Sam grew a little weaker, until Thor was within an arm's reach before Sam had managed to muster enough energy to pluck him up and throw him back again. Thor's head was bleeding from the impacts, but he kept coming. And coming, and coming, and coming . . .

The axe sliced towards Sam's face, and he had no alternative but to parry. His arms trembled as bit by bit his blade was forced towards the ground, and locked there. Thor's wild face was just a few inches away from Sam, and on his breath he smelled the sweet, sickly smell of decay. 'Where's Daddy when you need him?' asked Thor softly.

'Screw Daddy, Mummy, Uncle, Aunty and you,' Sam hissed, and kicked out at Thor's knee. The fact that Thor did not crumple in agony, as Sam had hoped, proved still further that he wasn't human. Thor grinned, and brought his elbow up. It struck Sam's face, and Sam reeled back, his grip slipping on the sword. His head was spinning, and when he lunged for the sword Thor's foot came down first and kicked it away. Sam began to crawl back, mustering his last reserves of magic for a final, heroic stand, like the kind he'd vowed never to have. Thor's axe darted downwards as Sam raised his hands, and stopped inches from his neck. Sam froze.

'So,' said Cronus in Thor's voice, 'you're supposed to save the universe?'

'Tinkerbell's behind you,' said Sam softly.

He saw doubt flash through Thor's eyes, and knew he was thinking of the last time he'd doubted Sam's word. He half turned, and Sam had the dagger out, not even bothering with his hands but pushing it with his mind straight up and through the air, spinning it round as it flew. He saw the look of surprise on Thor's face, saw him stagger a pace, turn and swing the axe down in Sam's direction. Sam flung his hands up and knocked Thor back one more time with a reserve of magic he didn't realise he had. Thor stumbled, axe falling from his fingers, struck a black marble wall and sagged. He looked with shock at the dagger in his side, buried up to the hilt. It wasn't quite where Sam had wanted it, though; it wouldn't kill. *No problem.*

He held out his hand, and the fallen silver sword flew

up into it. He reversed his grip on it and turned to Thor, who stared at him with wild, clear eyes. 'Lucifer . . .' he began. Sam leant down and pulled his dagger free of Thor's side, conjuring up a surprisingly womanish scream from Thor's trembling lips.

He pulled his sword back, levelled at Thor's heart.

'Lucifer!' screamed a voice in the darkness.

Sam turned. A darker figure stood at the end of the street, a drawn scimitar in one hand.

Seth.

Sam aimed the tip of his sword at Seth, feeling adrenalin and hatred give him new strength that couldn't last. *Better not waste it, then?* 'You're mine!' he yelled. 'If it has to end with your death, so be it! Everything else has been lost to me!'

And perhaps Seth saw that Sam meant every word, that he was bent on killing, because the dark figure at the end of the street turned and began to run. Sam hissed in hate and ran after, tossing a sphere of light and sending it ahead to orbit Seth's head, showing his path up even though he tried to bat it away irritably with one hand. Sam didn't know where they were headed. He simply knew that with Seth dead it would all be over. Cronus would sleep, the battle would be neither won nor lost and he could go free . . .

The black marble dome squatted in the fog. Sam saw Seth open the doors, and pelted after him. He ran into the dome, saw Seth look back, and heard the doors slam shut behind. He turned. Odin stood there, leaning heavily against the doors. Jehovah stepped out of a shadow, his face dark. Seth, panting for breath, grinned.

Sam looked from one conspirator to the other, before

turning to Seth once more. 'You,' he hissed. 'You brought it to this.'

'Deal with him,' snapped Seth to Jehovah and Odin.

Sam laughed. 'Thor didn't, and he'd sold his soul.' *But then, so has Jehovah, hasn't he?*

Seth simply shook his head and turned his back on Sam, walking slowly across the hall.

'Stop!' yelled Sam. Seth didn't stop. Sam flung out a hand, catching him in magic. The effort left him exposed. He felt magic slam into him from Jehovah's direction and staggered, struggling to clear his shields of the afterburn. Another ram of power from Odin and he fell to the ground, ice crawling across his skin.

Seth half turned in the doorway at the end of the hall and smiled. 'I've won, Lucifer.'

'You're a fool,' he managed to croak through his chattering teeth.

'And I've struck gold,' replied Seth.

'Oh, *you're* the stupid bastard who thought this was a good idea!' said a friendly, expansive voice from the door. Every head turned, except Sam, who grinned a wild, manic grin.

Seth frowned. 'Who are you?'

'Me?'

Sam managed to crawl round enough to see Tinkerbell clearly. He was holding his ever-faithful crossbows, both bolts raised to point at Seth. 'I'm the guy with the vengeance complex.'

For a blissful second, Sam actually believed Tinkerbell was going to shoot Seth and thought, *he'll shield*. Then, in a movement almost too fast to see, Tinkerbell spun and pulled the triggers. Both bolts slammed into Odin, whipped him around, picked him off his feet and knocked him down on the floor, blood seeping through the two holes in his chest. Seth snarled, turning back and starting across the floor.

'No!' snapped Jehovah, stepping forward to block his way. 'I'll deal with these two.'

Seth hesitated, then nodded. 'See that you do.' He turned and ran across the floor. Sam saw a hand descend to his eye height. He took it gratefully and leaned on Tinkerbell. 'Why'd you shoot Odin?' he moaned. 'You could have shot Seth.'

'Odin,' said Tinkerbell in a very quiet voice, 'was the guy Loki went to for protection and safety. Odin sold Loki to Time.'

Sam looked down at Odin with the two bolts sticking out of his chest. The man was hardly breathing, his eyes were shut, but Sam could still sense life there. 'Steel tipped?' he asked quietly.

'Yeah, but my axe is enchanted and should finish the job.'

Sam looked from the fallen Odin to Tinkerbell and finally to Jehovah. He staggered forwards a few paces, pushing Tinkerbell back. 'Odin's yours,' he explained. 'Jehovah's mine.'

He saw a flicker of fear pass across Jehovah's face. *Ah. For the first time you understand my power.*

'Let me pass, brother,' said Sam.

'You know I can't.'

'I'm going to kill Seth. Then there'll be no one left to free Cronus. It'll all be over. We can rest easy.'

'You've lost, Sam. The Ashen'ia are dying, so is Seth's army. Seth will free Cronus.'

'I'll stop him.'

'You know you can't.'

'I *believe* that I can. So get out of my way.'

'No. And I don't think you have the strength to force me.'

Sam's voice was on the edge of snapping, yet still he kept it level. 'Odin lies dying, Thor too. You stand between me and survival.'

'You never had a chance.'

'Jehovah,' said Sam, with a little sigh, 'I'm going to be frank with you. I can't win.'

Jehovah hesitated. He clearly hadn't been expecting Sam to say that. Sam beamed. 'But I can tell you something that may be to your advantage.' Purposefully, he sheathed his sword, slid his dagger into its sheath and approached Jehovah. Jehovah shifted uncomfortably from foot to foot, not sure how to react to this new side of Sam's nature.

Sam leant forward and whispered in Jehovah's ear. 'Always fight dirty.' He stood back, nodding at Jehovah eagerly, as if expecting feedback to this statement. When he didn't get any he shrugged, sighed, and brought his knee up hard into Jehovah's groin. As Jehovah crumpled with an indignant look on his face, Sam brought his elbow down across the back of Jehovah's head and kicked his shin. Jehovah fell to the ground, red face and cheeks puffed up big with the pain. Sam squatted down next to him and hissed, 'Sometimes it's down to sheer common sense rather than *strength*, brother. Might is not necessarily right, and don't forget it.'

He rose to his feet, glanced at Tinkerbell and smiled.

'Jehovah's weak spot. He always thinks in black and white.'

'You don't stand a chance,' said Tinkerbell, awe in his voice.

'I know,' replied Sam brightly, opening the door at the far end of the dome and running through.

NINETEEN

Seth

Whoever built Tartarus had made it easy for the attackers to get to the key. Deliberately so, thought Sam. All you had to do was raze the city to the ground, sacrifice a few thousand soldiers and, in the confusion, slip through the back door. But then Time would have known that Tartarus wouldn't keep a Waywalker out. He must have been counting on that fact.

Sam padded quietly down the long, dark corridors illuminated occasionally by a flickering torch, pausing here and there to push open doors as he passed. A few of the white people lay on the ground, dull red blood seeping from numerous wounds, but they weren't dead. Merely regenerating, like a Waywalker. Unlike Waywalkers, it seemed, they could regenerate injuries caused by enchanted blades. It just took a lot of time.

There were other bodies too. Some Ashen'ia, and a few demons. Clearly Seth had sent troops into the corridors before he dared enter, cannon fodder to clear his safe passage. Sam felt bile and shame rise at the thought that one of his *brothers* could do this. The deeper he descended, the thicker the bodies became until the entire place reeked of death. Seth had sacrificed thousands to get into Tartarus and didn't seem to care. Sam kept on walking, trying to shut his senses off from the bombardment of sights, smells and sounds around him, all of them dark.

A small, rather dull door was open ahead. He passed through it, and here the tunnels became more complicated, forking and dividing, twisting and turning like a maze. At every junction he came to, he chose the darkest, most foul-smelling one and ran down it with his eyes half-shut to try and not see what his brother had done.

He didn't know how long he ran through the tunnels, which seemed to get smaller and narrower and more claustrophobic with each turn until he was squeezed between two dark walls that pressed against his shoulders and seemed to suck the breath from him. He ran on, heart thumping in his head. *Don't panic, please don't panic, stay calm, oh Time have mercy, I want to stay calm . . .*

'Swing low, sweet chariot,' he sung quietly under his breath. *That's it. Music, calm, focus on singing.* 'Coming for to carry me home.' *Breathe, calm, relaxed, stay focused.* 'Swing low, sweet chariot –'

A door ahead. He pushed it open. Bright light beyond. Many torches burning with a pale cold flame. Wards on a heavy door torn to pieces, but Sam could see in just the afterburn of those wards that they had been thin, pale things to start with. Easy for a Waywalker to penetrate them.

And on a pedestal in a pool of still water, a single, small, brass key, tarnished by age. Seth leaning over it, reaching out hungrily.

'Seth,' said Sam, very quietly.

Seth glanced up and raised his eyebrows. 'Oh. You're alive,' he said, sounding disinterested. 'Manage to kill Jehovah?'

'Disable. Temporarily. You found the key, then?'

'Yes. Not that impressive, is it? But then, the smallest things are usually the important ones.'

'Doesn't it occur to you that it was a little easy to find, for such a small thing?' asked Sam, circling the pedestal slowly. Seth moved round the other side with equal wariness, his shrewd little eyes sparkling. His weapon was a scimitar, and Sam knew that somewhere about his person there was also a very small, neat stiletto. He still had the gall to wear his crown, though. A lavish gold thing, with spiky points and everything. *Mine never had spiky points*, thought Sam bitterly. *Bastard son . . .*

'I don't expect anyone thought I'd get this far,' replied Seth loftily. 'I admit the Ashen'ia were a surprise, but my army will deal with them. I thought Thor would slow you down, but I never had any illusion that he'd stop you. I know you far too well. You wouldn't let yourself be hindered by a simple thing like a Greater Power in a Waywalker's flesh. You've spent too much time learning how to fight.'

'You're an arrogant bastard, you are,' muttered Sam. 'But I'll try anyway, Time knows why. Literally.' He took a deep breath. 'You were *meant* to find the key. It's so that someone Cronus trusts will open the door to his prison.'

'Excuse me if I'm not entirely convinced,' said Seth in his urbane, easy-going drawl.

'Oh, you really are an idiot, aren't you? They *want* Cronus out, so that *I* can kill him.'

'Can you?' asked Seth mildly. 'Or should I say, will you? Perhaps I ought to have asked that before. *Will* you throw away your life on a random piece of guesswork, trying to stop a power that you can't even begin to understand?'

'You mean, will I throw away my life fighting, or will I let it be snuffed out while trembling? Daft question, really. But anyway, it's hardly my choice. I'm just a part of the plan.'

'Then I'd better make sure that I kill you first, hadn't I? That ought to throw their plan slightly.'

'I don't know why I bother,' muttered Sam, playing it as calmly as he could even though his fear was rising. 'That key has been put there deliberately! You're pawns in the puzzle, sacrifices to the enemy, just like me!'

'We're not sacrifices,' corrected Seth quickly. 'Those who die under my banner die fighting for a cause that we believe in. No more death. No more suffering. No more fate, no more destiny. You're just a face without a cause, too weak to fight your own battles, easy to con into fighting another's.'

'This is turning into a really bad million years, you know that?'

'It's a pity you didn't side with us,' murmured Seth from his own little world. 'You would have found freedom.'

'I used to think I was having a bad day,' continued Sam in the same easy tone, 'but every time something happens I find myself growing more thoughtful, and after a lot of contemplation I've come to the conclusion that the formation of the planets in the first place was a policy that needed rethinking.' He gave Seth a crooked smile. 'And I wouldn't have found freedom. For a thousand reasons that would take a French philosopher several hours and a particularly good bottle of wine to explain, I wouldn't have found freedom. I don't think I ever will. It's how you appreciate captivity that's the interesting question.'

A grin of triumph lit Seth's face. 'Ah. So you are your father's child after all.'

'And you're not?'

'I found freedom.'

'And on your grave they'll write that you died free and happy, I'm sure.'

'Will they give me a statue?'

'I know they won't give me one,' remarked Sam conversationally.

'They ought to give me a statue. I tried to change things. We're all so afraid of change. Time's universe is working fine, we say. Why bother to try a new system? Cronus is not the end, you see. He's just the beginning.'

'Is this the same Cronus who took possession of Thor and tried to educate me on the subject of being in two places at once?'

Seth wasn't listening. His eyes had the glow of a madman. 'We were always told that Cronus was the end of everything, but he isn't. He's the end of *everything as we know it*. A life prisoner is sometimes afraid to leave prison, because he doesn't know about the world outside. Doesn't know how wonderful it can be. Prison is all he knows. Prison is all he'll die knowing. He'll commit a crime the moment he's out to ensure this, because the world is so big and large and full of possibilities that he doesn't dare look, he's afraid.'

'Did you have a happy childhood?' asked Sam suddenly. 'Only you've got this nervous twitch in the corner of your eye . . .'

'Why don't you use the Light, Lucifer?' Sam said nothing. This seemed to cheer Seth up. 'Ah. You're already slipping, aren't you? Remembering things that are not from your mind, feeling things that you never felt, calling yourself names that are not yours, thinking thoughts that were born in another mind. You're just an insignificant spark in a fire. You're a pebble in the ocean. And you know it more than anyone else, because you've seen that ocean. You've seen the big, wide world and, like the prisoner, you're afraid of it.'

They were standing a few metres apart. 'Seth,' said Sam, 'I don't think we're going to be friends.'

Seth's smile widened. 'Neither do I.'

It was the old routine. Thrust, parry, slash, feint, duck, skip back and forwards like a Morris dancer on hot coals, search for an opening, aware of nothing but the regular rhythm. Clack, clack, hiss, scrape, clack. There was no magic, no fancy fireworks, no screams of rage, no cursing and no praying. Just the endless monotony, one, two, one, two.

Sam was fighting without a cause and no real passion. He felt so tired, physically and mentally, that he was hardly aware of anything but the weight in his arms and the scrape of his breath as it dug its way down his throat. He didn't know why he was bothering. One, two, feint to the left, slash to the right, lock, up, parry to the middle, turn, dodge, turn, thrust, one, two. He felt very detached. It wasn't him fighting, it was someone else. It wasn't him on the edge of death, it was someone else. It wasn't him dancing for things he didn't believe in, dancing with a partner who liked to dance with snakes as well as people. He'd been dancing all his life, and the steps were now automatic. He wondered whether he was going mad. He wondered whether it was physically impossible for a Waywalker to go mad, or whether, as a sadistic twist of fate, they'd been designed so that their brains were wired for sanity only. He wondered whether he could regenerate madness, like he could regenerate a burn. He looked at Seth and decided with a sigh that perhaps madness could touch even the great. He wondered whether he fell into that category.

One, two, cut, parry, thrust. Six basic moves taught in England, elaborated on in France, tweaked in Russia, expanded on in China. A hundred basic moves from a hundred countries were brought against Seth. Sam imagined that it was an impressive fight, to look at. But inside the wall of sharp silver he'd created for himself, it seemed only endless and futile. One, two, one and a half, if you count the feint, two, only by dint of a hasty step back and thrust down to catch a well-aimed blow from Seth on the tip of his sword. One, two, never a third step, because three was breaking the rhythm and meant someone else was counting the beat. Or if there was a third step, then you had to have a fourth already prepared, reading the other's mind without hearing their thoughts. One, two, three, four. Moves growing more complicated, a third meeting a second, where before the two would break after just a thrust and a parry and return to an opening move. Like chess. Heading away from the opening game, heading into the more difficult middle game. Thrust meets parry which turns to push which meets slash which meets block which meets stab. Rhythm picking up, growing faster, more risks being taken. One, two, three, four, five, six. Breathe. Always remember to breathe. Moves he'd never learnt, coming from memories that weren't his. Sensations that weren't his filling him, coming from feelings from previous battles that he'd never fought. Flow like the water, chop like the axe, stab like lightning, dance like the wind. Methods he'd never learned put into words he'd never heard, but he *knew* them nonetheless.

He looked at his own emotions with a feeling of detachment, and wondered. Should he discharge the Light? It would give him a break from his own morbid thoughts, at least.

He looked at Seth, and saw that his brother's face was pale and sweaty. But then, so was his. He was bleeding from a dozen shallow cuts, and so was Seth. He hadn't even felt the pain. Seth had, at some stage in the affair, drawn his stiletto, and Sam realised with a start he had his own dagger out. He looked at Seth. Seth looked at him. Sam felt the urge to laugh, and didn't know at what.

'Hi, brother,' he said, for want of something better.

'Hi,' said Seth.

One, two, three, four, five, six, step and duck and thrust and turn and stab and lunge. Reverse the grip on your dagger, bring it down as you turn, finish spin, sword up, bat aside blow, smash lunge away, kick, breathe, one, two, three, four . . .

There might have been sounds outside, but he wasn't sure. All that mattered was the silence, the peace of listening to his thoughts and feeling his feelings and wielding his weapons. Who cared that Seth was lunging down like that, and like that? The arms that belonged to Sam Linnfer were also coming down like that, and like that, and like that, and soon the left hand that contained *his* dagger, *his*, would come up like this, and like this, and like this, and *his* mind would think *his* thoughts and *his* eyes would see things only *he* could see and *his* heart would pump *his* blood through *his* body faster, and faster, and faster.

And Seth was staggering back, and opening his mouth and hissing, 'Why don't you die, bro—?'

And *Sam's* dagger was slicing through the air, guided by *his* calm mind, held in *his* trembling hand, and digging itself into Seth's heart. And Seth was staring at *him*, with wide, astonished eyes. And the scimitar was falling from Seth's hand, and Seth was grasping *his* arms, leaning on him for support and falling to the floor. Sam went with him, sword falling from his grip. Seth opened his mouth to say something, coughed, looked at Sam, looked past him, and smiled faintly. 'Well done,' he whispered softly. 'You've learned.'

'I'm sorry. It was . . . necessary.'

Seth grinned, a weak, pale grin. Sam hadn't realised how much blood they'd both lost, or how tired they both were. 'Tell them my last breath was something profound.'

'Sure. It's been a bad eternity, hasn't it?'

And Seth died. *No fireworks, no magic*. One second a spark of life, the next second nothing. Sam's knife was lodged in his brother's chest. He pulled it free, hands

shaking and bloody, but didn't feel strong enough to hold
it. Sam felt as weak as a child, and revolted by the
thought of handling weapons ever again. He washed his
hands in the water around the key, hardly aware of what
he was doing, and sat, staring at the door. Waiting for
whatever must happen to happen.

He knew it ought to be over, whatever 'it' would later
be named by those who cared, but his guts still churned
and his fingers tingled. His fingers. His memories. His
emptiness, waiting for something to fill it. The Light
stirred, eager to oblige.

A voice that was definitely his sighed inside the head
that definitely belonged to him, *Oh, do shut up.* He smiled.
It was nice to know there was still something inside.

The door opened. Jehovah stared down at him sadly.
Tinkerbell stood behind him. 'Hi,' murmured Sam, just
for something to say.

Without a word Jehovah stepped to the edge of the
pool, glanced at the key on the pedestal, and ignored it.
Tinkerbell helped Sam stagger to his feet. Sam sheathed
his sword and dagger, and leant against the nearest wall
as if it was all that stood between him and a collapse. 'We
won, did we?'

'Not yet,' murmured Jehovah, and for the first time
glanced down at Seth's small, insignificant body. One
more in the masses. 'Pandora is fading, though.'

'Is it? I hardly noticed. Though I do hope I've
managed to bugger things up for you.'

They said not a word as they helped him hobble
through the corridors. The pain of the fight was starting
to tell, but he ignored it. He felt too tired to do anything
about it and, besides, what were regenerative trances

for? They took him to the dome, and he looked up at the face on the ceiling. The woman's eyes were closed, but someone had drawn in a few tears, and she definitely looked unhappy. 'Hi. Miss me?' he asked it.

The face didn't move.

Jehovah gently guided Sam to the centre of the room and eased him on to his knees. He was wearing a kind, fatherly expression.

'I won, right? We can stop now. It's over.'

'No. You were two inches short.'

'Seth is dead, Odin is dying. What are two inches here or there?'

'The catapults are going quiet. The order has been put out to cease fighting. You've saved thousands of lives without noticing what you did.'

'I won.'

'No. Two inches, Sam, two inches.'

Sam looked round the dome at the empty walls, at Jehovah standing by his side, at Tinkerbell sitting quietly by Odin's body, and back down to the floor. 'I just want to sleep.'

'Soon, brother, soon.'

'Two inches, right? The two inches I needed to kill Thor, Cronus's last disciple?'

'Those are the ones.'

He looked at the doorway ahead. 'He's in those corridors?'

'Probably leaning over Seth's body as we speak. He hid as we passed him. Didn't you sense anything?'

'No.' Sam stared round the room once more, as though trying to familiarise himself with it again. 'How long?' he asked wearily.

'I'd give him five minutes to fight through the minimal defence that stands between him and Cronus.'

'What if it doesn't work? What if I don't destroy Cronus?'

Jehovah shrugged. 'We have to hope. Cronus, you see, isn't exactly the end of the universe. Just of *our* universe. Really, if he does win it's nothing to be afraid of.'

Sam smiled faintly, but his voice caught in his throat. 'Please don't do this.'

'I'm sorry.'

'Bollocks.'

'I am.'

'Then don't . . . then . . . stop . . .' His voice faded away, but his smile, automatic, fixed, as if he'd been caught that way when the wind changed, remained. In a whisper that seemed to take all the strength out of him he murmured, 'I didn't even get a last meal.'

'You will discharge, then?'

'You know I will. You've known all along, even if I haven't.'

In this quiet, thought Sam, *you could hear a mouse fart.* 'By the way, Seth said something profound when he died.'

'Really? What?'

'I can't remember. Not on such short notice. Ask me in a few minutes, when I've had time to think about it.'

Silence. Then, 'I've got a Mars bar, if you want it,' said Jehovah.

'You call that a last meal?'

'Better than sausage, egg and chips.'

Sam hesitated. 'Yeah, I suppose so. All right, give it here.' Jehovah fumbled in a pocket and Sam took the slightly spongy, melted chocolate bar. His hands trembled so much as he tried to get off the wrapper that Jehovah held out his hands to help him, but Sam waved him away and with his teeth managed to tear a way in.

'Keep the wrapper,' said Sam. 'If I'm lucky some occultist somewhere might preserve it as a holy artefact and mass-produce postcards of it for the especially pious.'

'Might be a little easy to forge.'

'You mean, as compared to forging a lump of wood from a crucifix, feather from the angel Gabriel, bone from a saint or stick from a burning bush?'

'At least I have holy relics in variety.'

'Really? Oh well, I can't be outdone by my own brother. Do you have a bottle of water I can drink from or possibly a flower I can torture in a particularly religious way? The holy Evian bottle, for which knights can go questing for in years to come, perhaps? Non-biodegradable. Could be a hit.'

No answer. Sam stared at the floor, his taut, hysterical voice silenced as the thoughts that he refused to think intruded again. 'How will we know?'

'We'll know.'

'Please . . .'

'No. What must happen will happen.'

'No back-up plans?'

'Not this time. You're very good at ruining the best laid plans of mice, men and monsters.'

'The plans of mice are too shallow, the plans of men are too obvious, the plans of monsters are too vulgar,' he replied firmly, waving a finger in the air. 'And the plans of deities suffer from arrogance.' Silence. 'Where's Thor now?'

'I don't know. Congratulating himself on a job well done, I expect.'

'Will he release Cronus? What if he smells a rat?'

'He'll release Cronus,' said Jehovah wearily. 'Deities are arrogant.'

'And monsters are vulgar,' agreed Sam.

'And relics are easy to forge.'

'Although carbon dating has its uses.'

'No one can ever be bothered.'

'True.'

Silence. 'Brother . . .' said Jehovah suddenly.

Sam raised a hand. 'Listen,' he whispered.

They listened. Nothing. 'Brother, I'm sorry,' said Jehovah. 'For everything.'

'You said.'

'There is a chance,' breathed Jehovah, so quietly that even Sam had to strain. 'A miracle.'

'I can't make miracles when I'm dead,' replied Sam, without malice or bitterness.

'I know. I'm sorry.'

Sam glanced up at him. Then, 'Call for Time, when it's over. Call him into your soul, let him possess you.'

'Why?'

'Please.'

'All right.'

Silence. Then, 'Listen,' whispered Sam. Jehovah rose to his feet, leaving Sam still kneeling, a tiny figure in a room too large for him. Sam turned his emotionless eyes up to him. 'Tell them I said something not only profound, but corny too.' He frowned slightly. 'Freya . . .' he began.

'Listen,' whispered Jehovah, raising a finger to his lips. And now they heard it. A sound like . . . children laughing. Like wings in an empty sky. Like thunder, heard far off. Like the clatter of a small bell falling to the floor.

'As for my off-the-record statement,' continued Sam, wide eyes staring towards the door. 'I have one word.'

A cold wind, rising from everywhere, tearing at hair and clothes, making pale skin paler. Sam rose from his knees, opening his arms out as though to embrace the world. His hands shook, he could hardly support himself, there were tears in his eyes and terror in his pale, pale face. 'Bugger,' he explained softly, as the world filled with the roar of an awakening god.

Every torch in the dome winked out, leaving Sam in darkness. He smiled. Darkness, like a lot of things, was breakable.

TWENTY

Bearer of Light

There had only been one discharge like it ever before, when young Sam, in search of the truth about his parents, had put on a silver crown in the Room of Clocks, and become the Bearer of Light.

This time, however, the Light had purpose.

On Earth they called it atmospheric disturbance, and in a few months to come an *X-Files* episode was based on it, in which not only did the protagonists prove conclusively the existence of witches, but the cast and crew got to go to France for the filming. In Hell the demons bowed down and begged for mercy. In Heaven, Loki looked up from the corner of his dark cage, and laughed like a child as the Light poured over him.

In Tartarus, Sam searched and found the mind of Cronus. It was small, he realised, made smaller by a few billion years with only itself for company, plotting and scheming and railing against Time, all to no avail. He searched, focused, and didn't need to do any more. The Light was already reaching, digging, searching for the right way to destroy this enemy. All Sam had to do was let it run, run out of control, pulling more and more minds into a whirlpool of power that sucked him and Cronus down into it.

No sensations, but that of thought. No smell, no taste, no touch. Just the ever-growing tide of minds, mounting like a mighty wave behind a floodgate, building up behind his mind, ready to smash the gates open and hit Cronus with all it had. Not his mind, any more. Their mind. He was just a memory left behind, one they all shared. It was the memory that held them back, not the man.

I could have offered you everything. I can still, whispered Cronus. The voice was everywhere, filling nothingness with sound. It was as kind and as fatherly as he'd always imagined Time's voice would sound, right up to the point where he'd heard it. It was the most musical and compassionate voice he'd ever heard. But he wasn't in charge. Not any more. Somewhere the mind of Sam Linnfer drifted, a tiny blot. And somewhere nearby the mind of Time himself also moved, no more significant than Sam's, no less. They spoke, and the world spoke as one with them. No individuals, just a huge personality formed of a huge number of personalities turning and fixing its full attention on the voice. On Cronus.

What could you possibly offer Us?

Freedom. Peace. Conclusion.

There is no conclusion. We are the intention and the act, the strength and the weakness, the light and the dark, the individual and the whole. We are life. You are nothing.

Lucifer, why do you hide?

The spark that was a name hears you.

He controls you.

Nothing controls Us. We are life. We are the power that finds a way, we end Greater Powers. For they are part of us. And we are everything to them.

If Lucifer can hear me, as I know he can, he should know that he owes no allegiance to his father. His father will see him die. His father will hurt him. His father has hurt him already. Expressions bound to Time, Time bound to him, eternity of imprisonment. Has, had, will. It is all he knows. He is afraid of change.

We are afraid of nothing.

You are afraid of me.

You are afraid of Us. We are life. You are not-being.

Time is death. He is your undoing.

Death is freedom. We are being. It is better that being and freedom should work together than that not-being should over-rule us.

Where is Lucifer?

No names. Not any more. A spark hides inside the whole, more afraid than Us all. The spark knows. The spark knows of Us and of you and of life and of death. We do not. The spark is frightened of what it knows. If knowledge scares the spark more than ignorance, then it is rational to desire that ignorance and innocence which it has lost.

You are afraid.

Always.

You cannot destroy me. You are life. Life cannot destroy.

Life finds a way. Life overrules. You are not-being. We are everything. You will become a part of Us. A spark. Nothing more.

Life has not the power.

Life ends and creates life. Life is everything.

Where is Lucifer?

The spark has forgotten its name. It is safe, while it forgets. It is free.

You dare not.

Always.

You cannot.

Always.

You will not.

Always.

Where is Lucifer? He controls you. He cannot deny me!

The spark hides within Us. The spark knew you'd come, and was afraid. The spark hides among the Many. The spark will not listen. The spark has forgotten how to listen, rather than hear you. You are nothing. We will prove it so.

You are not free.

Nor are you. But unlike you, We will endure.

Life cannot kill! Only Time can! He cannot beat me!

We can beat you. It is arrogance to assume otherwise.

You dare not.

Always. And for ever. And together. We are everything. You are nothing. We made you what you are. We made Time. We made Love, Hate, Greed, Suspicion, War, Peace, Envy, devils and angels, gods and goddesses, hopes and dreams and futures and pasts – and more. And all. We are life.

Lucifer.

The spark is gone.

Lucifer.

The spark is hiding. It will not hear you.

He hears me whether he wants to or not. He is an individual.

Not any more. No individuals. Just Us. What was a One is now a Many. The spark is gone. We are the whole and the individual. We are One. We are Many.

He is at your head. He leads you. Lucifer.
The spark is gone.
Lucifer.
Gone.
Lucifer.
Gone!
Lucifer!
Gone! Leave me alone, gone, leave me alone, gone!
You cannot deny me!
Leavemealoneleavemealoneleavemealoneleavemealone . . .
Lucifer. Lucifer? Lucifer!
Gone. Never there. We are the intention and the act, the strength and the weakness, the light and the dark, the individual and the whole. We are life. You are nothing. And there will be 'ands' and 'nows' and 'tomorrows'. We have ordained it.
Lucifer.
Gone. We are life. And we will have conclusion.
Lucifer . . .
Gone.

In a small hall in a small city in a small country in a small world, a small figure kneeling on a hard floor jerked as if pulled on strings, head tilting up and back. Its eyes were closed, and around it floated a still sea of burning bright light. The same burning bright light that covered the small world, and the small world a shadow's throw from it, and the small world a shadow from that world, and everything between and beyond. It shimmered like water. The universe held its breath.

The Light faded, darkness returned. Nothing happened. But somewhere on the edge of hearing, a tiny little voice, whispering to an empty world.

We are the intention and the act, the strength and the weakness, the light and the dark, the individual and the whole, the magic and . . . and . . . the miracle . . . and . . .

Leavemealoneleavemealoneleavemealoneleavemealone.

Lucifer . . .

Gone . . .

The tiny figure in a tiny world opened its white eyes and smiled a tiny, relieved smile as every strand of black hair began to turn white.

Lucifer . . .

Gone . . .

The jet of white light erupted out from his heart, outshining stars, as pale and cold as moonlight, but so bright that those who looked too close were blinded by it. It shot towards the darkness of a doorway, struck more darkness which occupied, for just a second, a terribly human shape twisted into something vile. The Light was silent, focused into a beam no wider than a heart and, after an eternity blasting at nothing, winked out. Measurable eternity, seconds, minutes, hours, days, years . . .

Lucifer . . .

Gone. Just like you.

Lucifer . . .

Gone. It's been a bad day, month, year, decade, century, millennium.

You're slipping, Sebastian . . .

Poisons in the blood . . .

And me.

And me.

And me.

And me.

No escape.

Not even the magic . . .

. . . and the miracle . . .

Poisons in the blood.

Lucifer.

Gone, slipping, drowning, darkness, poison, slipping, freedom, gone . . .

Lucifer.

Gone. Only the Father, the second, minute, hour, day, year, millennium, life, being, existence, death . . .

Lucifer.

. . . please don't do this . . .

Lucifer.

. . . the . . . the intention and the act, the . . . strength and . . . and the weakness, the . . . the magic . . . the miracle . . . the magic . . . the . . . the miracle . . .

Somewhere, in a small patch of darkness surrounded by fire and light, a tiny figure smiled at nothing, white hair falling loosely around his white face with its white eyes, and pitched forward.

Another figure rushed forward, dark as the power that gave him life, kneeling over the fallen body, calling names. Lucifer, Satan, Luke, Sam, Sebastian, remember, I am, you are, he is, she is, you are an individual . . .

. . . the second, minute, hour, day, year, millennium, life, being, existence, death . . .

A second figure, all grace and reserve, glides out of the shadows, kneeling down next to Sam's fallen body and gently lays a hand on the pulse. Nothing. He puts his ear above Sam's mouth and looks down the line of his chest. Nothing. Nodding, as if he's just been satisfied of something he already knew, he waves everyone else aside, and puts his hands over Sam's face, as if covering it from the world.

'You won, brother,' he murmurs. Magic grows up around his fingers.

There is a chance. Call for Time, when it's over. Call him into your soul.

Why?

Please.

Magic building, mind changing. Jehovah straightened, his eyes two translucent spheres, and looked round the room as though for the first time. Then, very slowly, face impassive, he raised his hands to his ears.

Things have reached conclusion. Rest. Freedom. Not alone, just not together. Never alone. Not any more.

Sam? Sam, what have you done?

In a tiny city on a tiny world a tiny figure leant over a tiny body, took hold of the man's limp wrist and whispered, *I hear you.*

I hear you too . . .

Where are you?

Everywhere.

Come home.

How?

I will show you the way.

Gone. No more. Not alone, just not together. Never alone. Not any more, it's been a bad day week month go away leave me alone year decade please don't do this century poisons in the blood millennium . . .

You're slipping, Sebastian.

Not even the magic can hold me up.

We are the magic and the miracle.

I will show you the way.

Call him into your soul.

Not even magic . . .

. . . perhaps Time?

Somewhere, Jehovah smiled. 'You clever bastard,' he whispered, before pitching forward to the floor beside Sam and leaving the Many screaming their delight.

We are the intention and the act, the strength and the weakness, the light and the dark, the individual and the whole, the magic and the miracle.

Lucifer, where are you going? Why do you hide?

I'm not going far. We won't be alone, you and I. We just won't be together. Never alone.

Now you see me, now you don't . . .

And at the end, there was just the silence.

TWENTY-ONE

Lucifer

There was a small flat above a newsagent in Clerkenwell. It could have been quite comfortable, and over the years had increased hugely in value as the city around woke up not only to what a pleasant, central location this was, but to what a fortune it might represent as a 'new and exciting development' or – the owner's worst nightmare – 'a dazzling, new concept-design penthouse'.

This, however, wasn't important.

There was a table in a sitting room, on which a strange and disparate collection of goods had been dumped. A battered old leather satchel that looked like it had been from a twenty-four-hour-sunlight desert to Siberia and back here again. A silver crown that looked pathetically dull and pale. A short silver sword, carefully cleaned. A shorter silver dagger, all the more sinister for being so plain – there could be no doubt, looking at this weapon, that it served any purpose other than killing. A copy of last week's *Time Out*. A pile of unread news-papers. A battered-looking chocolate-bar wrapper. An empty bowl stained with a substance that might have been baked beans *avec une sauce chimique* – this last object scraped clean by someone who obviously enjoyed the spicy tang of E numbers.

This, however, wasn't important.

There was a sofa. It looked like it had seen better days and may or may not have been at one time the residence of a polar bear on vacation. It had a rather forlorn flowery pattern on it and had been worn so thin and colourless that it was little more than a few tattered bits of string with some feathers stuffed inside. The owner claimed it was a family heirloom.

This, however, wasn't important.

There was a man lying on the sofa. He had pure white hair and his hands were folded over a tartan blanket. His eyes were closed.

This, thought Adam as he crept into the room, was important.

'Hi,' he said, sitting down on the edge of the sofa.

'Hello,' said the man, not opening his eyes.

'You survived, then?'

'Kinda.' Sam opened his eyes. They were pale grey, so pale they might almost have been white.

'You were rather clever.'

'Thanks.'

Adam shrugged uneasily. 'How'd you do it?' he asked, in a terribly disinterested voice.

Sam smiled, a tightening of his lips at not-so-distant memories. 'Time wanted me to give him my soul. When

I refused he tried to take it. But I'm not one person, you see? I'm so many different people now, it's all quite confusing. How could he take my soul when it's so scattered? But he – he is one person. I could take his, if I wished it. He tried to tear me open. I tore him open instead.'

'You could have destroyed him.'

'No. No point. I needed him in order to hide. I hid inside his soul. I wrote my own soul on to his instead of his on to mine. So that when my mind was scattered to a thousand directions, there'd be a place to come crawling back to. Jehovah was simply the catalyst. I possess Time, Time possesses him, he gives me the link through which I could pass back from Time to me. And live. Time didn't take me over, I took him over. He is, after all, only a One. And We are a Many.'

'You're not mad, are you?'

'As in angry?'

'No. As in stark raving bonkers.'

Sam considered. 'Don't think so.'

'What was it like?'

'Not as bad as it could have been. I didn't fight, this time. I knew there wasn't any point. So I just dived in. It was quite peaceful, in a way. The Light channelled everything, you see. Everything, not fear or anger or hate or anything like that – it channelled everything that makes up life. There was nothing else, you see, no discord in the music. It was . . . almost . . . beautiful.'

'Almost?'

'Right up to the point where I touched Time's mind and saw myself hidden inside him, like he hid inside Freya. I touched Time's mind last, you see. When I did,

I touched my own soul too, and for a second I heard my own voice standing out among the others. And my own voice was screaming denials against the Light, trying to break free.' He shrugged. 'But it was quickly drowned out, so that was okay.'

'I have a question. What was Time's mind like?'

'Surprisingly small, actually. He wasn't nearly as interesting as I thought he'd be. Just another Incarnate created by life, a tiny part of the Many. Admittedly a rather raucous member, but still only a One. I remember he was surprised. When I tore him open a second time so that I could use the imprint of my soul inside his to get me back home in one piece, I heard his thoughts. And he was surprised.'

'What'd he say?'

Sam smiled and folded his fingers together. 'He said, "Shit, I didn't see that coming."'

When Adam was gone he lay studying the ceiling. It wasn't a particularly impressive ceiling, and he quickly got bored with it. He heard a creak on the staircase.

Dad? I know you can hear me.

But of course. You are inside my soul, as I am inside yours, in a small way. How can we not hear each other? You joined yourself irrevocably to me.

Why'd you let me do it, Dad? You could have stopped me joining to you.

No, I couldn't. Besides, I might have a use for you in the future.

Dad?

Yes?

I don't think I like you.

Things change. At least you'll not be alone any more.

Not alone, just not together. Never alone. Not any more.

You're not slipping, are you? You're well and truly afloat.

I was afloat from the start, Dad. I got caught in some tricky currents, that's all. Dad?

Yes?

I don't think I like you. You're small-minded and selfish.

Things change.

Poisons in the blood?

I could be profound. I could say 'What is Time?', but you're not in the mood. I can feel that you're not in the mood. You're part of me . . .

. . . and I'm a part of you. And hell, you weren't expecting it, were you?

Can't say.

Dad?

Yes?

Go away.

Not alone.

No. Not alone. Maybe not together, but never alone.

He heard another creak behind him and half turned, smiling, to look up at Freya.

Maybe, he thought, it had been worth it after all.

About the Author

Catherine Webb wrote her acclaimed debut fantasy *Mirror Dreams* at the age of just fourteen, prompting extensive coverage in the national media and rights sales in France, Germany, Holland, Italy and Japan. Its sequel, *Mirror Wakes*, was published six months later, shortly after Catherine was named *Young Trailblazer of the Year* by *Cosmo Girl* magazine.

Catherine lives in North London and is currently reading history at university. As well as writing, she enjoys reading, badminton and chess. She likes cats, space (the stuff with stars in) and Fridays. She is less keen on drizzle, Hammersmith and the number 73 bus. You can find out more about her by visiting www.atombooks.co.uk.

MIRROR DREAMS

By Catherine Webb

Every dream you've ever had, and every dream yet
to come, exists somewhere in the Kingdoms of the
Void. Every nightmare, too. Because there had to be
balance – it's the rules.

Problem is, the Lords of Nightkeep aren't big on
rules. They're more into Conquest, Fear and Eternal
Darkness For All. It takes extremely powerful
wizards like Laenan Kite to keep them in check.

But right now Kite has other worries, and Nightkeep is growing strong. Its Lords hunger for power.
And they've turned their gaze towards Earth.

www.atombooks.co.uk

MIRROR WAKES

By Catherine Webb

The stunning sequel to Mirror Dreams

Deadly spells are igniting across Haven and the queen of Dreams is in mortal danger. The court is pointing accusing fingers at squeaky-clean Lord Rylam. But that's Haven's court for you – they start in on intrigue and lies well before breakfast. Or so Rylam would say. After all, how could a young noble with pots of loot but no crown possibly benefit from a suddenly vacant throne? Hmmm . . .

One thing's clear – Haven needs Laenan Kite. He's the most powerful magician in all of Dreams. He's the bane of Nightkeep and the protector of Earth's sleeping souls. And he's . . . on holiday.

Queen Lisana wants him found and on the case fast, because if Rylam isn't the enemy, then the Realm of Dreams is in some really serious trouble.

www.atombooks.co.uk

dream harder at www.atombooks.co.uk